WHEN WE
WERE ALL
STILL ALIVE

WHEN WE
WERE ALL
STILL ALIVE

A NOVEL

KEITH MCWALTER

Published by SparkPress, a BookSparks imprint,
A division of SparkPoint Studio, LLC
Phoenix, Arizona, USA, 85007
www.gosparkpress.com

Published 2021
Printed in the United States of America
Print ISBN: 978-1-68463-077-6
E-ISBN: 978-1-68463-078-3 (e-bk)

Library of Congress Control Number: 2020922574

Formatting by Kiran Spees

For Courtney

It is not a life we are living. It is life's reward, beautiful because it seems eternal and because we know quite well it is not.

—James Salter, Immemorial Days

NOW

CONRAD BURRELL, TWICE MARRIED, had long since learned that one shameful, unspoken fact about marriage is that at some point you're going to fantasize about your spouse's death, either as a very short-form version of divorce without the lawyers and the mess, or as a thought experiment, to imagine how your life might be different if that one enormous fact at the center of it were erased. And during his long second marriage, he had ample time to indulge such imaginings, which took the form of opportunities that life with Sarah had foreclosed—for travel to countries she regarded as failed states run by gangs, which eliminated Mexico, Africa, and most of the Middle East from their itineraries, or for new love, or novel sex, or simple solitude without attachments, without obligations to another human being.

But what could not be imagined, he now found, was that none of these opportunities, once presented by real life, would be any consolation. What could not be imagined was the deep habituated need he felt to talk to her, to say not only what hadn't been said, or said enough, but to say those innumerable things that came to his tongue each day like food he craved but could not eat. What could not be imagined was the profound emptiness that the subtraction of just one life can hollow out in the world.

The little crew-cut priest visits inevitably. Sarah, with her compulsive intimacy, had always called him Rick, though to everyone else he's Father Montgomery. He's built like a wrestler, pale as a librarian. Conrad reflexively calculates the man's age at around fifty, too young for his job; by Conrad's lights, a man should be on intimate terms with mortality if he's going to be a priest. They sit under the magnolia in the side yard, its buds like pink spears jutting out of gray bone.

1

A soft breeze, watery sunlight, the stink of mulch. Spring has come against all expectation and justice, the promise of resurrection's best shuck and jive. The priest is a no-nonsense guy; Conrad likes him, but wants this to be over.

"Come to church," says Father Rick. "There's comfort in community; I know it for a fact."

It must sound like a billboard slogan even to the priest, Conrad thinks. "I can't," he says. "I'd feel like too much of a hypocrite."

"Christians love hypocrites; it gives us someone to forgive."

Another slogan, but a funny one. Conrad smiles indulgently.

"What little faith I had has been severely compromised, I'm afraid."

The priest lapses into sincerity. "No one expects faith of you, Conrad. No one even expects to comfort you, believe me. We all get that there's nothing we can do. But I'm telling you that if you come and simply hang out with people who are open to you, with no expectations of anything, you'll feel better. That's my only claim," he says, his hands opening wide, the gesture of a politician. Conrad frowns; "hang out" is a phrase from his adolescence in the sixties, from before the priest was born.

"I'll give it some thought. I appreciate the sentiment."

"Sentiment is cheap," says Father Rick, thinking to startle with tough love. "Give it some action." Conrad half expects him to swing a balled fist through the air. "And if you ever need the actual religious stuff, prayer or anything, please don't hesitate to give me a call."

"I won't."

"Won't hesitate or won't call?" The priest grins. "I mean it. You never know."

"No, you never do."

"She was a wonderful woman."

At this Conrad raises his hands, palms outward. No one need tell him how wonderful she was. To talk of his needs is one thing; to talk of Sarah is to reify her absence, and he wants none of it. He's jealous of her memory, wants no one else to have it. If he could make her life and death a secret, wipe it from the record of the wide world, he would.

Father Rick changes tactics.

"What about a memorial service?" he asks.

"What about it?"

"Do you want one?"

In his prior imaginings of Sarah's death, the service was the thing he'd focused on, the wave of sympathy on which he'd ride up to the pulpit and say things that would make all the women cry and shame the men for not loving their own wives enough. Now it seems just another way of trying to bang the world into shape around her absence, of caving in to maudlin acceptance.

"No," he says to the priest.

"It might be good for you. Forget everyone else. Good for *you*."

"I'm having a lot of trouble worrying about what's good for me right now."

Father Rick sighs, leans back, ready to give up. "That's the point of these things, Conrad. That's why they're rituals, so things that should be done get done without too much thought. They're for events that people are bad at thinking clearly about. Marriage. Birth. Death." He pauses between each word to let the images form, as in a sermon. "They help us think about them in a coherent way. It might make a difference for you."

Coherence would be nice, he admits to himself. The priest has begun to refer to Sarah's death obliquely, like an undertaker, or a lawyer. Still, he's unmoved and sits quietly the way he would in a negotiation where he knows he has the upper hand.

"I have no idea what I'd say."

"You don't have to say anything," says the priest. "No one expects you to. I'll handle that. And you can let others speak, or not. It's up to you."

He hadn't considered a service at which he'd say nothing; it seems disrespectful. So there it is, a perfect conundrum: he can't speak, and he can't not speak. Impossible, just as it should be.

"What would Sarah have wanted?" the priest asks suddenly, as though the question had just occurred to him. Conrad sees that he thinks it's clever; he's saved it for what he thought was the right moment. The calculatedness of it offends him, as does the invocation of her name, with its soft syllables; a name, like the true name of God, that should be secret; a name that should be known only to him, foresworn by others. But the question pricks at him, troubles him. With the demented literalism that's become his refuge, he reasons that the question can't truly be, *What would Sarah say about a service if she were alive?* because if she were alive, her memorial service would be a morbid fantasy that she would never consent to discuss. So the real question must be, *What would Sarah want if she were somehow accessible, if she could speak to us now despite being gone?* And of course this is cruel nonsense, another kind of self-torture, because it implies her ghostly ongoing presence, which he can sometimes feel but which he knows he must stop feeling if he's to survive, and if he could actually receive Sarah's thoughts, there would be a thousand things he would want to know from her, and none of them would be about her memorial service.

Instead of all this, he says, "We never discussed it."

Father Rick sighs again. "But she was a churchgoing woman."

"I'm not sure what that means. We didn't go that often."

"She was a spiritual woman, don't you agree? The church meant something to her. She drew solace from it."

He feels himself flush. "Yes."

"So wouldn't you think that if she were asked—"

"Don't say that, please," he cuts him off, and it comes out as a plea that frightens the priest, who sits silently for a moment, his eyes downcast, then brushes off his black suit coat and rises.

"I don't mean to cause you pain, my friend. Call me if I can help in any way."

Conrad doesn't move. Then he looks up. "Let's talk some more about the memorial service," he says.

Of all the things he misses, all the things he loved, all the million facts of life with Sarah that were in an instant gone, what he misses most is something he thought not at all about during the days of his former life, something so incidental that he'd attended to it only in the act itself, at the moment when he and Sarah had settled into bed and turned out the lights, when the screens had been put aside and the covers pulled up, after he put the pink plugs in her ears to muffle his snoring, after they'd kissed one last time that day and she'd rolled onto her stomach, he would turn and rub her back for a few moments, the way she said she'd been comforted as a child, sometimes counting the strokes, twenty, thirty, from the nape of her neck down to her buttocks, and sometimes farther down on nights when he wanted to start something, that small span crossed over and over, making himself sleepy too, that stretch of skin the soft pale tablet on which their days were recorded each night, in the silent, complete complicity of a man and his wife. It had seemed unimportant, sometimes a duty, like washing the dishes. But he never failed to do it night after night, and now, when it was irretrievable, it was what he missed most.

We're all children when it comes to death. He talks with Sarah often, long conversations in which he plays both parts out loud, prays to her as though she were a protective saint, lifting his face to the sky as though that's where she'd gone. He asks her to return or, failing that, to grant him forgetfulness. The idea of her survival in some form torments him; he wants it to be true, and yet it's distasteful to think of her in some unnamable elsewhere without him or, worse, in some reincarnated future with no memory of him at all. He's surprised to find that he cares nothing about her spirit or what might become of that, how she might be found diffused in nature; the trees are still just trees, the sky just sky. What he wants is her, the corporeal thing that was his wife, the openings in her, the sweet inside of her mouth when he kissed her. Heaven is laughable; heaven is all he can hope for.

So what do they do then, these men for whom there's nothing left but the world's permission to stop what they've done all their lives? Most fall silent, as though embarrassed at having been caught at something; some stand and make great inappropriate noises and are regarded as cranks and coots, but most are silent in that stoic way they learned as persecuted little boys, and shrink, and do their best to become invisible.

The house, so old it still smells of his parents, is a sinkhole of memory; it drives him out into the streets of the town, to the coffee shops in the morning and the bars at night. Everyone pretends not to recognize him, for which he's grateful. People are helpless before a widower. No one knows what to say, which suits him fine, as he can't imagine what he would say back. When he was Sarah's husband he was often unnoticed because she drew everyone's attention, but now that she's gone, he's gone beyond invisibility and become a complete abstraction, beneath practical interest, like a mathematical problem of no relevance to real life. There are times, at the rare dinner to which he's still invited or at the bar in town where he sits with the other old men to watch a Steelers game, when he wants to shout out the heresy that they too will come to this, each a remnant of a finer life. But this would be the one unforgivable obscenity, so he stays quiet, sips his drink, and imitates the looks on their faces.

Over coffee and booze and with lawyerly order, he's ticked off all the possibilities: selling the house and moving away, becoming a drunk, and of course suicide, which suffers from the serious deficiencies that (a) he wouldn't be around for the consequent drama, (b) it was unlikely to actually reunite him with Sarah, and (c) death scares him now more than ever. He tries to imagine how he'll explain himself to people he might meet in his now-unimaginable future, who will wonder about this modestly successful older man who lives in a small town, alone. *My wife died in a car accident*, he will say. He tries the sentence in his mind, and it seems to work. He tries saying it aloud and can't.

Madeleine, his only child, tart fruit of his first marriage, grown now with a husband and a daughter of her own, leaves a long weepy message on his phone, barely intelligible, offering to come be with him for as long as he wants. It makes him angry, as though she were to blame for becoming the only woman in his life, for distracting him from Sarah through all those years. She's thirty-five, a lawyer like her parents, tall and thin like him, whip-smart like her mother.

Eventually he calls her back and they spend a few minutes telling each other how sorry they are, how unfair life can be. He longs to bring up the past, to apologize to her again, to try to explain once more why he and her mother broke up those decades ago, how they were right to do so, how it was almost necessary. She's able to listen now in a way that she couldn't when she was younger but is less willing to; there's just no point, she says. She understands as much as she needs to; the rest is for her parents, not for her. He knows that she comes closest to real anger at him when he tries to imply that the two of them share some sort of superior, conspiratorial agreement about the past that no one else shares or understands. The fact that he wasn't there for much of what she remembers, and that her mother was, divides them forever. She would never hurt him by saying this, and she's sorry that there's nothing he can do about it now, but choices were made, and as far as she's concerned, he'll just have to live with the consequences, his untimely widowhood being, by implication, one of them. In her voice he hears that she thinks she understands the gravity of choice and the precariousness of the world in a way that her parents never did, that she is exercising greater care than they did because so much had been given to them, things she has to fight for.

Her mother calls a few days later. "Megan" appears on his phone, and he stares at it as though it were a message from a distant planet, fearful of his ex-wife's pity, not knowing what he would say to her or how he could avoid sounding either too callous or too pathetic. He taps a button to make the call go away to voice mail, which he never listens to. A lifelong curator of ironies, she would want to talk about how she'd gotten through this when Vince, the man she married after him, had died, the peculiar fact of their joint survival and what that might imply. Maybe some other time.

A cop calls, asks twice if he's talking to Conrad Burrell, and says he regrets his obligation to convey the information (he must be reading this from a laminated card) that certain required lab analyses indicate that Sarah had been drinking on the day of the accident. He says he's sorry for Conrad's "loss" (that one reductive syllable, hollow as an open pit) and hastens to say that no one plans to press charges. Conrad sits stunned for a moment, then summons his best lawyer's voice out of the bile in his throat.

"And how could you press charges, seeing as how she's dead?"

The cop sounds like a very young man. "If she'd, uh, survived she would be DUI, Mr. Burrell," he says in his nervous monotone. "But her vehicle was struck from the side by the other vehicle . . ."

"T-boned, I think is the expression," he says bitterly. "I know all this."

"Yes, sir, but these lab reports indicate elevated alcohol in her blood, and under Pennsylvania law I'm obliged to inform next of kin when a driver . . ."

"Pennsylvania *law*?" he hears himself shouting. He seethes at the cop about how he dare lecture a lawyer about Pennsylvania law, and the boy apologizes and explains again his duty and tells Conrad to expect a letter in the mail, and before Conrad can arrange his mouth into words, the boy hangs up.

He takes all his clothes to Goodwill and keeps only a few white shirts and blue jeans, which he hangs with great care, evenly spaced, in the empty closet in the bedroom. The elegant suits from the years of his working life are given away, the dress shirts with their spread collars, the tight leather shoes with their laces, the belts and ties. Endless clothes, forgotten years of clothes, bales of it, stuffed into black plastic bags. And still he has too much. He boxes up her books in the study and takes them to the town library like a man taking his dog to be put down. He enlists some neighbor boys to help move furniture out into the backyard where Goodwill has promised to fetch it; he leaves just a chair or two in each room, his mother's piano, Sarah's dining table. Their friends fear he's punishing himself, but he's gripped by a manic sense of purpose.

On one night of this fever, he strips naked in the bedroom, emptied of all but their bed, and stares frankly at himself in the full-length mirror, sees a thin, tall man, tendons showing through the skin of his forearms, veins bulging from his long hands, cock shriveled in its graying nest, ribs protruding as they did when he was a boy, hair growing wild and lank, dry cracked feet a blasted yellow, eyes in their padding of sallow flesh evading even now his own frank stare, so practiced are they in self-deceit, flinching away like furtive insects; the skin of the neck flaccid over wiry cords, ears grown strangely overlarge and elastic, lobes sagging and creased like an old shirt. The stance is tentative, one heel raised as though ready to run, but above all self-conscious, self-presenting, faithless of acceptance. He searches the face one last time for some sign of courage, then closes the closet door on which the mirror hangs, and the image angles away, eclipsed.

Megan calls again, and this time he answers before he sees who it is.

"Connie, listen to me," she says, though he's said nothing but hello. "It gets better with time."

He can see her, the way she used to jut her face out like a hatchet when she was angry. "Megan, you don't have to . . ."

"It gets better." She hangs up.

BEFORE

1

HE WOULD NEVER HAVE met Sarah had he not lived in New York City, and never would have married her had he not been married before, to Megan. These were absolute requirements of his preparation, rigid as a catechism.

He recognized the city from the first; its smells, its sounds like lines of a song he'd learned as a boy, the steam rising from the subway grates, the restaurants filling up at dusk, the black garbage bags heaped by the curbs at night, the streets walled by buildings like byzantine rooms with no roof. His father had worked here, his mother; it was where adults went to become adults. They'd brought him to New York in the steaming summers of his childhood, this American city that was like a foreign country, its buildings like cathedrals. To walk its streets as an adult was to eavesdrop on a prior life he was sure he'd lived. He was twenty-six.

The Wall Street law firm of Dunbar Bell, old as the century, required new associates to rotate through departments, six months at a time: tax, corporate, litigation, trusts and estates. He met Megan Caldwell during the litigation stint; she had the carrel next to his in the vast law library on the forty-fourth floor, whose windows offered a distracting view of the harbor, Liberty waving her welcome, Staten Island, the distant curvature of the earth. He first fell in love with her mouth; not its shape or texture, but what came out of it: obscenity and opinion. He'd known women like her at Columbia, of course, but they were Seven Sisters girls, prep school valedictorians whose fathers were lawyers and judges in the suburbs and had made sure their daughters knew New York by heart. Megan had all their settled certainty but none of their jadedness; she was a city-struck Kansas girl, thrilled to be in Gotham, her impressions of urban life derived entirely from a lifetime of reading the *New Yorker*. She wore cheap skirts bought back home, blouses from Penney's in Wichita, her hair long and stick straight and parted down the middle like a folk singer's. She talked to the partners as though they were the state-school frat boys she'd grown up dating, from whom she would take no shit but whom she might fuck now and then. That was how she talked, language recently liberated from male domination, as she would have put it. She would quote feminist-socialist doctrine at the slightest provocation, and no one could understand what she was doing working for a law firm largely made up of Rockefeller Republicans.

"I wanted to see New York," was her shrugging answer when he finally asked her this over dinner. Nine o'clock, the work day only just ended, the heat of summer still radiating from the brick of the apartment houses. He took her to a cacophonous Greek place in Chelsea where the souvlaki was good and the ouzo strangulating, the windows open to a warm, fetid breeze off the Hudson.

"You'd never been to the city before?" he asked.

"Never. We never went east of the Mississippi. My father thought New York was fucking communist headquarters."

"Well it is, you know."

"Yes, and I'm here to help."

"How did they find you?"

"One of the partners went to Notre Dame Law, probably the only one who did. He came to campus and interviewed me, and I guess he liked me." She gave him an insinuating smile, her mouth soft and thick, as though injured.

"What does your father do?"

"Drives a gas truck."

"Natural gas?"

She laughed, a short, sharp snort. "No, the kind you put in your car. Except in his case, in your farm tractor. Aren't you going to ask what my mother does?"

"What does she do?"

"Dead."

"I'm sorry."

"Not me."

"Sorry for that too."

"It's okay. I'm here now; I escaped."

"You an only child?"

"One sister, still at home. You don't talk much, you know. Are *you* an only child?"

"I have a brother, but I haven't seen him in years." It came out plaintively, as though he wished he had more to offer.

Sticky summer nights in Manhattan, racing through a supermarket on Sixth Avenue at midnight, buying pizza and cookies and cheap wine after receiving their first paychecks from the law firm. Grownup money, funny money, all of it unreal. Through the warrens of the Village streets, thin caged city trees bending over the sidewalks like a benediction, back to her disheveled apartment, Van Gogh and Jimi Hendrix taped to the walls, Vermeer's girl on a coffee mug by the bed, books and magazines scattered everywhere, better things to do than clean. She smoked; her mouth was bitter when he kissed her. The screenless windows thrown open and facing south, on a floor just high enough to see all the way down to Wall Street where the office buildings rose into the checkered night, to the looming towers of the new World Trade Center, like monstrous twin mesas, so brazen that you wanted to laugh the way you would at an arrogantly muscled man.

Megan had the sort of face people called interesting rather than pretty, cracked bawdy jokes, was serenely unimpressed by the self-proclaimed elitism of their law firm and was too good at everything she tried not to hedge her bets. He would later believe he was something to try. They were married in her apartment in the spring by a young city judge they'd met at a party, a few friends crammed into the tiny living room, their parents with their backs in the corners, uncomprehending and largely ignored. They would learn a few weeks later that she was already pregnant. Or perhaps it was Conrad who learned.

Their ending, too, was as natural as rain: two careers, parenthood, the centrifugal force of the city, of youth itself, two aging children of different worlds behaving as though they had invented themselves, their stories defining them even as they pretended those stories meant nothing: she from a family rooted in the plains, he from itinerant corporate stock; he all about standards, she all about attitude. Their law firm suddenly merged out of existence, and their common ground was erased, the two of them searching for new jobs in the indifferent city. She found one quickly, in a small Midtown firm run by women; his search took longer, dragged at him. He felt he was that most commonplace thing, an overeducated young white male in New York City, too privileged to be pitied, too lucky to be helped. He grew sullen, resentful, enrolled in school again thinking he needed another degree, withdrew into the world he'd known all his life, where all that was required was diligence. That they lasted four years would come to seem surprising in retrospect.

John Lennon was shot in the lobby of the Dakota the night before they finalized their divorce. While their lawyers traded papers in a dingy Midtown office, they fell to consoling each other, grateful for the solace that their failure was small in comparison with the world's routine depravity.

Megan insisted on full custody; Conrad would have Madeleine for two weekends a month. She behaved as though there were no other conceivable outcome, worldly in her remove, and when she remarried a few years later, he would feel a pang of jealousy as lucid as a piano chord in a distant room. It was all shut away, a world he'd never again be admitted to, that brief dream of family, Tom Paxton on the stereo in an apartment in the Village, the crib next to the dining table, Dry Sack over ice, the night of city summers wafting in through screen-less windows, the first real failure of his life, the tangled demands of profession and parenthood he couldn't meet, the exile his daughter might never forgive him for. He'd settled rather than fought. He hadn't asked for enough.

2

A HEADHUNTER CALLED; a West Coast firm named Mason & Gannett wanted a young transaction lawyer of Conrad's general description, and when he consulted Megan, she seemed relieved that he might remove himself from their weekly child custody skirmishes. So he went.

San Francisco, its hills wrapped in morning fog, the braying of the sea lions drifting up from the wharves in the mist, the town's subordination to nature the opposite of New York's monumental artificiality. From every corner, staggering vistas, out over the sprawling red bridge, out to where the great gray prison sat in the bay ripped white with wind. It was a socially guarded town if you were over thirty, and he never dated, found it more convenient to say that he was still getting over a divorce. His apartment was on the top floor of a building in Russian Hill, a one-bedroom he paid too much for, New York prices really, but it had a deck on the roof where he would sun on warm fall days, and the bedroom faced Coit Tower, and from it he could walk downhill to his office in the looming brown monolith of the Bank of America building, where the law firm of Mason & Gannett was housed on the fortieth floor. He was given the office of a mogul, floor-to-ceiling windows taking in the entire bay in one great sweep, bridge to bridge, a desk made of glass, a languidly voluptuous secretary with a British accent inherited from a senior partner who'd retired. The work seemed easy, the hours shorter than in New York, as though he'd returned from some war and deserved special treatment. He wondered if every newcomer to San Francisco felt that way.

A few fleeting years of this, the flights east to New York for business and visitation, the desultory, self-important obsessions of one's thirties. Then, in one of those absurd ironies so typical of the working world, the firm opened a New York office, and he was a natural choice to join the dozen or so lawyers being shipped off to staff it. He sublet the apartment in Russian Hill, shipped his recently purchased Mercedes east, and paid valedictory visits to his favorite restaurants. It was simple, really, like leaving a woman whose companionship he'd enjoyed but had never intended to marry.

Manhattan seemed twice as expensive as when he'd left, and the firm paid associates by their year of graduation from law school, regardless of where they lived. He heard of an apartment on Gramercy Park that was about to be vacated by a young partner who was getting married, a one-bedroom, on the small side, dark, with windows that looked out on a brick wall, but it was in a doorman building whose entrance gave onto the north side of the park where the trees caught the sun, the neighboring townhouses were like grand old dowagers indifferent to time, the Lex stopped at the corner, and rumor had it that the place would soon go co-op. He signed the lease.

He celebrated with Madeleine that night at a Japanese place in Soho, and to his surprise, Megan joined them. They'd just moved across the river into Megan's doctor boyfriend's brownstone in Park Slope. His name, they told him, was Vince Van Siclen.

"Nice alliterative name," he said. "Dutch?"

"Nice alliterative guy," said Megan. "His mother's Italian, which is what matters to him. His grandfather was Dutch."

"Making him Dutch. Old New York family." He was thinking of

money, of Madeleine's tuition and the four-figure support check he wrote to Megan each month.

"You'll meet him sometime," she said. "You can decide for yourself." She was more at ease than he, at home in her city, her face calm, her dark eyes newly fringed with fine lines that made her seem mirthful. She wore no rings yet seemed married in a resolved way he'd never observed when it had been to him. Their daughter, her arms crossed, watched the two of them warily, as though at any moment they might pull weapons or burst into tears. He sat and sipped his sake, as though this family, these two who subtended the arc of his life, convened like this every night of the week. He'd be forty in a month; his scalp had become visible through his thinning hair in the light over the sink in the mornings. He was already late to whatever professional distinction he'd once dreamed of. He'd put one foot in front of the other since he'd left his parents' home, and it had led him here.

"Have you met Vince's kids yet?" he asked Madeleine, groping for a neutral topic.

"They live in New Jersey," she replied, as though that explained everything.

"His daughter is married and has a baby girl," Megan elaborated with a reproving glare in their daughter's direction. "She lives in Saddle River, so he sees her every so often. His son seems to have disappeared."

"How does one's child disappear?" he asked, though he could easily imagine.

Megan hesitated. "After college he moved to Peru and stopped communicating. Then they learned he was back in the States when a lawyer in Arkansas who said he was representing him called and asked for bail money. He was busted for some kind of possession, amphetamines, I think." They both glanced at their daughter, gauging how much of this she should be hearing, hoping to see shock in her face, which they did not. The story of Vince's son had an arc that Megan and he had discussed often, the downward mobility of privileged children of whom so much, yet somehow not enough, had been expected.

Madeleine piped up. "Did Vince get him out of jail?"

"Yes," said Megan. "But he never made his court appearance and disappeared again. Every once in a while, Vince or his ex will get a letter from somewhere in South America, usually asking for money. It's very sad."

"Don't worry, I get it," their child sighed dramatically. "Be like the daughter, not like the son. No tattoos, no meth labs, no jail time."

"You don't have to live in Jersey, though," said her mother. "Brooklyn will be fine."

"Mom, please. I'm only applying to colleges in California."

Conrad dropped his chopsticks and clutched his chest. "Could you wait just a darn minute! I just got back!" he cried. They managed indulgent smiles.

When they finished he walked them to the curb and hailed them a cab, kissed each of them on the cheek and watched them go. Wind had sprung up, sluicing down the side streets toward the river, lifting trash like leaves. He looked around in a daze, reckoned his location in the grid of the city, and turned north.

Life in a law firm passes like life in a family. The offices of Mason & Gannett were on Lexington Avenue in Midtown, on four high floors in a modern building whose glassy façade mimicked the color of the sea. His office looked out over the East River and across the rumpled plain of Queens, not the bay view he'd enjoyed in San Francisco but impressive nonetheless, its desirability carefully calibrated to someone on the brink of partnership and yet from out of town. He was exotic; few lawyers moved between offices of the same firm as he had, fewer still had been so-called lateral hires. He was an odd blend of both coasts, old to be only now coming up for partner, but soon he had a small team of helpers, smart and diligent, better than he'd been at their ages, receptive to suggestions, tolerant of the exactitude he'd learned from his mentors and demanded of them in turn. They composed summaries of terms, drafted segments of the thick lease agreements, wrote the closing memos that were the roadmaps for where the money would go; sorted the blizzard of documents on the long tables at closings, chased down signatures. You could tell who had a talent for what, who would rise, who would drift away from the firm and into smaller practices, corporate life, parenthood. Clients liked him, he knew, because he met deadlines and his billing rate was lower than a partner's. It was already past the time when personality won or kept business, and he was inoffensive and efficient. When he finally made partner—without ceremony, just a handshake and a pat on the back in the hallway late one night—it felt more like a concession than an accolade.

The city was a backdrop, the stage he traversed among the fixed points of his life: work, dinners, weekend outings with Madeleine, his apartment. Occasionally friends would arrive in town on vacation, and he would take them to a show or to the MoMA or to Central Park, but for the most part the city was like a coat he wore without thinking about it until someone commented on how oddly it was tailored.

There were women, of course, scattered and passing like summer rain. There was the client, a straitlaced airline executive, who without preamble kissed him in a cab they were sharing on the way back from a closing dinner downtown. He skipped his stop and went with her to her hotel room; she left town the next morning before he awoke and left the airline soon after. The investment banker, southern and young, whom he'd met on a plane and then pursued through a dozen cordial, inconclusive evenings until he realized he was a placeholder and she too polite to tell him so. The older woman in the steno pool, a green-eyed, black-haired, third-generation Irish Catholic from Staten Island, who blurted one night that she would have gladly left her husband and children for him if he'd wanted, but contented herself with appearing at his apartment door once or twice a year in the dreaming dawn, after night steno had closed. The doormen knew her; he'd hear her gentle tap on the apartment door, and when he opened it she'd be standing there in only her bra and panties, smiling, in her perfect middle-aged body, her office clothes draped neatly over one arm. And there was the neighbor, a tall, ethereal, full-lipped blonde he'd seen walking inside Gramercy Park, to which only the residents of the square had keys. He'd struck up a conversation and learned she was an aspiring cabaret singer living in the old women's hotel on the southwest corner of the square until she found an apartment she could afford. He invited her up to see his. Her shoulders smelled of soap.

In these ways, years passed, as though they were endless. On certain weekends when Madeleine was willing, they'd go on overnight visits to friends in Westchester, on the train up past the Harlem tenements where he imagined himself living if all came to nothing, windows like wounded eyes in the brick façades, then the string of towns along the Hudson called out by the train conductors with stentorian reverence, the platforms passing like the stations of the cross. Yonkers. Hastings. Dobbs Ferry. Ardsley. The stately old homes full of children again, reclaimed from decline, from the fading past. Men and women, married couples he knew from school or work, comfortable in their skins, living as their parents had but with more money, certain of their children's love, of the correctness of the world they inhabited. He saw only the surface of it, knew that it must be flawed, yet it stunned him, made his solitary life seem insubstantial and fraudulent. He had no idea how they went about it, how they knew to choose this place to live, this mate, this almost careless way they had with their children. The crowded tables at mealtimes, the comfort of the upstairs rooms. Madeleine in her bathing suit, giggling with a younger girl by a luminous blue pool in a summer dusk, the sky a salmon pink, the smell of cooking, the soft song of ice in glass, laughter, while he stood at the edge of a broad dark lawn. It was a world he was sure he would never belong to, a foreign country where at any moment someone might ask for his papers and he would have none to present.

3

IN A PHOTO OF Sarah that he kept on his desk at work, she's in a bassinet being pushed by her sister and brother down a sidewalk in a suburb of Philadelphia, the older children smiling at the camera, Sarah's small face serious and framed in lace and tilted up at the sky as though staring at the sun. Born Sarah Bergman in Gladwyne, on the Main Line, to a self-made man and a dramatically beautiful woman of what was then called independent means, she was doted upon as the child who had not been planned, born prematurely, a curled thing in an incubator, clinging to life.

Everyone thought her father was a Jew because of his surname and financial success; it had been a matter of some concern to her mother's parents, though they'd been assured he was Episcopalian. Still, Sarah's mother made it a point early in most introductions to strangers to make mention of her husband's church, so as to avoid confusion, and advised Sarah to do the same.

Sarah's sister, Frances, had determined that Sarah would be the sweet, feminine girl that Frances, from the first, had no intention of being. She begged for money from her mother so she could buy clothes for Sarah and dressed her like a doll, her cheeks daubed with their mother's rouge, and would prop her up in the living room to be admired while Frances escaped to the woods with the neighborhood boys to climb trees and fashion makeshift weapons.

Robert, the middle child, took his little sister more seriously, as though he understood she was at risk of being turned entirely into a vessel of others' expectations. As soon as she was old enough, he would take Sarah with him to the Franklin Institute downtown, where he would sit in the darkened planetarium with her, teaching her the names of the constellations, the moons of Saturn, the order of the planets from the sun. He wanted to be a doctor or a botanist; he couldn't decide which. Once, when they were a bit older, she went as Robert's date to the wedding of one of his best friends, a boy from the neighborhood whose number had come up early in the first draft lottery and who was marrying his high school sweetheart before he left for Vietnam. Sarah and Robert danced together at the reception, the way he had taught her to dance, her left hand poised on his shoulder with just the fingertips, her chest always an inch from his, never touching, knowing his next step, anticipating it, but waiting for him to take it. The way a lady danced, he said. She saw the older girls watching them, envying her, and realized that her brother must be handsome.

He was strangely quiet on their last trip to the planetarium together. The program was about comets, the Oort cloud, all the objects that were not planets but still answered to the gravitational pull of the sun in their millennial orbits, their oracular reappearances when humans had all but forgotten them. She sat in the dark and held his hand as she had when she was younger, already knowing these stories, having learned them from him long ago. He was inattentive, frowning, and when she asked why, whispering under the narrative of the comets, he said nothing and pulled his hand away. Riding home on the train, she asked again, and that was when he said something she would not remember clearly, about his being different, about hers being the only hand he could hold, the only girl he felt comfortable with. And why should that be, he demanded of her suddenly. Why should that be? Late that night, thinking to calm him, Sarah led him into her bedroom and made him practice kissing a girl.

Sarah could not mention this to her mother or father, and Frances said to ignore him; he was being dramatic. Frances was going off to college and would never return, Sarah was sure; she was only waiting for the moment when she could leave them all behind. She had grown into a striking young woman with wavy black hair and piercing green eyes and had learned to dress in a way their mother thought proper, but she still had the cunning of a boy, a recklessness that Sarah both admired and worried over. She was no help in matters of delicacy, advised Sarah that Robert's problems, whatever they were, were his alone.

Their father, George Bergman, commuted every day from Philadelphia to New York City, rising at five to catch the train at seven, then once in Manhattan sprinting down the stairs at Penn Station to the subway that took him downtown to his offices at the Bank of New York, One Wall Street. At the end of the day, he arrived home at eight or nine o'clock with the look of a man who had crossed deserts and hastened to make himself a martini. Alice, his wife, made the children wait for dinner so he could join them. This went on for years, six days a week, as the Bank of New York expected its executives to work on Saturdays. No one questioned it, and the children came to think of their father as merely away, at work, a perpetual state of absence that filled them with longing and curiosity.

At dinner one night, Robert announced that, unlike his elder sister, he didn't want to go to college. George and Alice looked up together as though slapped; Sarah stared at her brother while Frances studied her fork. He saw no point in it, he said, especially while there was a war going on and half his friends had been drafted, some of them already killed and shipped home to graves he had visited. Their father sat looking at his only son, unguessable thoughts playing across his smooth face, his beautiful gray hair perfectly combed back, and with a steely evenness said that nothing needed to be decided just then, that Robert's graduation was over a year off, that the war could come to an end by then, and all the craziness that was going on, the rebellion and the marches and the drugs, could seem foolish in a few years. So the thing to do, he said, was to proceed as though none of it were happening and do what would give Robert the most options later, which was of course to apply and go to college.

Robert had used all he had in him to make his opening statement and lapsed into silence, as they all did. Utensils clicked against plates; Sarah glanced from face to face and found no eyes meeting hers until Robert looked over at her from under his long hair and winked with a flicker of an eyelid so quick that she wasn't sure she saw it.

Frances was gone by that fall, Sarah was sent to a Catholic girls' boarding school in Connecticut, and Robert's draft number came up around the same time he was accepted to Oberlin. It was a number, uttered on television by men in suits who'd plucked it from a spinning cylinder, that meant he would go to war after all, his father's wisdom notwithstanding, and Sarah stuck close to her brother for as long as she could. Whenever she was home, they went to movies together, new ones about adventures in outer space with robots and romance in them, scary ones about monsters that hid in the bowels of ships for centuries, waiting for humans to come and find them, beautiful ones in black and white about grown-ups in big cities who were in love and therefore just as foolish and confused as any child. They disturbed her; the idea of fiction, of narrative itself, disturbed her, as it seemed another way of lying. Her first question to Robert as the opening credits rolled (and years later, to Conrad) was "Is this true?" He was never sure how to answer, for of course they were someone's fantasies, and yet they were true. She could never have watched these things alone, without Robert. In some crucial way that her parents did not, he had made the world available and understandable to her, there in all the darkened halls of the waning years of their childhoods.

So when she sat on a broad curve of grass on a college campus years later, the sun in her face and her senior thesis on the art of

Edward Hopper in onion-skinned sheaves around her, and watched the dean of students walk toward her with a piece of paper in his hand, there was something in the pace of his steps, the way he held the paper before him, the look on his face, that pulled the breath from her lungs like a sword drawn in anger from a scabbard, and she leaned forward on her knees with her knuckles in the grass and waited for the dean to cross the green space between them and tell her what she already knew, that her brother had loved his friends too much, had gone to war once too often, and that it had finally claimed him and what little she knew of rightness and order. So that even before the words were handed to her on the piece of paper, she had gathered the pages of her thesis up and held them to her chest, and had stood, and had vowed to never forget him, to find a way to love him by loving the world he had abandoned her to more fiercely than he had ever imagined she could.

It fell to Sarah to make arrangements and track down her sister. Frances had graduated from Beloit and had immediately disappeared into the Pacific Northwest with a man she'd met in college who was evading the draft. Friends at home who were still in touch with her said that they'd planned to escape to Canada. Sarah followed the chain of her sister's addresses to Seattle, where she'd apparently worked for Boeing as a secretary, then to a sheep farm in the San Juan Islands and eventually to Vancouver, where a high school friend swore she'd seen her on a skiing trip in Whistler the previous winter. Sarah called the telephone company operator and asked for information in Vancouver and, after talking to another operator, was given the phone numbers of three women named Frances Bergman who lived there. The first spoke only German and French, and after a few seconds of trying each, hung up. The second was her sister.

"Frannie, it's about Rob," Sarah said after they exchanged guarded hellos, and she waited for her sister to begin to guess, but the silence went on too long.

"He's been killed, Frannie, he . . ."

"I know that," her sister said suddenly, angrily. "Why else would you be calling?"

"Yes," said Sarah simply.

"How?"

Sarah knew that there was no point to this question, that it was a play for time, but she went through the story as the Army had told it, the sniper's bullet in the jungle near Bien Hoa, the heroics of the medics, the overwhelming loss of blood, his body unblemished but for the single small wound, shipped home and waiting for them on a dock in Philadelphia.

"Bastards," said Frances. "All of them."

"Yes," said Sarah.

"Stupid bastards. He should never have been there. He was too good for them. All of them."

"You have to come home," she said finally.

"No. They'd arrest Carl."

"Just you, Frannie. You come. They're not after you."

"Yes, they are; I'm an accessory, an accomplice."

"They don't arrest girlfriends, Frannie. Come home."

"No. I can't."

"Yes, you can," Sarah said, steel finding its way into her voice. She gripped the phone, wanted to smash it down on her mother's kitchen table in front of her, wanted to rip it from the wall and drag her sister with it. Rain was falling in the backyard of her parents' house, a dense straight rain that fell as though hurled from above, pooling at the roots of the sycamores.

—

They stood by the grave arm in arm, apart from their parents, leaning together. A cloudy, chill day. Sarah wore a black suit, Frances a pair of dark slacks from her mother's closet and a simple white blouse. It was not a military burial, but a young uniformed Army officer came anyway and presented the folded flag to Alice Bergman with a quick salute. Sarah had to restrain Frances, who wanted only to walk up and hit the man in the jaw. It had rained for days and the ground was soft beneath their feet as they walked away, friends scattering, smiling at one another in the vague benign way of people at funerals, the smug survivors. Sarah and Frances lingered under a tree near the grave, and Sarah turned and leaned against her sister, felt the sinews in her strong arms as they enclosed her, and wept as she would not weep again in her life, not at the death of her mother, not when her husband told her he wanted no children, not at her divorce, not at the news of her father's death, not even when Conrad asked her to marry him many unforeseeable years later, those tears of relief that would redeem all the others. She wept until her throat was raw and her eyes dry, hearing only the beating of her sister's heart.

Later they went to a bar together and drank and talked into the night. It was the first time Sarah had ever been drunk, and she was surprised at how it made the pain go away.

4

SARAH FOUND WORK AFTER graduation in a gallery in SoHo that was owned by a friend of her father. She was paid next to nothing and had to draw on her trust fund to help with rent on an apartment in the East Village that she shared with two other girls. It was dull work, typing the names and addresses of artists and the names of paintings and their prices into a database on a clunky beige computer, letting workmen into the gallery to hang new pieces on the white walls, take away ones that had been sold or, more often, had outlasted their consignment. But she loved the art itself, big abstracts in bright colors, the occasional piece that was vaguely representational or intentionally primitive. She was alone in the gallery for hours at a time, and it was a great thrill when customers—usually women in pairs, one an interior designer, the other her client—actually came into the gallery in the long afternoons and would wander languidly through the adjoining rooms, stopping to discuss how this or that piece would go with the color scheme in a dining room, asking Sarah for dimensions as she followed them a few paces behind. She saw that art had become beholden to people like this, people with money who were decorating.

One of them was Paul Stinson. He came in alone one day near closing time, when she had already shut down the computer and had put on her coat. She could see immediately how he looked at her, as though something had collapsed inside him, stealing control of his face. He approached her like a man trying to formulate a question in a foreign language, searching for the right tense. She had briefly considered addressing him in French when he finally blurted out, "Do you work here?" He was just a bit older than her brother would have been.

He was carefully dressed, like a lawyer—she heard his name as "Paul Stuart" and had to ask again, sure he was kidding—and of course that's what he turned out to be, a new partner in the Midtown branch of a West Coast firm, a single man with more money than he knew what to do with, just returned from two years in Paris where he'd learned French and discovered art, trying to buy some that he liked without being had. He told her most of this in the first five minutes with a nervous candor that made her feel protective toward him, and she walked him through the rooms of the gallery, pointing out the work of those she thought would last, gauging his likes and dislikes among them, describing for him the general terrain of the New York art scene, even going so far as to suggest other galleries that might be more accessible to someone just starting to collect. As she said this last, she realized that it might sound condescending, but he seemed grateful to her in the way of someone who is paid to give advice.

By the time she locked the door of the gallery and had declined his offer to share a cab, they had exchanged their entire personal résumés in a volley of frank questions, from place of upbringing to education to the critical question of where each of them lived. He was the first man she'd met in New York who'd asked her these things, to whom they seemed important. She'd given him her phone number, scrawled on a piece of notepaper, and he'd given her his business card. She hadn't looked at it but put it in the pocket of her coat as she walked north toward the subway station, fingering the embossed lettering of his name.

Their wedding was at the Cloisters on a hot day in June. There's a photo of Sarah in her dress with an astonishingly long and impractical train standing next to Paul in a garden with a fountain at its center, surrounded by friends only some of whose names she would later recall, the women looking relaxed and sensual in long summer dresses, the men sweating and uncomfortable in their suits. They're affecting a look out of Fitzgerald, and succeeding in this, as in life, to varying degrees. Her parents and his attended; it was the last time she would see her mother outside of a hospital room. What she remembered most of that day was the enormous pride that radiated from her father, not just in her, but in what he saw as the quality of the life he had created for her, that had led her and all of them to that moment in that beautiful place. That it was fleeting, that its beauty was borrowed and the relationship they were celebrating was based entirely on the whim of two people inexperienced in intimacy—none of that mattered. It was a lovely wedding, and she felt Robert would have liked it, would have liked Paul.

They moved into his co-op in Murray Hill, a two-bedroom in a prewar doorman building that had slivers of views of the river. The apartment was on an upper floor, with high ceilings and big walls on which Paul encouraged her to hang whatever she liked. She bought a huge oil by Homura for the living room after asking several times if they could really afford it. The block was lined with elms, the neighborhood had a nice grocery and fine restaurants, and Paul could walk to work. She perceived that their life was enormously expensive, while avoiding the blatant ostentation of Park Avenue. Still, the city wore on her, the constant need to be alert and careful, the ceaseless, braying traffic, the crushing crowds in the Midtown blocks, the absence of gardens. She used to say that Central Park was too big to be a real park; it was more like an airport with trees. And in the back of her heart was the knowledge, unspoken but as certain as her name, that she wanted a child and this was no place to raise one.

Paul was the kindest adult man she had ever known, but also the hardest working. On the long summer weekends when he had to prepare for a trial, and she went with girlfriends and their husbands to Fire Island or the Hamptons, she was grateful she'd had a father who'd shown her what a career demanded of some men, what some men would sacrifice for it. They had sex perhaps twice a month, infrequently enough that she began to doubt her attractiveness and to dress more provocatively. Paul seemed not to notice; he was as consistent in this regard as in all others, though when they did make love he was diligent, the way he was at work.

She was shown the house in Dobbs Ferry by the friend of a friend to whom she'd mentioned her wish to leave the city. They conspired about it, knowing as women do that sometimes men have to be led. The house sat alone at the end of a quarter-mile lane, had been empty for years, the roof ruined and the shutters hanging at odd angles. It was like seeing an old friend, one who had come on hard times but who had never lost faith in her, who knew she would help. There was an overgrown English garden in the back and deep woods nearby, places where a child could go and be with herself when ashamed or lonely.

Paul had agreed that they could move as long as he could keep a small apartment in the city so he wouldn't have to commute every day, and they bought the house in Dobbs Ferry. It was in this house that she made her first true home, filling the rooms with fabric and color, shells from trips to the Cape, scented candles, fresh flowers in Chinese vases that had belonged to her grandmother, etchings of animals, vintage chairs and tables that she scavenged from the shops up in Brimfield. There was a purity to this effort that she had never known, making a life for herself out of nothing. Slowly the house took shape, became itself. They tore up the carpeting to expose the original floors and added a sunroom on the western side where Sarah could read and knit. Paul liked to swim, so they bought the empty lot next door and cleared away the honeysuckle and put in a pool behind a whitewashed lattice fence. She would sit on a wicker sofa by the pool under a pergola covered with wisteria with a glass of wine in her hand and watch him swim laps, quietly cheering him on and trying to understand what gave him such energy, what could be so important as to make him want to be away from this place, from her. They got a dog, an ungovernable black Lab they named Box, to keep her company there at the end of the lane.

She began to drink more, to appreciate wines; she would empty a bottle in an evening whether Paul was there or not. It imbued her with a great serenity, she found, a great deep thoughtless peace. She took up plein air painting, then running; she and Box would leave the house near dusk, the scent of jasmine in the air, the metronomic pace of her footsteps on the gravel back roads like the soothing beat of a great heart, the dog running by her side, tireless. They would run for an hour or so, or until she knew she would sleep well that night, after her wine. She grew thin and strong, ready for the next act of her life.

Over the years the house had become a jewel; friends from the city were always thrilled to be invited there. They slept in the guest rooms overlooking the pool, and she learned to cook for them, how to dress a table, how to entertain. It was in the bedroom upstairs after one such dinner, after the final guest had driven off and she'd had too much to drink, that she'd finally had the courage to tell Paul that she wanted a child, and it was there that he confessed to her that nothing frightened him more than being responsible for bringing another life into this world. She had felt like someone afloat in a warm ocean under a beautiful night sky who knows she lacks the strength to reach land; everything benign and beautiful, everything fatal. And it was in the garden behind the house, glorious with peonies and jasmine on a day in her late thirties, where she stood with her back to the sun and the phone to her ear and heard her father remind her that life is not a dress rehearsal, that if she was unhappy, she needed to make a change.

–

After she married Conrad, Sarah always lit a *yahrzeit* candle on the anniversary of her father's death, as she'd learned from an aunt that George Bergman had been, in fact, a Jew. She hadn't been particularly surprised and began to wonder what else she didn't know about her own family, whether Robert really had been gay, whether her sister was too. These gaps in her own story frightened her. "Don't look back," she often said to Conrad. That was the lesson she drew from her past. But it's one he never learned.

5

IT WAS A TIME of life that Conrad dimly recognized as the passing chance that it was, and took it.

Madeleine was about to graduate from law school, and he was living in the apartment on Gramercy Park, working late, and eating dinners alone. The neighborhood was just beginning to be gentrified, and there were small places to eat where a solitary man was made to feel welcome; white tablecloths, good food, a cold martini brought quickly. He would read an associate's memo by candlelight, mark up a document over a glass of wine and something from the fish market downtown. There was a luxuriousness to this solitude that he resisted, since he believed in marriage and family as the way life should be lived. But he also foresaw that it would pass, and had the inkling that he would look back on those days as the secret treasure they were, a great interregnum, an ellipsis between two marriages, when the world opened up to let him in.

When Madeleine was a child, he'd arranged scuba instruction for her at a smelly YMCA downtown with the thought that diving with her would allow him the watchful presence that he'd been denied for most of her life. Now, over her spring breaks and after her summer internships were done, he took her diving in Hawaii or Belize or Bermuda, staying in the sort of places he might have taken her mother or, later, would take Sarah. On the long flights and in the restaurants when they arrived, people would look at them in a slightly scandalized way, as though Conrad might be dating too far out of his age bracket. It saved them that she dressed like a student and they looked so much alike.

She was at that perfect age one never recognizes when it is being lived, the moment only a parent sees. On her certification dive in Belize, eighty feet down, Conrad knelt like a supplicant on the sandy seabed, hands crossed like a martyr, utterly still, breathing in the conscious way one does underwater, and watched as the dive master had her remove her tanks and mask and then put them back on again and clear the mask, all with the languid calm of a lover. Their breaths visible, loud as surf in their ears, the deep, slow breath of the dreamer, the mystic, the slow metronome of life in air. Tracers of sun from the distant surface like the rays of light through thunderclouds, like the light planned by long-dead men to fall on cathedral floors. They drifted, never touching, conscious of the other's place.

They celebrated her impending graduation from law school with a dinner at La Grenouille; Conrad had invited her mother and stepfather, but they wanted nothing to do with his fatherly sentimentality. The high ceilings with their pink glow, giant urns sprouting enormous bouquets, the assuring calm of the waiters in their tuxes. Madeleine was dressed in a masculine suit and had cut her hair short, her face less like her father's by then, more womanly, her manner more confident, a bit brash, unimpressed with the world. The maître d' seated them with a smile and addressed her sardonically as "Madame." They were side by side in a banquette, looking out into the big room, leaning together to murmur commentary on the other patrons, the wealth and presumption of Manhattan parading before them. They talked of her anxieties about the working world, her wish to have a family of her own, and he groped for the exotic syntax of loving a grown daughter, pretending to read the menu through a thin veil of tears.

It was not long after that Conrad met Sarah Stinson. The two events would always be linked in his mind, since the occasion was another expensive dinner, this one in the home of Mitch Jeffries, one of the senior partners of Mason & Gannett who thought of himself, not incorrectly, as a Brahmin of old New York society and who liked to have younger partners and their wives up for an evening at his estate in Ardsley. The house was vast and lit up like an ocean liner on a sea of green, its broad lawn running down through a corridor of trees to the great river's edge. There were five couples and Conrad in the chandeliered dining room around an impeccably restored, thick-legged oak table that Mitch claimed had belonged to Lafayette, the men in sport jackets and ties, the women in cocktail dresses. As the only single man, Conrad was seated between the host's leonine wife, Frieda, a former district court judge whose frame loomed ever larger from the ankles up, topped by an enormous lacquered black helmet of hair; and Sarah, so slight as to be almost unnoticed in a green dress that plunged a bit in front, across from her husband, Paul Stinson, a sleek, sardonic litigator who Conrad knew only noddingly from partners' meetings. Paul had had a couple of martinis, one of which sat in front of him next to an untouched glass of Ornellaia. His eyes flitted up and down the table, reckoning relationships, hierarchies, who liked whom: a tactician's eyes. He rarely spoke, playing off something someone else had said, careful to have the last word. His wife was the opposite: guileless, questioning, leaning into conversations with a smile that dimpled her chin. They were one of those couples you could imagine in bed but not in the kitchen.

"What's Madeleine up to these days, Connie?" asked Frieda, trying to keep the single man engaged in the proceedings. She'd written a letter of recommendation for Madeleine when she applied to law school and had asked after her ever since.

"She graduates this April. She hopes you'll come."

"We'll see. I'm getting too old to come into the city. Then what?"

"One of the downtown firms, I think. She hasn't committed to anyone yet."

"Are there any downtown firms anymore?" she asked rhetorically. "She wouldn't dream of M and G, I'm sure." A thick band of hair had come loose from her coif and dangled distractingly over her plate of veal marsala.

"Dear, I wouldn't *let* her dream of M and G," said Conrad. "I can't imagine a worse fate for a child than to be in the same firm as her father."

"Hell, that's how I started," Frieda said with sudden intensity, holding the errant lock of hair in one hand and her fork in the other. An enormous emerald protruded from a ring on her forefinger. "I had to leave eventually, but it wasn't a bad way to start. Of course this was in the dark ages when there were no women in law firms."

"You were friends with Ruth Bader Ginsburg, right?"

"Connie, please. I'm not *that* old. She taught one of my classes at Columbia," she said with mock indignation.

Conrad laughed, pretending he knew it all along. "Con law, I hope?"

"Contracts, actually," Frieda said, smiling. "She's a better judge than she was a law professor. She was too quiet. I used to sit up front because we could barely hear her." She paused. "But she did help me get my first clerkship, so I love her forever, despite her politics."

This happened often, the presumption that everyone around a table shared the same ideology.

"Pardon me. Conrad?" He turned from Frieda Jeffries' craggy, bespectacled face to find Sarah Stinson touching his arm with a tiny, perfectly formed hand. It was like emerging from a dim room into full sunlight; he blinked.

"Did I hear you say your daughter is graduating from law school?" There was delighted awe in her voice.

"Yes. From NYU, this spring. Very gratifying. Her name is Madeleine."

"That's so wonderful, congratulations. You don't look old enough to have a daughter graduating from anywhere. You must be very proud."

"I am." He could only nod and smile, so truly pleased did she seem. She would always seem to him unlike other women in this way, without any instinct for emotional disguise.

"Paul and I have no children." She took a sip of wine and glanced her husband's way. "I can't imagine what it must be like to see one fully grown and off into the world like that, but it must be one of life's greatest joys."

He could think of nothing clever to say, and nodded and looked at her, wanting to see her smile again. "Certainly one of the best things I've ever done was to be her father. Not that I did it very well."

She watched Conrad eat for a moment as though this were an unexpected talent. A roar of laughter went up from the far end of the table, Mitch Jeffries telling a golf joke, Paul Stinson barking something clever in response. She looked that way, looked back. "I'll bet if I asked her, she'd say you did wonderfully well."

"Please don't. I want to retain as many of my illusions as possible," he said. "That's one of the advantages of not having children. No one to tell you how wrong you've always been about your own past."

"Yes," she said. "I can see how children wouldn't leave much room for illusion. And where would we be without it? Every marriage depends on it, don't you think?" Another sip, another smile. He smiled back, waiting. "If you're childless, you think you're the end of the line," she said. "You're what everything led up to. If you have a child, you're reminded that you're just a part of a much longer story." Her hand remained firmly on his arm as though to convince him of something.

Jefferies had hired limousines to take the city dwellers back into town, and Conrad shared one with a very drunk couple, a tax partner and her husband who lived on the Upper West Side and fell immediately asleep as the car pulled away from the big blazing house into the arboreal darkness. The long glide through the hushed, shuttered suburbs along the river, and then the bridges, and finally the staccato of lights along FDR Drive, staring out the window remembering the moment when he said goodnight to Paul and Sarah Stinson and bent to kiss her on the cheek and instead learned that she was one of those women who would have none of that, and turned her head at the last moment so that his mouth met hers. They'd ducked away in opposite directions, waving.

He took more interest in Paul Stinson after that, said hello to him in the hallways of the firm and watched for ways to refer work to him. The two men began to sit at the same table at the monthly partners' dinners at the Yale Club and play cards and smoke cigars together afterward, falling into conversation on the sidewalk as they waited with their vouchers for the cars to take them home. Having nothing in common at work, their talk was about the city: the new restaurants and shows, what exhibit had opened at the MoMA, where to find the best sushi, how high the rents had become.

"You ought to come up to Dobbs Ferry," Paul said one night as they parted. "We'll take you to a great new French place, better than any place in the city. Bring your daughter."

He hadn't thought Paul knew he had a daughter. "She's never available, but I'd love it." And they were gone into their separate lives.

Late fall, dusk ebbing, Madeleine and Conrad on the northbound train along the Hudson, leaves falling in great yellow clouds from the trees on the banks of the river. A Friday night, the work of the week over, her first month at her law firm ending, the newness of all of it bubbling out of her, the long hours, the odd coworkers, the partners, cautious, thorough men like her father. Her mother had of course heard all this already; they talked every day, had murmured constantly to each other since the day she was born.

Lawyers of all stripes had become more interesting to her now that she was working in a firm, and Paul Stinson was someone they all read about in the legal press. He'd recently been on the cover of *The American Lawyer*, having won a victory over the Justice Department in a huge antitrust suit against one of the country's biggest telecoms.

"He's a bit of an odd duck," Conrad explained in the fading light of the crowded car. "He's aloof from everyone, but I guess you have to be once you're that well known. Not that I know him all that well. I think he's a frustrated artist. When he's not at the office, he's up at the Met. Or so his secretary says."

"Maybe he's got a mistress, ever think of that?"

"Lord, I hope not. His wife is the sweetest thing in the world. Why do you always have to be so cynical? It's sad in someone so young."

"Because it's the safest bet, Dad. How do you know she's sweet? Do you know her?"

"Only met her once, but believe me. Sweetness all the way through. You don't find it anymore."

"I've noticed this about you," she said with a finger in the air. "You always assume women are nicer than they really are. That's what got you into trouble with Mom."

"You'll like Sarah," he said to close the subject.

"I'm sure I will."

There are nights, he'd learned, when life pours itself out like a husbanded wine. The restaurant was small, half a dozen tables, the owner and chef a young Provençal Frenchman, his pretty wife the hostess, the chef's sister the only waiter, darker and less pretty but more sensual with a big, pouting mouth. The tables in simple white linen, the menu in chalk on a wheeled blackboard, lace on the windows looking out onto the river. Paul with his hair still wet and slicked back from an afternoon swim, looking more like the head of an acting studio than a lawyer, relaxed and tan and self-satisfied; Madeleine was instantly intrigued. Sarah, rather startlingly transformed into a redhead since the night at the Jeffries', in turn focused on Madeleine as though she were the only one at the table, dipping her head to murmur to her conspiratorially.

Dinner came, exquisite, classic: bouillabaisse, a mesclun salad with zucchini flowers, breast of duck in a lavender sauce, tiny vegetables delicately arranged, a Côtes du Luberon that the chef had chosen at Paul's request. The sister, whose name was Clarisse, decanted it tableside with great sardonic flourishes.

"It is like we are in Avignon, *oui*?" she asked as she poured.

"Better than that," Conrad said. He waited for Sarah to raise a fork and then tasted the duck, closed his eyes.

"I told you," Paul said quietly.

There had been a bit of a controversy after the presentation of the menu, when Clarisse had carefully explained in her partial English that certain dishes, like the duck, were masculine, and others, like the salt-crusted sea bass, were more feminine. Sarah beamed, delighted at this information, but Madeleine visibly reddened.

"How can the French think that a plate of food is masculine or feminine? It's so sexist!" she said after Clarisse withdrew with their orders. "What, the heavier foods are masculine, and the lighter ones feminine? Is this so we maintain our figures?"

"Now, Maddie," Conrad said, "give her a break. She just got off the plane."

"It's a language thing," Paul said benignly. "When you name the world with masculine or feminine nouns, as you do in the Romance languages, you begin to believe that's their actual nature. And it carries over to everything: food, books, furniture, wines. It's charming, really."

"It's an expression of their passion for life," Conrad said grandly, waving his wineglass around. "If she didn't care, she wouldn't try to teach us."

"I don't want to be taught when I go out to dinner, though," said Madeleine. "Certainly not about masculinity and femininity."

"Seems like a perfect time for the subject to me," Conrad said. "Clarisse can teach me anything she wants." Madeleine whacked his arm. Sarah giggled.

"She certainly helped me," Sarah said. "Though I think she was making it all up to be nice to us clueless Americans who have no idea what we want."

She was precisely what she appeared to be. What at first seemed a studied kindness was in fact all and everything she had to give. Looking across the table at her sitting next to his daughter, Conrad felt the world shift suddenly, like a great lock falling open.

Later, when the place had emptied, the chef-owner came from the back, and he and his sister drew up chairs and sat with them, and opened a bottle of Armagnac. His wife, he explained, had had to go home to check on the children. Paul responded with something in French, and they were suddenly off on a long, detailed conversation of startling fluency. Listening, ignored, Conrad looked around the table. Double worlds sprang open in his imagination, of the conjugal life of this young chef and his days at market in the mornings and in bed for long afternoons with his young wife, the palpable jealousy of the sister who lived with them, the children growing up amid the strangeness of America; and of Paul, perhaps more involved in all of that than they knew, perhaps funding the restaurant, perhaps involved with the sister. The vapors of the Armagnac flooded him. Sarah watched carefully. She leaned over as her husband chatted on in French.

"They sent him to the Paris office for two years after he first joined the firm," she whispered, picking up Conrad's hand and holding it under the table while Madeleine glanced back and forth between them. "I have no idea what they're saying either."

On the train back to the city, a bit drunk, Conrad and his daughter agreed it had been a fine evening, one of the best dinners ever, anywhere, and that Paul and Sarah were a peculiar match, looking well together but seeming to be from different worlds, as though their pairing had been devised for effect by someone who knew neither of them well.

"Sarah likes you a lot," Madeleine said, her head against the window strobed with light, the shabby car empty.

"She'd had too much to drink."

"She does drink too much," she said. "But she likes you."

Months passed before Conrad saw Sarah Stinson again. A brilliant spring day, steel blue behind the Midtown buildings, the city rousing itself from winter, the sidewalks along Madison Avenue choked at lunchtime. They met at a little place in the seventies, Collette's, that served only soufflés and salads. It was crowded and noisy; in his annoyance at the close quarters, he ate too quickly and burned his tongue. He remembered not a word of what was said, only that she seemed to have dressed more carefully than was called for. And that afterward, on the sidewalk, the sun blazing down as she looked up at him, shielding her eyes with her small hand, she had said, "I would do anything for you, you know." He almost laughed and then caught himself, seeing the pain in her face.

He kissed her glancingly on the mouth and watched her walk away in her tailored pink suit and hurried back to his office and sat at his desk unmoving, empty of thought. It was only when the phone rang and he reached to answer it that he saw his hand was shaking.

—

They were married two years later in Gramercy Park, the iron gate on the east side of the fabled square opened with his own key, the ceremony allowed only by special petition to the trustees of the park, a fusty band who insisted it last for only a half hour, and that much allowed only because he was a resident of the square. A cloudy day in deep summer, threatening rain, warm as the tropics, breezy, the leaves of the huge old oaks turning their silvery undersides toward the sky. Sarah in a lavender dress that went below her knees, heels that sank in the gravel paths of the park, pearls he had bought for her on a trip to St. Barts. Megan and Vince were there, and Madeleine, and the Jeffries, a dozen partners and friends. Paul Stinson had moved to LA to run the firm's office there, and that had been the end of that; there were rumors at the office that he'd promptly remarried, but Conrad didn't repeat this to Sarah. No one of the circle they would later count as closest friends was present, as they knew none of them yet. It was the first time Megan and Sarah met face to face, and though he'd worried about the moment, when it came Sarah beamed at his ex-wife, and they fell into each other's arms like long-separated siblings.

Sarah kept the house in Dobbs Ferry and they spent weekends there in the summer by the pool under the elms, though Conrad never felt comfortable in Paul's former bedroom and preferred the city. They went occasionally to the little French restaurant; the place had become known and reservations were hard to get, though never for them, who were remembered there as friends of Paul Stinson.

When he would tell this story to the friends they were to make, Sarah would protest that the suit she wore that day in Collette's had been plum rather than pink, and that the idea for the lunch had been hers.

6

HE WAS IN CHICAGO for meetings with an airline when the phone rang in the hotel room. It was his mother, who'd called his office in New York and demanded that she be told how to reach him.

"David . . ." she said, then stopped. For Helen Burrell, a deeply reserved woman, to utter his father's name over the phone as if he were an acquaintance was a sudden and unwelcome intimacy, like the time when, as a six-year-old, he'd stumbled into their bedroom one night and caught her naked.

"David died last night," she said finally. "It was an aneurysm."

He was dead by the time they got him to the hospital. He was eighty-six, Conrad's mother a few years younger. He could hear that she was weeping in what he assumed was shock rather than actual grief; theirs was a marriage that had gone on too long.

"Have you told Walt?" he asked, staring out over the lakefront, the plains beyond the city, not knowing what else to say.

"No, I was hoping you'd do that," she said.

"Mom, that's not my place. You need to call him."

"All right. In a while."

He pictured his mother alone in the old house in Western Pennsylvania that he'd advised them not to buy. It was broken down and in need of paint, the wiring unreliable, the naked oak floors splintering, in the pretty little town not far from where he'd lived when he and his brother were boys.

"There will be a service," she was saying with great deliberation, "at the Presbyterian church." He told her he'd be there as soon as possible, made some sounds of comfort and regret, and then hung up and called Sarah and then Madeleine, then made more calls to excuse himself from the day's meetings. Finally he called his parents' lawyer in Pittsburgh, whom he'd met when they'd executed their wills, and asked that his father's estate documents be sent to him. He knew what they said—everything to his mother and, on her death, to him and his brother equally—but now he wanted to hold the pieces of paper in his hands.

His father's father had died when his father was a teenager growing up in Glasgow, Scotland, a fact about which he and his brother were too cowed to ask. His mother, on the other hand, was a shrill and, to Conrad's eyes, rather unbalanced woman who lived into her nineties, giving his father the opportunity to ignore her for more than half her life. Whatever had happened—or not happened—between his father and grandfather, it had not passed down a warm family feeling.

Upon her husband's death, Conrad's grandmother threw herself on the mercy of relatives in America, who resentfully passed her and her son around from household to household up and down the Eastern Seaboard until they washed up at the home of her uncle, a successful Chevrolet dealer in Birmingham, Alabama. Uncle Angus was quite well-off enough to have no trouble supporting these two freeloaders, but parsimonious enough to resent it deeply all the while, and to make sure they knew it. Eventually, as the country was clawing its way out of the Great Depression, he allowed his nephew to earn tuition for his bachelor's degree in theater by working at one of his less profitable Chevy franchises, the one on the Black side of town, thus turning young David Burrell into a Ford-loving bigot in a single stroke.

So it was that Conrad's father came to adulthood, and to his sweetheart Helen, without a clue as to how a husband or father might behave, or what a real home might feel like, but he concealed this deficit behind a carefully constructed façade of salesman's joviality and thespian bombast that she took, tragically, for warmth. After a courtship that Helen dutifully persisted in portraying in winsomely romantic terms until his death, David Burrell proceeded to go about the machinations of an adult life that he fundamentally loathed, selling first his uncle's cars, then auto parts for a Pittsburgh steel fabricator, and finally high-performance tires made by a big Midwestern conglomerate, all the while wishing he could quit and open up a little theater company somewhere. In the last twenty years of what he ruefully referred to as his "employment days," he came to specialize in "aviation rubber," as he called it at cocktail parties, which meant airplane tires. Hence his family eventually moved from Pittsburgh to Long Beach, California, to be close to the Douglas Aircraft Corporation, and later to Monterrey, Mexico, where he learned to sell airplane tires to Aeromexico in very bad Spanish.

Helen, a Jersey girl who'd never been west of the Mississippi, loved California and never wanted to leave. She'd take her sons to the ocean on days when her husband was away or working late, taught them to swim and eat sushi. On arriving home at night, David would make himself a martini or two and fall asleep right after supper in a chair that she had strategically placed in the dining room for that very purpose. Walt and Conrad would clear the table and then burst outside into the gathering desert dusk, happy to be free and unnoticed by him in general.

Occasionally he'd take a vagrant interest in one of them and take them along on his calls, which entailed driving up and down Route 1 in his "company car," a Pontiac Super Chief, visiting the airfields and schmoozing the Douglas procurement personnel. The boys would stand in the open hangers, enormous beyond their imaginings, and look up at the gleaming fuselages, the props big as windmills, awed not so much by the uses to which such machines might be put as by the machines themselves, so sleek and huge and mutely powerful.

Conrad outgrew this romance with aircraft, but Walt was a goner from the start. All his imaginary play revolved around dogfights, crash landings, and the pursuit of altitude records in experimental planes like the X-15, which was making the news. Every penny of his allowance was spent, often in advance, on model aircraft of every stripe, from World War I biplanes to modern commercial airliners like the bizarre, whalelike, double-decker Viscount, or the majestic, sinuous Lockheed Constellation. He'd cement one together in a few hours of intense, hunchbacked work in their bedroom, hang it from picture wire strung across the ceiling, and by bedtime be lusting after the next one he planned to buy. In his teens he turned to the infinitely more difficult motorized model planes, simpler in design but harder to build because they were actually supposed to fly. Each was constructed of balsa wood, tissue paper, and carefully applied lacquer, so numbingly laborious in detail as to actually depress Conrad as he lay on the upper tier of their bunk bed and watched Walt from above as he worked, his X-Acto knife slowly carving out the small, fragile pieces of flimsy wood that would form the thing's intricate endoskeleton. Finally he'd attach an oily little kerosene engine to the nose, take it out to the empty lot across the street, and have Conrad release it into a tight, dizzying orbit with Walt at the center, clutching the tether wire and turning, turning in place as his brother ducked out of the way. "Dumb," Conrad would mutter as he backed away from the scene, though he was secretly proud of his brother, who would eventually become a commercial pilot and then a salesman like their father, taking rich men on joyrides in the private jets they were thinking of buying.

So when his plane crashed in Colorado a few months after their father died, and Conrad saw the pictures of the crumpled fuselage in the snow, he felt, in addition to the customary grief and sense of abandonment, a nagging guilt for having been his brother's accomplice in his obsession with planes and flying, and wished that he'd not been so pleased for him when he got whatever he wanted, which from Conrad's perspective was pretty much the story of his life right up to the moment when it ended.

But that was still months away when Walt flew himself and his wife and their sullen teenage boys to their father's funeral. Conrad met Sarah and Madeleine at Pittsburgh International and drove them down separately. Sarah smiled out the window of the rental car, delighted by the little town, its corridors of trees, its churches in white clapboard.

"It's beautiful," she said. "I could live here."

"You'd be bored, dear," Conrad said as they peered out at the cobbled streets. "And the winters are terrible." Madeleine sat in back, ignoring them and tapping on one of the new pagers Conrad had considered getting; it seemed ridiculous for someone so young.

Conrad was the elder son, the one whose work involved words, and Walt wanted nothing to do with the eulogy. His challenge in delivering it was to avoid the sentimentality that would have made a liar out of him and a caricature out of his father, while somehow honoring the man, the artist who had ended up a salesman. Already his mother had repressed her memory of most of their rather fractious marriage, during which she'd increasingly assumed the mantle of caretaker and disciplinarian, preventing her husband from drinking as much as he would have liked. Her recollections were now focused on early scenes of his courtly pursuit of her, his thwarted theatrical pursuits, his love of Shakespeare, his natty wardrobe. It was an act of hagiography that Conrad found almost as charming as it was preposterous. Not that these things weren't true of David Burrell, but so much had been edited away. Conrad remembered too well the violent temper, the black moods of the man sitting at the dinner table with his eyes closed and his jaw working at his food, shutting out the disappointing world. He was older than Conrad's friends' fathers and had no interest in sports, so he and Walt hadn't learned any. On the other hand, he'd never raised his hand to his sons or his voice to their mother. He drank, but he didn't smoke. He could be loud and volatile, but he was never vulgar. There are worse things, Conrad thought, to say about a man.

Sarah, Madeleine, and Conrad's mother sat in the front pew while he stood in the pulpit and spoke of his father in factual terms: childhood in the old country, college at what was then called Western Reserve in Cleveland, love of the theater, attempts at writing plays, a late marriage to Helen, the many friends of their young suburban lives, some of whom sat before him in the pews as old men and women. He looked out over them and recited from memory a passage from one of his father's favorite poems:

> *Life is real! Life is earnest!*
> *And the grave is not its goal;*
> *Dust thou art, to dust returnest,*
> *Was not spoken of the soul.*

He told the old family story that when he was a toddler, his father would trot him out in front of dinner guests to recite these lines, and he felt a kind of rueful symmetry in reciting them again as an adult and at his father's funeral, to finally join those vacant, memorized words to their actual meaning after their long servitude to David Burrell's sense of theater. Madeleine held her grandmother's hand, looking so much like her that it made his eyes brim; the congregation thought the tears were for his father. Walt, mere months from joining him in oblivion, looked up at Conrad from the pews, his face a mixture of incredulity and relief.

Only after they had returned to New York would it dawn on Conrad: they should have had bagpipes.

Six months later, Walt's plane crashed with him at the controls, trying to land in a snowstorm in Telluride with a group of skiing buddies, all of whom were killed as well, making six sudden widows, a dozen fatherless children, and a heap of tangled metal just short of the runway. It was then that Conrad became gifted with a compulsive imagination about death, a need to visualize the private final moments of others, to understand what the end must be like, to make it real and somehow intelligible. He imagined his brother's struggle as the plane went down, determination turning to panic as control slipped away, the silence or shouting in the cabin, depending on what those men were like, how they'd learned to present themselves to the world and one another, and no time to unlearn it. He imagined silence.

In another few years, he was sitting in his office immersed in a document when the call came from his mother's doctor, a man of Conrad's age. A bad cold had worsened into pneumonia, potentially lethal to a woman of eighty-six. She'd been hospitalized, and her doctor thought Conrad should come. He went alone, thinking he'd be back the next day.

Again the short flight to Pittsburgh, the drive through the suburbs. The grid of the little town on a late fall day, sun lancing between heaped clouds, leaves piled on the curbs. In the small hospital the nurses and orderlies were solicitous, the doctor respectful. Fellow professionals, standing in a brightly lit hallway, discussing how things should proceed.

"We've had to put her on a ventilator," one of them said, "but I assume you don't want any heroic measures taken."

It was only then that he realized what was happening. "No, no heroic measures," he said numbly. He'd read his mother's living will and knew her wishes from her own mouth: Helen wouldn't want to live like a vegetable; Helen wouldn't want to be poked with needles and manhandled by orderlies. She would rather be dead.

He stood over her, bent and kissed her forehead, papery and cool. She slept on. Her thin arm was bruised where an intravenous needle had been inserted; even this struck him as brutal. He sat by the bedside, stroked her steel-gray hair as she would never have permitted in all their long lives. In that moment, as he never had before, he longed for his brother's company, someone to share this with, this strange new nakedness, and he wept at his absence for the first time. He saw that his entire life had been conducted in the shelter of his parents' and his brother's existence in the world, and saw that time would enter through the needle in his mother's arm, and that he had somehow failed to anticipate that this would happen, that it could not be stopped.

He convinced Madeleine to go with him to San Francisco, and on a blustery Mother's Day they drove a few miles south and west to where the peninsula meets the edge of the Pacific. He had a particular place in mind, one he'd visited during his California days, one his mother had never seen but he'd imagined showing her one day, before she'd forgotten their life together on this coast. The drive followed the ridge of the coastal hills, fog continually cresting over them from the west and dissipating to the east, cedars looming over them, rocking in the breeze. They parked in a nature reserve and for two hours climbed a high hill that stretched upward into the headlands. It was an arduous climb, but from its peak they turned west and looked out over the Pacific, turned east and took in all of San Francisco Bay and, beyond, the green continent from which they'd all come. "It's perfect," Madeleine said. The day glistened; the wind beat at their backs; their breaths came in deep draughts. They pulled his mother's ashes from a knapsack and scattered them where they stood, the long grasses swallowing the grey flakes like rain, lost in a second, taken into the earth as though they had never been.

Far over the horizon in the little Pennsylvania town, his parents' house stood empty.

7

LATE LIGHT SLANTING THROUGH the kitchen windows, the smell of spices and chopped onion, Sarah running her hands under hot water. She is thin and fair, her hair cut short; other women like it, they tell her, envy its ease. Knives and measuring cups surround her, cutting boards here and there covered with the ingredients of dinner, the day's first drink at hand. She is thoughtful and thoughtless, her mind spinning lightly, content. This is how he would come to remember her, but with a soft blur where her face should be, because in these remembered moments she is simply Sarah, his wife, a concept that inhabits a part of his brain where there are no pictures, just an oceanic peace. Friends say she's still beautiful, impossible to photograph unflatteringly. Her thoughts are all of people she loves, or wants to love better: Becky Sternberger, Felix McCaffrey, Meg Franklin most of all, whom she thinks of as having a heart most like her own of all the people she knows. She misses Meg even when she's seen her the day before, an odd ache that reminds her of being a little girl and yearning to go out and play.

Most of their friends are younger than they are, all married couples in the little town. Sometimes just one member of the couple or the other is close to Sarah or to Conrad, and the other can't quite ever appear or can't be stood when he or she does. Other times they are four or six people around a dinner table who all seem to be in love with each other, leaning into each other's words, and that, Sarah tells him, is as close to heaven as we're allowed on this earth. The other couples have children ready to go to college or already gone, radiant with youth, who have known Sarah and Conrad long enough to see that they love them as a facet of their love for their parents, without their parents' anxiety for them. Sarah often tells Conrad how lucky they were to have found this place, this circle, after so little in the way of friendship in the big cities on the coasts. Was it just that simple? That people didn't care there and here they did?

They joke that they like their houses old and their friends young. She wears the house around her like a favorite coat. They'd built it back from the run-down place it had been when Conrad's parents owned it, made it fit back into the old town in the way it had when it was new and the town had no sidewalks and the Civil War was about to begin. They saved all the ancient doors and floors; everything else was new but didn't look it. The house is full of things drawn from their former lives: artwork Sarah and Paul had bought when they were married, some of it old and valuable, of Paris scenes in the rain, a chaise lounge from the bedroom in the house in Dobbs Ferry that Conrad can barely remember but in which the first half of Sarah's conjugal life transpired, Persian rugs from Conrad's old office in New York that the firm let him keep, an inlaid mahogany dining table inherited from Sarah's grandmother, crystal from her mother, silver from Conrad's mother, an étagère that Megan hadn't wanted. Somehow it had all worked together, these strands of one another's lives; there had been a place for everything. The one thing Sarah misses from her former marriage is Box, the black Lab, long dead now, who had followed her everywhere and was terrified of storms. She can still feel his heavy triangular head on her knees when she sits at the mahogany table.

She is lean, almost sinewy, in silk and denim, her hands small as a child's. She goes upstairs, makes the bed. A quilt that Megan made when she was married to Conrad goes on last, its pattern dark and richly geometrical, like shattered onyx. She can't imagine having the patience to plan the design, let alone execute it. Conrad tells her that there's something incestuous about his ex-wife's blanket covering their bed, but Sarah loves the old quilt, loves the woman he married first, for giving him a daughter and occupying him until she was ready, for being so different from herself as to make jealousy seem silly.

In the mornings there are twigs and strands of dried grass on the porch outside the back door, collected at the base of the column that, like its two brothers, hold up the eaves and the porch roof and the sky. She sweeps them away, assuming they are bits of the world that the wind blew in. But the next day there's more stray vegetation at the base of the column, and she sees the mark of intention in the strands of grass and doesn't disturb them, so that after a week or so the twigs and dried bits have been elevated to the top of the column and woven into a nest. If you wait and are patient, she says, sometimes these things happen, the world orders itself. It's not all the entropy and decay that her husband tends to see.

She has lunch with Becky Sternberger and Meg Franklin and Christine McCaffrey once a week at the restaurant in the little town's inn, a relic from before the war when steel barons would spend week-ends there and golf at the country club nearby. Conrad is semi-retired, barely working, and on this frigid day has nothing better to do, so he joins them. The women are tolerant of him, let him sit in silence while they talk. He thinks of himself in these situations as a sort of honorary woman; his willingness to be led is familiar to them. The women rarely drink during these lunches but talk as if they did, one reckless trusting revelation after another, about children, their marriages, gossip of the town.

"Rex and Bea Wachtel are finally getting divorced," Meg says.

"Finally?" asks Sarah, always the last to know.

"I never knew how they made it work; he was gone all the time anyway."

"I thought they'd be married forever," Sarah says. "What on earth will they do with that house and all those cars of his?"

"Oh, he'll take the cars, and she'll get the house, and he'll move to the city," says Meg. "That's how these things go. Apparently Bea has a boy, and finally told Rex."

"A boy?" asks Sarah.

"Well, a guy of some age. Right here in town, though I don't dare ask who."

"Bob DeForest," ventures Becky, who avoids gossip but always has an opinion.

"No, he's gay, isn't he?" says Meg. "I see him at the pub with younger men all the time."

"Doesn't mean anything; he always had the hots for Bea, ever since he redid their driveway." Conrad knows this story better than the women do, having golfed with some of the male protagonists. The Wachtels had the largest home in the town, a rambling Craftsman that required constant upkeep. Bob DeForest was the biggest building contractor in their part of the state. Then he and his brother, who co-owned the company, had a dispute that meant a good deal of debt had to be prepaid to buy the brother out. Rex, one of Bob's best friends, had helped Bob pay the debt in exchange for some services, which included replacing Rex's long and winding asphalt driveway and, evidently, keeping his wife company while Rex visited his far-flung real estate investments. Did any of this matter? Not in the least. But they all knew it like the history of the republic.

"Really, ladies, this is beneath us," says Becky. "How are your beautiful boys, Meg?"

"Never hear from them, but thanks for asking. College kids don't call; they text. When I was in college I felt bad if I didn't call my parents once a week, and this was way before cell phones, of course, when you had to scrape together a lot of quarters and go down to the pay phone in the lobby of the dorm and wait your turn. Now they have these devices in their pockets but can't be bothered to speak to you."

"Hostages to fortune," Becky murmurs into her teacup.

"I've never understood that expression," snaps Meg. "Who are the hostages, them or us?"

Conrad looks around at them, beautiful women losing their looks, the lines that radiate from their eyes beginning to deepen into fissures, the pale, perfect skin of Meg's neck collapsing over tendons that protrude like ribs in the ceiling of an elegant cathedral. He loves them for the vulnerability they share, this being borne along together on the face of time. Like a good lawyer, he's always thinking ahead: he looks at Sarah and imagines her standing with him over Becky's grave on a beautiful sunny day, or Becky standing with him over Sarah's. Sarah's hands are folded on the linen tablecloth while the other women talk, like his mother's hands lying like felled birds on the sheets of her hospital bed in the weeks when she was dying. She sees him looking at her, pulls them down into her lap. The talk of others' children always stills her, though she loves them as her own, calls them her babies to their faces, which always makes them laugh.

She would have given anything for to have had a child with Conrad, but it was just barely too late, her body too unreliable, and both of them too set in their ways to recreate the world in that way. It's the one true regret of her life, though she has his daughter, and there is the chance of Madeleine becoming a mother and of Sarah's watching all that from up close. It has become her life, to watch, to help, to take pride in other people's children, to make her very barrenness a gift.

Christine McCaffrey is childless too. There is no wistfulness about it in her; she makes it a point of pride. "I forgot to have one," she'll say when she finds herself in the midst of mothers talking, and they'll all laugh, so comfortable is she with the fact. She's blonde and regal with eyes light as sand, almost as thin as Sarah, though wonderfully buxom; all the women comment on it, and the men are silently appreciative. She and Sarah are often mistaken for sisters and when left to their own devices will act like teenagers, taking turns farting as they walk down the street arm in arm. "We'll be old bag ladies together," Christine would say. "A bag lady alone is a sad thing, but a bag lady with a friend is a party in the park." Sarah has noticed that Christine calls something or other a "party in the park" all the time; it must be an echo from somewhere in her youth, from some lost lexicon, something she mistakenly thinks everyone says. She, too, had lived in Manhattan, though long after Sarah and Paul did. She had met and married Felix McCaffrey there when they were both working in the muni bond department at Goldman Sachs back in the roaring nineties when, as Conrad says, Western civilization reached its high-water mark, though nobody knew it then.

Sarah had learned the quirky vectors of friendship in the little town, how some women don't socialize with others for reasons no one speaks of. She's realized that some of her friends don't spend time with Christine because of something she said or did in the past, something Sarah doesn't particularly want to know. It's not that Christine isn't liked, just that no one makes the effort to be with her. Sarah has trouble accepting that they all can't be together at once, since she loves them all. She'll make up guest lists for dinner and Conrad will have to remind her that so-and-so doesn't get along with so-and-so, and that therefore there would have to be two dinners, or none at all. She knows that men don't have these scruples; they can always find something to say to each other, even if it's only about sports. She reasons that this is because men's hearts are elsewhere, that they don't make any new friends after childhood, but learn in their offices simply not to make enemies.

Christine's husband, Felix, is a bit of a mystery to Sarah. He travels a lot and works in some aspect of finance that isn't clear even to Conrad. He almost never shows up with Christine at a party; people joke that he's with the CIA. Sarah allows herself to think that he's the most handsome of all the men they know. At dinners he's always to one side with a scotch in hand, talking with one of the women.

"Felix and I are giving up alcohol for Lent," Christine announces to the group. "Last week we got pulled over by the highway patrol, and I thought for sure we were going to jail."

Sarah stares at her, equally appalled by the idea of giving up alcohol and the idea of Christine getting arrested. "Did I tell you about the time I went to jail?" she asks, glancing at Conrad to see if he will try to stop her.

"I was in Santa Fe and got stopped coming back from a party. Paul was on a trip somewhere. The cop—he was a young jerk, full of himself—made me walk the line, and I did it perfectly, but he said I'd flunked it and wanted me to blow into the breath thing . . ."

"Breathalyzer," corrects Becky. "When is this?"

"Right, and I refused. This is fifteen years ago. I remembered Paul telling me that you didn't have to do that unless you'd actually been arrested, which I hadn't. So they take me to the station and they want to take a blood test, and I refused again. So they put me in jail."

"Oh, my God, Sarah. What was it like?" asks Meg.

"Did you call Paul?" is what Conrad wants to know, feeling cobwebby fraternity with his ex-law partner and his wife's ex-husband.

"Of course I used my one call to try to reach him, and of course he was in some Asian time zone. So I left a message on his cell and they put me *in* a cell. Just an ugly little room, kind of like a dorm room, with no window and the toilet down the hall; you had to use this awful phone on the wall to call someone if you had to pee." She holds her thumb to her ear and her little finger to her mouth. "My main memory is of this other girl who'd been picked up for vagrancy or something, young girl, maybe sixteen, and how badly she smelled and how she cried the whole time. I'm in my de la Renta so she thinks I'm from Mars. I wanted to comfort her, but I don't think we exchanged five words all night."

The other women are transfixed. They all know she drinks. Earlier that week Conrad had suggested that perhaps she needed to cut back. She vaguely remembers that that night he'd had to help her up to bed.

"But how awful," Christine says. "When did you get out?"

"They let me go the next day. I had to get the car out of some awful compound and went home and took a two-hour bath. Of course the point was I was going to lose my driver's license, so we had to go to court. Paul was furious about the legal fees."

"Did you win?" Conrad asks.

"The cop never showed up to testify, so they had to dismiss it. Luckiest day of my life. More or less."

"Dear God," says Meg.

"I've often wondered what happened to that girl, though."

8

THEY GO TO ALL Souls Episcopal in the little town, two hundred years old, spare, almost Quaker in its simplicity. A small latched door guards the entrance to each pew, which Sarah finds deeply comforting, as though that tiny barrier would protect them from everything. The choir is composed of high school students and retirees. There aren't enough of them, and Conrad has thought of joining just to fill out their ranks, though he can't carry a note. The priest is a vivacious little man with a crew cut who introduces himself at every service by saying that he's a sinner and he'll be leading them in prayer that day. Conrad appreciates the sentiment but Sarah finds it a bit too flippant for church. She drops her chin and crosses herself and genuflects slightly as the cross goes by, holds his hand as they recite the Nicene Creed, the Lord's Prayer, the Confession of Sins.

The sermon is full of abstruse metaphors usually lost on Conrad; his mind wanders to others in the pews—Becky Sternberger and her husband, Stu, and their teenaged boys; Agatha Webber, beautiful and reserved and startlingly tall, and her lawyer husband, John, and their daughter and son, who occasionally come here when their Baptist church in the next county seems too far away; Fran Templeton, the aging doyenne of the town, who's called The Dowager behind her back. Conrad thinks they really must have Fran over sometime before she dies.

Time is light in their hands. The day is long, the hour is over; they walk the two blocks home, and Sarah goes back to planning the evening, when Becky and Stu are coming to dinner along with Christine and Felix McCaffrey. It's her favorite mix of couples; each person seems to like all the others. There's even a bit of sexual frisson between Christine and Stu, though Conrad says she's imagining it. There will be rack of lamb, a salad Becky will bring, and some root vegetables Conrad has promised to prepare.

But the evening is different than they expected, Becky not at all her usual unconquerable self, brooding over her eldest son who has just announced in his junior year that he wants to drop out of college, Stu almost manically animated as if in compensation, Christine and Felix strangely quiet, almost spectators. Conrad is reminded of the delicate chemistry of friendships, the intricate minuets of long-married couples. Sipping his wine, he recalls a book he'd read when Sarah and he were engaged, which suggested that every marriage has seasons like the seasons of the year, some persistent enough to seem permanent, just before they change.

After dinner Sarah serves the coffee and drifts behind Becky, stopping to bend down and kiss her on the top of her head. Becky reaches up to her. They can think of nothing to say about her boy, whom they've known for years. Christine has roused herself to tell a story, intended to comfort Becky, about a niece who stayed in school at the insistence of Christine's brother, finished college as directed, but then immediately eloped with a man her parents had never met, left the country, and had not been heard from since.

"Damned if you do and damned if you don't," concludes Christine. "As far as I can see from my position of happy inexperience, you can't possibly control what your children do."

"No, you can't," says Becky. "We raised them to question authority, and that turns out to include their parents."

"*Never take advice, including this,*" Stu quotes, extending his glass toward the last of the wine. "It's the family motto." Christine, seated next to him, leans over to rub his back in sympathy and keeps it up as the conversation goes on. Conrad feels a twinge of vicarious jealously at her easy intimacy with someone else's spouse; Sarah wouldn't do it in front of him.

"It's no tragedy," says Becky. "It's not as though he's become a drug addict or wants to marry someone wrong for him. My God, what a first-world problem to have, that your son merely wants to drop out of college."

"But you can't help but remember all the pain and suffering he and we went through to get him in," says Stu. "None of it was a waste, but I just wish he'd decided this two years ago." They all laugh. He moves his shoulders sympathetically with the massage Christine is giving him.

"Before you dropped eighty thousand dollars," Conrad offers.

"I wish it were only eighty." They laugh again.

Sarah's eyes are on Felix McCaffrey, who has said almost nothing tonight. He looks tired and, as always, a little sad, his arm draped across Becky's chair as he listens, glancing briefly from face to face as though trying to take them all in, to understand something. She tries to think of a question that will include him, draw him in, but nothing occurs to her; the talk at the table has veered into politics, a subject she firmly believes should be avoided at dinner. Felix is in his mid-fifties, Sarah's age, but he looks older, a bit portly, like a senator or the mayor of a prosperous city, his hair thick and gone completely white, his eyes a penetrating blue, his face still smooth and pale as a birch. He's away in New York every week for his work, almost never comes to dinners like this, pleading fatigue or migraines. Sarah has said that he reminds her of her long-dead brother, but to Conrad he resembles her ex-husband, the long, soft fingers, the resonance of his voice, the persistent, impenetrable melancholy.

There is a code among all the couples in their life, unspeakable and unbreakable, and they dimly realize that they are friends, in part, because each of them believes the others all know and understand this code. To express it would be to transgress it, but it involves the old etiquette of reciprocity and care, of unquestioning service to the duties of friendship that trump convenience, and a profound trust that the boundaries of each marriage will be respected from without even more than from within. This is clear to Conrad when he thinks, as he sometimes does, how much more horrible it would be to jeopardize someone else's marriage than your own; your wife might understand, but no one who knew you less completely ever would. They openly admire one another's spouses, even flirt with them, and are admired in turn, from the safety of a deep communal belief in the sanctity of their pairings and the sufficiency of things as they are. To Conrad this isn't religious, merely practical. Part of it is the wisdom that age brings, the knowledge that desire is often best left unfulfilled, and that they've already been luckier than they could have hoped. To want more is forgivable; to take it would be greedy.

Yet he can see, as a husband will, that something about Felix touches his wife. He's handsome, yes, but only in a conventional way. It has more to do with his reserve, with his near silence. His hands are immaculately manicured, his manners fastidious. He stands when Christine enters and leaves the room, pulls the chair out for her when she sits. He appeals to Sarah, not by comparison to anyone else, and certainly not to Conrad, but in himself, like a lovely and graceful animal she might see in the wild. Occasionally, at Sarah's pleading, Felix will bring his guitar, a beautiful old gut-stringed Martin, and play something by Villa-Lobos while she fixes drinks, sitting in the next room where no one can watch him too closely. It's the road not taken for him, the last strand of a branching in the path of his youth that led him away from music and into the safer world of business. His pale skin is translucent as he bends intently over the strings. In those moments Conrad can sense that Sarah, already a bit drunk, wants to rush in and hold him in her arms, but the Main Line girl in her knows that nothing could be more pointless. That they are all together, that she gets to see him regularly, that Christine loves him more than Sarah could dare and in a way on her behalf—all this is more than enough.

"Has anyone ever been to India?" Felix asks in a lull in the conversation, apropos of nothing, and Sarah starts as though someone had called her name. She gets up quickly and goes to the kitchen to get him another scotch.

"I suppose someone has," says Christine, ever the syntax cop.

"Never," says Stu. "No desire to, really." He looks at his wife, knowing what's coming.

"I went once," says Becky. "When I was in college. Filthy. Wonderful. I almost died of dysentery. Loved every minute of it."

"I'd go in a heartbeat, but no one ever asked," says Christine, leaning back and looking at her husband.

"Have you been, Felix?" Conrad asks.

"Just recently, actually, on business, which isn't really being there. You're in a cocoon; you don't get to see anything except the inside of limousines and office buildings and hotels. I'd like to go back and smell it this time."

Becky nods knowingly. "The stench is overwhelming. And the poverty. Mobs of children clutching you, hands out everywhere. But the colors! Colors like you never see anywhere else. It's their form of wealth. My only problem with it is you end up feeling like a colonialist."

Felix turns to his wife. "I'd go again if you'd go with me," he says, accepting the scotch from Sarah, the calluses on his fingertips brushing her hand.

He turns to Becky. "What made you go there?"

Becky is smiling her ingenue smile, a specialty of hers. Sarah watches her with enormous pride, as though she were a beautiful, brilliant sister. Becky is in fact stunning tonight, carelessly sensual, in tight jeans and a cashmere sweater that clings to her breasts, her hair wild and fine. "Why a man, of course. A boy, really. He was a follower of some maharishi, and I was in love with him for at least a week in my junior year at Bryn Mawr. That was all it took. I learned more about him than about India."

"I'm sure you learned everything about him," says her husband. "A true scholar." They exchange lascivious looks, lean together, kiss.

"What does Bryn Mawr mean anyway?" asks Stu.

"It means a fine education, of course," says Becky, chortling into her drink.

"No, I mean the words *Bryn Mawr*. What a strange name. Is it Gaelic?"

"It's Welsh for 'big hills,'" says Becky, thrusting out her chest. Christine is watching Stu with an indulgent smile. They all laugh. This is Sarah's idea of heaven, these people, the long table with its empty bottles, napkins scattered like fallen leaves, the candles guttering.

They've said goodnight and locked the front door and are loading wine glasses into the dishwasher when he pulls Sarah to him and kisses her, his tongue finding hers in their familiar way. They're usually more deliberate, making appointments in the late afternoons for this, but their urgency tonight reminds Conrad of their early times, the furtive nights in the apartment on Gramercy Park, the way she would dress for what was to come, the lace and black leather and high heels. They chase each other up the stairs like cats and fall onto their wide bed in the moonlight, clothes scattered, slowing now, deliberate. He feels their separate pasts with them in this room, the near-forgotten lovers, the two people, far away, who were their first companions in marriage; all that was learned from them and given to them are present. His fingers find her there and her mouth is on him, the smell of her. Soon—she knows when it's coming—in one movement he's above and behind her, pinning her wrists to the sheets, his tongue tracing her spine. She's shouting animal syllables, and he hisses in her ear to be quiet, but she shouts anyway, and after a time, not slowing, he reminds her that that she'll scare the neighbors' children. She laughs and turns and pushes him down on his back and encloses him again and looks down at him, still beautiful, ageless, her stomach flat, her arms downy like a schoolgirl's, her mouth stark as etched marble in the moonlight. His hands are on her hips, holding her by the bend of her waist. "I'll try to be quiet," she says, moaning between words, rocking. "I'll try." In the end she's unaware that tears are streaming down her face, and when she's finished he has to pull her down to him, kissing her, holding her like a stricken child until she stills.

In the middle of the night he wakes as though from anesthesia and lies reassembling the evening, watching the patterns of the windowpanes track with celestial slowness across the walls. It's snowing again; he can hear a plow scraping a distant street. Lobos' *Concierto de Aranjuez* is running through his head, the brush of callused fingers across strings. Felix's hands. Sarah lifts her fingers to her mouth, breathes her own sweet scent.

Meg Franklin asks Sarah to join her for lunch. They meet at a sandwich shop on the edge of town, a place with jackets of old rock albums on the walls, a wine bar at one end, simple food. Meg looks old. The lines in her face have deepened, and she's put on too much makeup. She's grown heavier. There's something off about her, Sarah thinks; she's holding her body in a self-conscious way. She asks after Meg's father, who's been ill. No sooner did their children leave home than the parents of their friends have become replacement objects of anxiety, obstreperous as their children had been and as resistant to advice or help, yet incompetent to live alone.

"My mother called last week, and it was like a loop of recording tape," Meg says. "She kept telling me that she couldn't open the garage door. I said that's good, because you shouldn't be driving. She'd change the subject, and two minutes later she says all over again that she can't open the garage door."

"She's in her eighties?"

"They're both eighty-eight. No way in the world they should be driving anymore. The expiration date on all driver's licenses should be in five years or age eighty, whichever comes first."

"How's your dad doing?"

"He's fine; it was just another cold. He has prostate cancer too, but the doctors say it will kill him so slowly that he'll die before it does. No point operating. That's funny, isn't it? That we won't live long enough for a lot of things to kill us?"

Sarah doesn't trust doctors; hospitals scare her. Conrad had a prostate scare a couple of years ago; the biopsies were supposed to be minor affairs but meant weeks of blood in his urine, his semen.

"On the other hand, there's me," says Meg, looking down into her coffee. "I found a lump in my left breast a couple of months ago." It's said with the deliberation of something long prepared. "They did a needle biopsy, and it's cancerous. It needs to come out, but they want to do chemo first, so I'll be starting that soon." Her voice is steely, but the rims of her eyes have reddened suddenly; Sarah reaches across the table and takes Meg's hand from around the coffee cup and folds it into her own. Fear races through her, the memory of her mother's death, the tubes, the machines, the lethal whiteness of the hospital rooms.

"Margaret," she says softly, "I'll be with you every step of the way."

"No, I couldn't have that. I have to tell Bill." Her voice is failing.

"You haven't told him?" Sarah asks, horrified.

"Not yet. I wanted to be sure."

"But you have to tell him." Sarah tries to imagine keeping something like this from Conrad, realizes that yes, she might. His fear would only magnify her own. She finds herself wishing for a drink.

"I know, I know. I wanted to be sure, and now I am," she whispers. Sarah grips her hand.

"They don't want to do a . . ." Sarah hesitates, not wanting to utter the word.

"Mastectomy, no, not yet. They want to do the chemo first. Maybe radiation after that, we'll see. This runs in my family; my aunt died of it."

"I'll be with you. We all will be." She means for the treatments, but the words hang in the air like open arms that would embrace more; the slow dissolution, the long decline.

"I know," says Meg, freeing her hand and turning away, reaching for her bag. "I'm not so much afraid as I am angry." She's weeping now, her fingers clenching a handkerchief. She stares at Sarah. "I thought I'd done everything right. We all think we're different, don't we?"

9

SARAH'S MOTHER HAD DIED this way, but quicker. It had been too late for surgery or chemotherapy or radiation, and the doctors, smug and efficient and no older than Sarah at that point, had contented themselves with making her mother comfortable, as though that could happen in a room like that, white and blank as a stone, five degrees too cold. She kept bringing her mother's things to her in the hospital room, the playing cards, her bracelets and earrings, her glossy fashion magazines, but they only annoyed her, reminded her of life outside the room, the life that had left her behind. In the end she had Sarah take it all away.

It was her mother's final and most complete evasion, the last in a series that had included not really wanting to be pregnant, not nursing Sarah as an infant, leaving her behind with nannies while she and Sarah's father went on their month-long vacations to Bermuda, drinking too much to be able to prepare dinner for Sarah, who would then craft a meal out of cold soup from a can, sending her off to an upstate boarding school when she was only fourteen, neglecting to attend the rehearsal dinner at the Plaza the night before she married Paul. Her eyes would fill when she told Conrad of the hundred nights when she would phone her mother, far away, both of them weeping pitifully, to beg her to come home, or to allow Sarah to come home. There was always a reason why this was impossible, why both of them had to be strong. Even later, grown and loved, she was still the girl by the window, clutching a phone, left behind and willing herself to remember her mother's face.

Meg Franklin's doctors want to shrink the tumor with chemotherapy before performing surgery. They think they can save her breasts. Sarah drives her to the clinic once a week and sits with her while the machine pumps the fluid into her vein. For mysterious reasons this sometimes takes several hours, sometimes just an hour. Meg's husband is at work, her sons at college. Meg says she wouldn't want them there for this anyway. Sarah sits with one of Meg's books, usually a historical novel, and reads to her. Meg closes her eyes and sometimes seems to be asleep, but Sarah has learned to keep reading. Meg is stoic, cracking jokes about losing her hair, her breasts. Sarah laughs with her, but it seems sacrilegious. It's not so much the physical decay that troubles Sarah as the thought of no more time.

In moments like this she resents the comforts of her life that allow her to skate across the surface of the world, keep her at a distance. Her life is so easy, and the distances between sick and well, rich and poor, have become so great and can happen so suddenly that nothing can bridge them. She knits scarves for cancer patients in the local hospital, but what did that do? What if she and Conrad gave half of what they've saved to charity? What would that do? What if they gave all of it? She tells Conrad that this is what Christ would do—give all of it—and yet she know that it, too, would do nothing, the chasm is so deep. She knows this, knows that there are people out in the world who would hate her, want to hurt her, no matter how much she tried to love them. Conrad reminds her of this every so often. Still, she wants to do something to close that distance.

"Do you ever think about dying?" Meg asks during one of the chemo sessions. Her head is thrown back against the faux leather of the treatment chair, which reclines as though they were in a spa or on a transatlantic flight. Meg has not yet noticed that a patch of gray hair has come away from behind her ear, and Sarah is touching her there as though staunching a wound, deciding whether to point it out.

"I won't hear you talk like that," she hisses, looking around furtively.

"No, really. I don't mean thinking about how you might die. I actually don't think I'm going to die from this. This is too obvious. It will be something later, something unexpected. I mean what death itself is like."

Sarah stares at her. "That's just morbid, Meg—stop it."

"It is literally morbid, yes, but don't you wonder about it? Shouldn't we be allowed to wonder about it? It must be like sleep but without dreaming. Like being under permanent anesthesia. Which could be nice, I suppose, except you never come out of it. I often think about people who die in accidents. One second you're alive, thinking of loved ones, screaming probably, and the next second—what? The film ends, no credits, just blackness for eternity? Actually, that's not it either, because blackness suggests you're there to experience it. It's more than blackness; it's nothingness. It's really quite unimaginable." Her hands, which have been hovering like a question, drop into her lap.

This line of conversation makes Sarah angry. "That's because we're not supposed to imagine it."

"Well, I can't help myself; I try not to think about it, believe me. But I do." There is an oddly pleading look in Meg's face, then it sharpens. "Tell me you don't actually believe in heaven."

Sarah has wanted to say it, to put an end to this nonsense. "I do, Meg. Or something like heaven. I believe we go on in some form."

"Oh, my dear Sarah. I do love you. I forget you're a churchgoer."

"I believe we never really die."

"I know, dear, I know," says Meg, taking Sarah's hand. Tears pool in Sarah's eyes; Meg's are dry and clear. "The heaven I believe in is this one," Meg says.

"We live on in the hearts of our families," says Sarah. It comes out as a recitation, stubborn and willed.

Meg arches an eyebrow. "You must admit that's a pretty feeble way of living, wouldn't you say? I'm remembered, therefore I am?"

"You've got to have faith." She presses Meg's hand with her own.

"I do, my darling. I have faith in you."

"Faith is the assurance of things hoped for, the conviction of things unseen," Sarah recites.

"Well, I see you, and I have faith anyway. And that's from the Torah, isn't it? I thought you were a Christian." Meg is smiling, closing her eyes.

"I don't know where it's from," says Sarah. "It's true."

Afterward Sarah drives Meg home through the twilight. Magnolias have begun to bloom in the yards; daffodils are rising through the loam: the signs of spring, of Easter. Sarah is fifty-five.

10

IT'S ONE OF THOSE commonplace days before everything changes. Time, if not a friend, is at least not yet his enemy. Deep winter
on the edge of the Appalachians, new snows coming at intervals just
far enough apart to make you think that each must be the last, the
grayness threatening the soul. It will relent only when you can stand
no more, and you can always stand a little more because you're from
there, you grew up with it, stamped your feet praying for the yellow
bus that was only a degree or two warmer than the day, the bare
limbs of trees on the hills like black fissures in the sky. It was on days
like this that Conrad had Sarah remind him why they chose to live
here, what it was about the place that called to her. The little town, of
course, the stately old homes, the prim streets aligned to the cardinal
directions, the imagined lives behind the glowing windows. But it's
the people that kept them here, the friends she couldn't abandon.

The roads are clear and dry despite the night's snows. Conrad's old
Mercedes, forest green, with its license plate frame from the dealer
in San Francisco where he bought it, accelerates up the ramp to the
interstate, northbound. He loves the car, dotes on it as an embodi-
ment of memory, though it's growing old and expensive to maintain.
Like him, he thinks. The little town falls behind, its neat squares, its
churches. The highway unspools ahead, the fields and strip malls and
nameless towns streaming by on either side.

Someone's secretary in the New York office has told him what to do this day: go to a certain building in town and present himself to be interviewed for admission to the Pennsylvania bar. It's a nuisance, but necessary if he's to continue to work.

Why would anyone have settled here? he thinks. Iron and coal just beneath the grass, the trees dusted with it. Why not keep going west, out to the plains, the real mountains, out to the sun? He would have. He did. His mother's ashes are part of that hill in California where he and Madeleine scattered them, his father's bones in a graveyard he never visits, though in a few miles he can see it from the interstate. This was the life they had all lived, strewn about the continent like bits of straw.

The sun has begun its brief dolphin's leap above the horizon. He hates these mornings, fears the dark of winter mornings as though it might kill him. Without looking he always knows what time it is within a few minutes. These short days depress him; Sarah makes him take vitamin D. He can taste her lipstick from when they kissed goodbye. Her laughter is still a little girl's, her mouth opening up to heaven. She can't keep house, but he doesn't care. He's long since decided that she's simply blind to disorder; to her it must look normal, objects in space without relation, whereas he scans a room and links things by their categories as if preparing for a later quiz. A lawyer's tic, he thinks. He roams the house turning off lights she's left on, picking up the remains of her afternoon drinks.

He never leaves her without a twinge of foreboding, the cellular knowledge that disasters happen, that a routine parting might in retrospect be limned in regret, but he trusts that the fear itself is prophylactic. It strikes him that he would never have thought this way when he was younger, when he and everyone he loved were immortal.

After he and Megan divorced, he'd read dozens of books about marriage. A little late, he realized, but there you are. One of them said that you could predict with great precision the success or failure of a marriage by the number of positive or negative interactions the couple engage in during a day. The valences are not equal, the book said; it takes half a dozen positive interactions to counterbalance a single negative interaction. By this measure, his first marriage was a predictable failure, and his marriage to Sarah certain to succeed. To be told daily how you are loved, how proud your spouse is of you? No self-respecting adult needs to be told this, and yet how he secretly loved to hear it, how it made him want to earn what he was sure he hadn't. These were things that must have been said to her as a child, recited like a bedtime prayer. Did she say the same things to Paul Stinson, he wondered, and if so, what did he make of them, and why was the book's glib ratio wrong in that case? Who can know another marriage, even when you've inherited half of it?

He'd awakened that morning thinking of his mother, the continuation of a dream in which she'd asked him something about their life in California, whether they never should have moved away from there, expecting a response at the moment the dream ended, his mouth forming words he struggled to remember. The interior of the old Mercedes smells of cigars smoked long ago. None of that now. His back aches in its usual way, and there is the customary pain in his side, long undiagnosed but unlikely to kill him, according to the doctors. They can't find out what it is, only what it isn't. These afflictions have become familiars, like patron beasts in a medieval story. He's accommodated himself to them, to the lined face in the rearview mirror, the chin beginning to crumple beneath the mouth. He's formed the habit of never looking himself in the eye, so as to see only the periphery, what he needs to see, the hairline, the jaw, just enough to shave. Despite the aches and what the mirror proves, he feels as fit as he did when he was forty, or thirty, though he suspects this is an animal trick, that if he were suddenly transported into his thirty-year-old body, the differences, the thousand subtle recoveries, would be like an electric shock. His daughter is thirty, exactly half his age this and only this year, one of those odd milestones that often pass unnoticed. She still seems absurdly young, a child, not yet the vessel of a life's story, but serious, hardworking, a litigator, the hardest specialty to practice and still have a life. He'd warned her against it, but as in so many other matters, she'd quietly gone about her life regardless. Just as he can't tell if Sarah is still beautiful, he doesn't know whether Madeleine is pretty, though he believes she is, the way he believes in God, as an arbitrary choice. She alludes occasionally to a man she's seeing, an investment banker who works for one of her clients, though he suspects she's invented him to keep her father and mother at bay, and Sarah is too wise to ask about such things. He wants to meet the boyfriend and dreads meeting him, has no idea what he'd say to someone who was sleeping with his daughter. Congratulations? Keep up the good work?

Across the road, a mass of starlings bursts up from a winterberry tree like an explosion, circles, circles again in a way that seems unnaturally precise, the edges of the black flock as defined as a school of fish. Their thousand wings cut the air, dense with cold. The earth is no longer the black floor of the sky; snow has made it luminous, like a window to another world. The flock rears up, growing, coalescing; they rocket across the highway and are gone. He exits the interstate and takes the slower route, through the towns of his childhood, the old names like a familiar song: Washington, Thompsonville, Mount Lebanon, Dormont. Towns settled by mid-level steel executives amid elms and sycamores that have stood as long as the republic, brick homes with slate roofs, basements full of coal torn from nearby hills. People who had made enough to move out of the city, people who never lived in the city, people whose parents had worked all their lives in the mills, people, like his parents, who came from elsewhere and stayed because the schools were good and the homes were affordable and the commute to Pittsburgh was manageable. He can see the pockets of loss where there had been no recovering from the end of the mills, like craters left by bomb blasts: hollowed-out towns, homes built a hundred years ago and now abandoned, blocks of devastation that the highway flew over. But then other, reinvented places, the shiny office buildings far back from the highway, the shopping malls beckoning to it.

He considers driving through his old neighborhood, decides against it. The house they all lived in, a split-level ranch, was in one of the first subdivisions built this far south of Pittsburgh, almost too far out to commute from, almost rural. Farmers had seen what was coming from far off, like a bad winter, and sold their land to developers; the highway was widened, the speed limit went up, a new high school was built out of corrugated metal painted bright blue like a plastic toy. This was the way the world was going, to ease and color and carelessness. Couples who had married after the war streamed southward out of the city to raise families, the neighborhoods filled up with children, and he and his brother spent their summer days roaming in packs of other boys across the seamless lawns and hills of what had become, underneath their feet, a suburb.

He swings the old car up over a rise and then steeply down through what would have been a deep green valley a hundred years ago, now cleft by the highway running through it, thronged with cars funneling toward the tunnels that pierce the mountain ahead. In the flickering light of the tube lined with white tiles stained with exhaust, cars rocketing along in their lanes like bullets in a gun, he's smiling even before they burst out again into the air, yellow girders arching over them, the rivers leaping away to either side, and the city, like a child's idea of a city, looming up ahead, shining in the winter light, ice floes drifting where the rivers meet. Pittsburgh.

His application is collected in a big binder that sits next to him in the passenger seat like a skeptical in-law, proof of his admittance and past practice in New York and California, the recitation of every place he'd ever lived, every job he ever had, over forty years of adult life, most of it beyond memory, lost. He had to call Megan to help fill in the blanks. They've developed a tolerant, knowing air with one another, like veterans of a long-ago war. She remembers everything, every address, the nuances of how they lived, neighbors and friends and coworkers of the time, furniture, street names, restaurants — things he never paid attention to for one moment after they ceased to be part of daily life. He's wearing a suit he bought back then; the lapels are a little too wide. Sometimes he'll scroll through the contacts list on his computer and there will appear a name he hasn't thought of in thirty years, longer than some lives, and a memory from that long ago will come back: a face, a meal, a kiss, a random night, an embarrassment.

He wants to keep working if they'll let him. A check arrives from the firm every month, pension money and his share of whatever hours he's billed. They remember him in this fashion, the old partners, WASPs and Catholics and a few Jews, older than his dead father would have been, living on in their genteel way, with no idea of what they'd do with themselves if they quit working. When he joined the firm, the place was like a men's club, unapologetically elitist, riding above the economic tides. Now it's struggling, strictly a business, the collegiality stripped away, everyone angling for advantage. He receives, with the check, the minutes of the monthly partners' meeting, where this decline can be traced between the lines. There is talk of a merger with a larger, Midtown firm with a big international practice, a death knell, he thinks. No one asks his opinion of such things. His e-mail inbox is less and less full, the clamor and static of working life slowly receding like a parade moving on down a village street. His career in retrospect looks less like a litany of successes than like a series of risks avoided, not least of which was the threat that he might have been revealed as knowing less than he should have. Now it doesn't matter; no one looks to him for answers, no one pays him for his thoughts.

He parks in a multistory garage, checks the directions on his phone. Pittsburgh has become a tidy, livable city, like an aging bachelor recovered from a debauched youth, dignity and handsomeness at last revealed, unpretentious and quietly accomplished, well-off but simple in taste, needing no one's praise. He's at home, unthreatened, an hour early.

His appointment is in a tower built in the middle of the last century, just after the war, all granite facings and Gothic arches, a businessman's church. In the last decade its lower levels have been hollowed out to make room for a huge shopping mall, smelling of candy and hamburgers, with a Macy's at one end. It takes him half an hour to find the elevators, where an ancient Black doorman, imperious as a pharaoh in his perfectly pressed blue uniform, tells him which bank to take, and that he'll have to switch to another set of elevators on the thirtieth floor. He wonders briefly about this elegant man's life. They make eye contact for a moment, two old survivors.

The second elevator reminds him of those in Europe, barely large enough to bury someone in. He can read the firm's reception area like a scorecard: middle-aged receptionist with a pleasant but reserved air, perhaps a half a dozen offices down the carpeted hall, antique maps and prints of Civil War vessels on the paneled walls. A small firm, with some niche specialty to keep it alive (he guesses bankruptcy or tax), compact offices squeezed into the upper set-backed floors of the musty old building, just enough for two or three partners, one of whom is the founder and probably pays all the rent out of his own pocket so they don't have to move and he can get out of the house every day and say he works downtown. Conrad exchanges small talk about the weather with the receptionist, dressed in plausible knock-off Chanel, while he waits on a slightly broken-down divan. A window looks out over the rivers below, the sports stadiums on the far bank, distant gray snows.

"Mr. Burrell?" a voice asks, a cracked voice, verging on timidity.

He stands and extends a hand. "Mr. Thompson."

"How was the drive in?" Thompson gestures down the hall and leads him into a small conference room, where he takes a seat facing the window, the interviewee's side, the supplicant's.

As they arrange themselves he steals glances at Thompson, a small, round, balding man with a cheerful face and bifocals, more casually dressed than he is in a blue blazer and a button-down shirt, even that probably more than he wanted to put on this day. Conrad relaxes slightly. He's known a hundred like him in a hundred different firms, men whose basic competence and doggedness have had to make up for so much. He likes him instinctively; this will go well.

That night, he and Sarah sit by the fire, a single glass of bourbon passed between them in his latest gesture at getting her to cut down.

"How was it?" she asks, swirling the drink.

"It was fine."

"Were they nice to you?"

"It was just one guy. He was very polite, no big deal. It went well."

"I'm so proud of you," she says with that naked sincerity that always pierces him. "Oh, and Madeleine called. She misses you." The quaint idea of his daughter missing him is touching, but it's one only Sarah would find plausible.

Snow is falling again, the latest in a string of snows, heavy and deep. Nothing is moving in the streets of the town. A dog barks briefly down the block, asking to be let back in. They face each other, flanking the fireplace, no other light. She finishes the drink and holds the glass out to him. He hesitates, then rises and kisses her on the cheek on his way to the kitchen. He tells himself that he loves her too much to deny her, but suspects it may be that he loves her too much as she is, with all her well-mediated love and self-medicated calm.

"So what else did Madeleine say?" he asks as he hands her the fresh drink. His daughter's life is something he feels he must conjure by sheer inference and the accumulation of this kind of sparse data.

"She said she's working too hard, of course," says Sarah. "She asked that you call sometime. But Connie, you really should go to New York and see her, and you could stop in and visit the firm too."

"I don't want to visit the firm," he says. "It depresses me. They're so painfully polite. I'm just an interruption in their day."

"They love you."

"Darling, whatever they feel for me—those who remember me at all—it's not love. Not the way you mean."

"Still, you should go. Remind them of who you are."

11

THEY FLY TO NEW York together. The planes are all small now, always full. First class makes little difference. He remembers the days when he could fly between San Francisco and New York and place a call from a phone built into his seat. He catches himself telling these stories to Sarah, fearing he's become one of those men he's pitied all his life, aging blowhards that Sarah calls "previously important people." She listens as though she hasn't heard it all before. She's dressed well, as though they were going out to dinner.

The flight from Pittsburgh to LaGuardia takes them over downtown Manhattan, the absence of the World Trade Center still like a missing limb, something the eye can't avoid. He picks out the building where he and Megan worked at Dunbar Bell, a black monolith so close to Ground Zero that it might have been crushed by the falling towers had they not collapsed down into their own footprints like the dying witch in *Oz*. He was living in California when it happened, staring at a screen in disbelief, thinking of the times he had stood in those immense lobbies, of the teeming thousands he had passed on his way to work, of the Olympian view from the restaurant on the top floor, human spaces that had seemed the essence of the city and impervious to time but in an instant could cease to exist. He thought for the hundredth time how lucky they've been to have lived when they have, through years punctuated only by isolated wars far away, somehow spared the nuclear carnage that everyone feared when they were growing up, their little pocket of time in which what must surely be the last sweet coda of the human song played out. He expects that this luck cannot possibly hold, that the end will come down like a hammer.

They check into the St. Regis, but their room isn't ready.

"I'm supposed to meet Madeleine in half an hour," he says to Sarah.

"I'll go over to Madison and shop for a while. I'll see you here later."

"You're sure you don't want to come?"

"You should have the time with her. Tell her I love her."

Madeleine Burrell walks into the Armani store on Fifth Avenue and strides briskly toward the elevator at the back to avoid being approached by the sales people. She would never shop here, but it's close to her office and she knows her father likes the restaurant on the second floor, all chrome and leather with a view of the street. She is thirty-one, tall and thin like her father, beginning to go gray as he did in his thirties, dressed in a pantsuit with a short toreador jacket that she thinks could have come from Armani, but in fact was purchased online for a third that much. Clothing is of no interest to her. She and her father differ as to whether she is pretty. She wears no jewelry except a pair of pearl earrings that she really must get cleaned and submits to conventions of self-beautification only by applying a bit of eyeliner on mornings when she has time. Men are puzzled by her, some would say threatened, but she doesn't think that's accurate; it's just that they can see that she isn't trying to please them, and this simply doesn't fit into most young men's equation of how the sexes interact. She forgives them for this but prefers the company of women, where less artifice is called for. She lives on the West Side even though it would be far more convenient and no more expensive to live uptown on the East Side. Her walk to work takes thirty minutes on a good day, but she counts it as exercise, and forces herself to leave her office every other day to spend another hour in the gym in the Peninsula Hotel, an extravagance she knows she really can't afford. The hardest thing in her life is to prevent work from becoming her life. The work itself is easy for her, but it's consuming in a way that she finds as insidious as an overly handsome man hitting on her in a bar. The city is full of Madeleine Burrells, and all of them are different.

Her father is already seated at a table by the windows overlooking the avenue. He stands when he sees her; she knows he would do this for any woman joining him at a table, but the look on his face—that mixture of pride and concern and something like yearning—is one she knows well because he always wears it when he first sees her. The look embarrasses her slightly, which in turn annoys her, but she suppresses the feeling and hugs him and presents her ear to be kissed.

"You look great," he says as they sit.

"You too, Dad." In fact, her father looks old to her, the new thickness around the eyes, the hair thinner and gone completely gray; most of all the hands, which she holds across the tablecloth for just a moment before reaching for the napkin in its silver ring, hands still soft, white-collar hands, but thicker now, veins and knuckles bulging, skin papery and wrinkled.

She looks at him appraisingly, the way she would at someone she had just met, a client perhaps, a well-dressed older man, comfortable in this expensive environment, modestly successful or had been, decorous and slightly shy, still thin, careful of his body, not yet stooped. If she didn't know him, she might have noticed him across a room and wondered briefly who he was, whether he was married, what his family was like, whether it included a wife or a daughter like her. He looks like most of the men she works for, and that only reminds her of what she's left back at the office, the motion she must still draft, the conference call with opposing counsel later this afternoon.

"How's work?" he asks, reading the distraction in her face.

"Crazy busy, I'm afraid."

"Thanks for doing this."

She pokes a finger at his arm in answer. She knows how he likes her to touch him, even in irony. She's always thought the phrase "broken family" to be overly dramatic; in her view, her family had broken open, allowing her to escape. Her anxiety about being with her father is triggered by the sentimentality and regret that emanates from him like a damp fog, his longing for that imagined alternative history, that impossible, obliterated world where they had all stayed together, he had tucked her into bed each night, taken her on tours of colleges, arranged family ski trips each winter and diving trips each spring, helped her with her homework, taught her to be more like him. She would have eventually escaped that life too, but while within it, his love might have become oppressive, and she less like herself. It's enough that she's had to deal with her mother's fierce embrace. As it is, she only looks like him, their faces sharing the stamp of certain chromosomes, and she's become, she believes, a true child of divorce: her own woman.

"Are they treating you well?" he asks.

"They pay well, though not nearly enough." She stops, thinking how spoiled she must sound.

"What are they telling you about partnership?" he asks.

"Another couple of years before I come up. I'm not sure I'll be there then."

"Oh?"

"I get calls from headhunters all the time. I might like an in-house job where the hours would be better."

He nods at this; it's a choice he might have made. "Sarah sends her love."

She smiles with a nod and a tilt of her head, a habituated gesture that she uses on the male partners at her firm; it always puts them at ease. His life with the woman he married is of minor interest to her, and only vaguely imaginable. She knows that Sarah cares for him with an intensity that neither she nor her mother could have managed over time, and this great stroke of fortune has absolved them both.

A waitress with an Eastern European accent comes and pours water into crystal, and they stare at the menus, printed in an elegant script on heavy ecru paper. Madeleine makes a few quick decisions and then puts her menu aside and looks out the window at the crowds on the sidewalk below while she waits for him to catch up. Her parents' fascination with restaurants and menus mystifies her. She understands fine cuisine and appreciates it—God knows they exposed her to enough of it in this town—but her mother drives her crazy by studying menus as though they hold the key to her fate, and as a child Madeleine had copied her, often unable in the end to make any choice at all and falling into a paralyzed fit. When she left home, she'd trained herself to scan quickly for one or two things she could eat and be done with it.

"So," he says, putting his menu aside and leaning toward her. "How's your mom?"

"She's okay. Vince has been sick, which makes her a bit crazy. But she's okay."

"What's wrong with Vince?"

"Something with his heart," she says, putting a hand over hers. "He's had an issue since he was a child, something congenital. He may need another operation."

"Sorry to hear. How old is he now?"

"I think he's late seventies." Her stepfather is considerably older than her father; she used to fret about it, back when having a mother who was dating seemed an unfair compounding of the general curse of adolescence.

"Where's he being treated?"

"Mount Sinai."

"Good," he says. All that can be done is being done; he can add nothing.

Her stepfather's health worries her because she can't imagine what her mother would do if he weren't around. She has grown to love him over the years, his wit and gruff protectiveness, so unlike her father's needy camaraderie. Vince makes no effort whatsoever to treat her like an adult, which charms her. She would be saddened to lose him, but her mother would be devastated and would turn to Madeleine, so she hopes he'll live forever.

"Give them our love, will you?" he says. This has always been her role, the shuttle diplomat. He waits a few beats, sips water. The waitress returns, and they order; he asks if she'd like some wine, and she declines. An attractive couple is being seated nearby.

"Do you think they're married?" he asks. This is an old game of theirs, making up stories about strangers. Madeleine glances at them, looks away.

"No, he's being too polite. It's a business lunch. They're both in the fashion business. Retail. You can tell by how they're dressed. She's got a new line; he works for Nieman's and might be interested."

He tears a roll in two, dips it in oil. "They're tourists from Texas. She has Texas hair."

"What is Texas hair?" she asks, knowing full well but wanting to be feminist about it.

"They're staying at the Carlyle, going to the matinee later."

"It's too late for the matinee. They may be going to his apartment later, though."

"Which reminds me, what happened to the guy?"

"That's a salacious segue, Dad. Which guy?"

"Is there more than one? Weren't you dating somebody?"

"Lloyd Davidson? I'm not sure 'dating' is the word I would use."

"Do I want to know the word you would use?"

"We see each other some weekends. We're both very busy."

"Of course. So it's nothing serious?"

"Don't know yet, Dad. I like him a lot; we have fun together. We're not pushing things, which is fine with me." She tries to keep her face open, neutral.

"Remind me where he's from?"

"Grew up in Camden . . ." she starts to recite, singsong.

"Oh, right, you told me . . ."

". . . Williams undergrad, Tufts for business school, works at GE Capital."

"So he's out in Summit?" It comes out sounding like Siberia.

"Morristown, but he has an apartment in Chelsea. He reverse commutes." She watches her father consider this, his brow knitting involuntarily as he visualizes the place in Chelsea, the faux bohemian flat near the High Line, the windows open in the summer, the unmade bed.

"I'd like to meet him someday."

The nodding smile again. "I'm sure you would, and I'm sure you will."

"We should all have dinner."

"He's away right now, but maybe next time."

"I'm going to have some wine if you don't mind. You met him at work?"

"At a conference on patent trolls. He was a speaker, actually."

"I love the notion of a patent troll. I imagine it living under a bridge in Silicon Valley."

She smiles indulgently; she's never considered her father as funny as he thinks he is. "I don't think there are any there."

"Trolls?"

"Bridges."

"I'd really like to meet Lloyd," he repeats, not wanting to let the subject go just yet. "I used to know a lot of people at GE Capital. I did a lot of aircraft financings with them back in the day." He starts reeling off names that mean nothing to her, men who have probably retired like him, replaced by men like Lloyd. Her thoughts are elsewhere, flickering involuntarily to their last night together, her bed like an animal's nest, the smells, her hips under his hands.

"Maddie, could you pass the salt?" She hands it over, straightens her jacket.

She relaxes slightly, seeing that this is going to be another one of those conversations they keep safely superficial. A cold green soup arrives; they sip it in silence. He glances at his watch.

"While I have you," he says, "Sarah and I have redone our estate plans, and I want to make you a trustee, if that's okay with you."

"Of course." She tries to think of questions to ask, so they can feel like fellow lawyers collaborating, but nothing comes to her. She hated trusts and estates in law school, just as her father says he did, the consanguinity charts more impenetrable than the periodic table of the elements.

"You'd administer a trust for Sarah's benefit after my death." He watches her eyes as he says this, something he rarely does.

"Sure, no problem," she says. She hates that expression, but feels herself reverting to the blithe detachment she mastered in her parents' presence during her adolescence. They had a conversation like this the last time her father rewrote his will, shortly after he married Sarah, when the prospect of his eventual death had seemed the stuff of a law school hypothetical. Now she sees in a way that she did not then that it will all come true, that those documents are vessels of inevitability, that his hand is trembling slightly as he brings the spoon to his mouth, that he's asking her not only for her future services as a trustee, but for something else, something she cannot give.

"Is Sarah okay with this?" she asks finally.

"It was her suggestion, actually."

Her imagination flashes to this, she and Sarah in a conference room somewhere in the future, her father dead, his money in her care, comforting his widow. The two women discussing how things should be, how much the older woman will need to live comfortably. She will be kind and generous; Sarah has been nothing but loving toward her, expecting nothing, hoping only for her acceptance. She will be the competent one, of course, knowing what to do, unaffected by sentiment; getting things done is her gift.

Afterward, on the sidewalk, he watches her hurry away; she's become a woman of the city, all rush and focus, serially obsessive. He's helpless to slow her down, make her stay. He waits to see if she will look back at him or if her mind is already elsewhere, and at the last moment she does, lifting a hand as she turns the corner and disappears. He tells himself he would have felt no differently if she had not.

Because he's standing still and staring, people begin to glance at him warily, as though he might be a well-dressed lunatic or panhandler. He finally turns and threads his way among them back to the hotel with that dodging city rhythm he learned long ago and has never forgotten. He waits for a light to change, and what he can see of the sky among the rooftops is a cerulean blue, like the day he met Sarah for their first lunch alone together not ten blocks from where he's standing.

Sarah wanders back down Madison toward the hotel. She has no goal other than to pass the time. She turns east on 57th Street just to admire the shops, knowing she will buy nothing, walks the long block and turns back on the opposite side. Winter is waning, but the days are still short, the sun already plunging toward the Hudson. She hopes that Conrad will be smiling when she sees him; she knows how his meetings with his daughter affect him and can read his face in an instant. It worries her that Madeleine may not understand that she holds Conrad's heart in her hands, thinks him far stronger than he is. Sarah knows differently, wants to protect him, but knows there is nothing she can do; part of him was lost to her long before she met him, on the day Madeleine was born, and then another part when he and Megan separated. How strange that those two women, so unlike her, are as bound to her as though she herself had borne one and married the other.

The city is cleaner than when she lived here; the gutters have been swept, the shops brimming with endless luxuries, the homeless people moved out of sight. She thinks of Clara, the woman of about her age who cleaned her house when she lived in Dobbs Ferry; she came up on the train from the Bronx every Tuesday. Sarah had inherited her from another woman who'd gotten divorced and moved away, and she worked hard for what now seemed very little money. Then Sarah herself had gotten divorced and moved away and had to let Clara go. There was never any discussion of what Clara would do next. Sarah wishes she'd given her more, wishes she would see her now, down the street. She would run up to her and hug her and press something into her hand, tell her how much she valued her work and her companionship, how much she misses the home they both cared for. She straightens her back as she walks and studies herself in the passing storefront windows. The woman she sees is not young anymore, no longer has the margin for error allowed to the girls in the photos in the shops, the infinite forgiveness that beauty confers. There was a time when she thought that, as the population aged, older women might become fashionable, but the models are all younger than ever, children really. The stores are all shrines to youth, relentless and uncompromising. Other women hurry by, their heads down, their eyes averted, something desperate in their bearing. She has avoided the uniquely feminine disaster of being middle-aged and alone. How could she have been so lucky as to be in this place in this time, walking in the dusk back to a beautiful hotel to rejoin a loving spouse? What more could anyone reasonably hope for? She lowers her face and murmurs a quick prayer.

She had gone out to shop for gifts for Meg and Christine and Becky; they expect nothing, of course, will be confused to receive souvenirs of her trip to New York, but this is a habit of her childhood, when her parents always brought her something when they returned from their long absences. Scarves would be perfect, they all wear them now to hide their necks, and anything more expensive would embarrass them. She'll go to Bloomingdale's tomorrow when Conrad is at the office. She glances at her watch—almost cocktail hour, thank God. To make her husband happy she's been trying not to drink until after sundown, not always succeeding. She loves the calm that first drink lends her, the quieting of all her heart's voices, before the buzz and blurriness of later in the evening.

As she turns back onto Madison, she sees Felix McCaffrey a block away on the opposite sidewalk, leaning forward and peering into the window of a fancy electronics store. His coat is open, draped around his shoulders, and his white hair glows in the dimming light; he's like a bright buoy in the sea of people rushing around him. Her heart suddenly accelerates; though she knows he's in New York all the time, this seems too lucky, a coincidence so contrived that it must tell her something fateful. She starts across the street as the yellow walk/don't walk counter reaches zero and has to run the last few steps, dancing on the toes of her high heels while the traffic honks at her. He's still there; he hasn't seen her yet. She will run up and grab his arm; he's her height, so she could surprise him with a kiss. He wouldn't even have to bend down to her as Conrad does. As she approaches, he's in profile, studying something on the other side of the glass, so handsome and calm, his skin so pale she believes she can see the delicate bones shining beneath. She doesn't want to startle him, but she knows he'll be pleased to see her, as surprised at this good fortune as she is. She knows she's still beautiful; men have been looking at her all day. There's still time before she's supposed to meet Conrad. She could suggest a drink; the Peninsula Hotel is somewhere nearby, all art deco and demure, its entrance off the avenue. Her intimacy with Felix has till now consisted of complimenting each other on how they're dressed and glancing kisses on the cheek, but this can change in an instant. She's striding quickly down the block, closing the distance between them, conscious to appear not too hurried or undignified in case he should look her way, and in those few seconds she can imagine a different life where years unfold in his company, how Paris would seem when shared with him, India through the prism of his blue eyes, or sitting at a bar somewhere in the tropics where he plays his guitar for tips, the pure human elegance of his fingers on the strings, on her, no one knowing except she who he really is, who they are. To have time enough to learn his world, to be lost with him that way, perhaps in a future life, in a past life, who knew? There's a vertiginous moment when her thoughts seem plainly adulterous, but was that true? No, not when it's a separate life, one where he'd met someone else, found his happiness in another way, or where Christine and Conrad had simply not existed, or ceased to exist. This last thought is troubling to her, and she looks up to see that he's turned toward her and of course it's not really Felix, that the white hair and pale skin and nice clothes had fooled her, that she had almost kissed a stranger. She smiles at him nonetheless without breaking stride and he smiles back in a knowing way, his eyes not even blue, but calculating, seeing that she's not from here, no one here smiles at anyone on the street. She slides past him quickly and hurries on down the block, back across the street at the next corner, the crowds now a comfort, a camouflage, bearing her along like a tide.

12

THEY INVITE MEGAN AND Vince to join them for dinner, but Vince is indisposed; his operation is the following week. Megan suggests a smart new restaurant in Brooklyn with what she describes as a stunning view of lower Manhattan. They're seated near the windows, cantilevered open to the river breezes, the jagged profile of the city like a cardboard cutout against the violet sky, the bridge a necklace of light. Megan is simply dressed in black, her hair silver verging on pure white; Sarah is all geometric color. She and Sarah embrace and sit next to one another across from Conrad, where he can look at the two women who have defined his adult life. He doesn't want them to see that he thinks of them this way, so he studies the skyline. It's yet another night, another moment, that he could never have imagined.

They ask after Vince and his health. They haven't seen him since Madeleine's graduation from law school.

"Let's talk about something else," Megan says, her eyes downcast. Sarah and Conrad glance at each other. "How is our Maddie?" Megan asks.

"Don't you two talk every day?" Conrad says, trying not to sound peevish about it.

"Sure, but she never tells me anything, really. Did you discuss Lloyd?"

"His name came up, but I wouldn't call it a discussion."

"Same with me. Which makes me think it's serious."

They pause while a waiter serves drinks: a chardonnay for Sarah, Lillet blanc on ice with a slice of orange for Megan, a Gibson for Conrad. Conrad can't suppress a smile; Lillet is what he and Megan drank in their garret in the Village thirty years ago.

"I don't know," he says. "Wouldn't she tell us if it were?"

"I'm sure she would," ventures Sarah, looking at Megan for permission to say it.

"I have no confidence of that at all," Megan says. "Her private life is very private. No visible relationships. For a while I thought she was gay."

"Madeleine couldn't be gay," he says a little too quickly. "I mean, it would be fine with me, but she really doesn't seem the type."

"Anyone's daughter can be gay, and there is no type, trust me. But maybe she just doesn't care about sex in general."

"What do you mean, in general?" Sarah asks, flicking a look Conrad's way.

"Oh, you know," Megan says, waving a hand, "there are people who just don't need it, can't believe sex can ever be an expression of love, don't want to confuse the two, so they avoid both."

Megan had always made Conrad feel as though he'd wandered into a final exam for a course he'd never taken. Her face is wearily serene, her brow deeply furrowed, a face he knew as well as his own now stamped with age, a continual shock to look at, a rebuke to his delusions about his own appearance. She's unadorned, without jewelry or makeup. Her hands are rough, the joints swollen; even when they were young they joked that she had a farmer's hands, a fishwife's hands. He can remember almost nothing of the details of their conjugal life except one or two inextirpable images: sitting on a battered secondhand sofa in the living room of her apartment in the Village, the windows open to the hot summer night, glasses of sherry in their hands, a song on the stereo about diamonds and rust. And the day

Madeleine was born, racing in from LaGuardia where he'd been about to board a plane, to St. Vincent's Hospital, gone now, to the room where Megan lay, her feet in the metal stirrups, doctors impatient, waiting for him to arrive, and the moments that followed that would join them forever in a way that mere marriage never could.

The rest, incredibly, has been washed away. The thousands of hours together, the lovemaking, almost nightly then; he can remember something about the feel of her mouth when they kissed and how her long, straight hair draped about them like a veil as she sat astride him, but nothing of the other details that had intoxicated those days, nothing of the texture of those blind intimacies. It was like drowning, but how the water felt is lost. He can still see the woman he loved in her face and understand why he did. One of Sarah's aphorisms comes to him: people don't change; they become more themselves.

Megan and Sarah have moved on to the subject of summer houses, Fire Island versus Cape Cod versus Block Island on a set of criteria that involve restaurants and the attitudes of the locals and how one likes to spend one's afternoons. Conrad has nothing to say, but is most content in moments like this, watching others at ease and enjoying themselves, with no expectations of him. Observing, ignored. In the confluence of his old working days, that fast-rushing river whose banks he only glimpsed as they swept past, there had been rare islands of time like this one, where the present fully invaded him and made the world plain, without judgment or even longing. He'd reached a point in life where those moments presented themselves more frequently, or perhaps he was better able to recognize them. The women talk, and he sits back and looks down at his hands and then out the window at the city across the water, almost embarrassed at his good fortune.

A man in a jacket approaches the table suddenly, startling them. It's Vince Van Siclen, looking flushed.

"Don't get up. I'm sorry. I was sitting in the apartment, and I said,

'Why am I here when they're out having a good time?' I hope you don't mind." Conrad stands to shake his hand; Vince leans down to kiss Sarah on the cheek. He's one of those older men who seem perpetually tanned, as though just returned from a beach. His hair is receding and oiled with something fragrant and combed straight back, the exact silver of Megan's, and he has an impeccably trimmed moustache that covers more of his upper lip than Conrad remembers. He's wearing an expensive checked shirt, possibly bespoke, and a knit tie hastily knotted. It seemed that men like Vince populated Conrad's life. His father was one, with the ease of a professional who knows how good he is, all erudite bluster and reminiscence. Smiling across the table at the older man, Conrad thinks they might have been close friends; it's only the reason that they know each other at all that makes them wary of each other. When Madeleine was in high school they fought over money, who should pay what percentage of her expensive education, but those days are long past. Sometime around her graduation from college, Conrad came to understand that Vince's intrusion into what should have been issues for Megan and him was an expression not only of male territoriality, though it was certainly that, but of Vince's love for Megan and Madeleine, and that this was not only as it should be, but good for all of them, including Conrad. Meanwhile Vince had long since ceased to view Conrad as a rival for the affections of the women in his life; they've come to see each other as two fathers rather than two husbands.

"I know you've been talking about me; my ears were burning," Vince says, gesturing for a drink to a waiter in the vicinity, who scurries off. He evidently has no need to specify.

"Actually, not at all," says Megan. "But now that you're here we can."

"Let's get all the medical stuff out of the way first," he says. "Who has questions?"

Sarah reaches across the table and takes Vince's hand. "How are you feeling, my dear Vince?" Conrad winces inwardly; only she could get away with this, though Vince plainly loves it.

"Never felt better. But that's what all my patients say just before they drop dead. I've found that how you're feeling is a very poor diagnostic tool."

"When is the operation?" Conrad asks as Vince's martini arrives festooned with a sprig of rosemary, which he removes, sniffs appraisingly, and tosses aside.

"Next week. It's just a bit of plumbing. Anyone could do it, but a colleague at Mount Sinai volunteered. He's a bit of an ass, but you want that in a surgeon."

"How long will you be laid up?" asks Sarah.

Megan leans forward. "He will tell you two weeks, but that's a lie. This will be—what, Vinnie?—his third heart surgery, and each time the recovery is twice as long as they say, and getting longer."

"They should pay me, the practice I've given these guys. I'm a one-man clinical trial. Have you ordered wine?" He gestures at the waiter again.

Vince used to perform surgery himself, but no more. Now, Conrad hears, he consults, he confers, he teaches. He's Conrad's senior by ten or twelve years, which now casts Megan's choice of him in a different light than when they were in their thirties and she took up with this established older man, a cardiologist rich in contacts and money, at home in the city, at the top of his game. The remorseless passage of time has changed the implications of those choices. Conrad realized that of course the same might be said of Sarah's choice of him; she, too, married a considerably older man at an even later stage of her life. Would she come to regret it when he no longer could be considered distinguished, but merely old, when his doctors, too, begin that long war of attrition that can have only one victor? Regret was surely too strong a word. Resentment, perhaps, that the cost of those choices had not been disclosed and is so high.

All this was utterly foreseeable—that word beloved of lawyers—yet utterly beyond the heart's belief: the slow, relentless flow of time. He glances across the table at Vince and silently wishes the man well. He looks like a Sicilian lord, all broad gestures and geniality; in an odd, inexpressible way, he's become as dear to Conrad as a brother. He wants Vince to outlive Megan, just as he hopes to outlive Sarah. He wishes life and health and time for Vince Van Siclen, as proof that they can be his as well.

"What on earth are you eating?" Vince asks, peering at Conrad's tournedos of grouper, which look nothing like fish.

"Don't know, but it's delicious."

"Needs a white." He summons the waiter and orders a "Pooly," the way a man would order a beer. It takes Conrad a few moments to realize he's ordered a Puligny-Montrachet and must do so with such frequency that it's acquired a nickname.

"There's something we should talk about," Vince says. They look at him, utensils hovering. "There's a possibility, small but real, that I won't survive this operation."

"Vince, stop right now," says Megan, a familiar brittleness in her voice.

"No, we should talk about it. You two are her only real family once I'm gone." He's pointing his fork Conrad's way, though Conrad is uncertain whether the second 'you' refers to his wife or his daughter. "I want you to know that I've provided for her . . ."

"Could we please not talk about me in the third person while I'm sitting here?" says Megan, her voice rising.

". . . and that you and Madeleine won't have to worry. My own children have their own money, so everything will go to Megan. Everything. The apartment, the place in Montauk, all of it."

"Stop it!" Megan's fists thump down on the table.

Vince ignores her, something Conrad never dared. "There's only one hitch."

Megan stands abruptly. "Excuse me," she says, making it sound like a curse.

"Would you like company?" offers Sarah.

"No, thanks." She stalks off.

"Just as well," says Vince. He tops up their wine glasses. "The problem is that my ex-wife died a year or so ago, and the children of her second marriage have no money. Their father is a drunk and hasn't worked in years. They have huge student loans, expensive cars, typical spoiled kids."

"Didn't your support obligation end when she remarried?" Conrad asks, not seeing where this is going.

"Of course. But that didn't stop her from asking for money over the years. Sometimes I would give her some. Not huge amounts, but some. This went on up till the time she died."

"I'm still not seeing the problem."

"There's a bit of an ambiguity in our post-nup about whether her kids would have a claim on my estate, despite the fact that I'm leaving everything to Megan."

"Really?"

"My lawyer is a nice guy, but he's conflicted, as you lawyers say, because he also wrote the post-nup way back when. I need somebody to look into it objectively and see if there's anything we can do to make Cheryl's damn kids go away."

"Go away? You mean they're after you now?"

"Let's say there have been insinuations. Cheryl obviously told them that I'd been giving her money all these years, and they're trying to carry on the family tradition."

"But you're in no way related to them," says Conrad. "That would be like your kids coming after me."

"Ha! Right! Maybe I should suggest it to them!" Vince smacks the table gleefully; Conrad chuckles awkwardly. Sarah stares at them, appalled.

"Like I say, the only reason this could be a problem is because of the wording of the post-nup, which my idiot lawyer says isn't a problem, but he'd be the last one to admit it."

"He must be right, though."

"I just want to be sure," says Vince, the energy suddenly gone out of him, replaced by a kind of resignation. "There's little enough to be sure of. I thought since you sort of have an interest in this too, you might recommend someone."

When he was a young lawyer, Conrad learned that the hardest thing is to inhabit silence, to let a question hang in the air. Everyone wants to fill a vacuum. He forced himself still, looked out the window at the city, now a wall of black perforated with light. He's flattered that a man like Vince would ask this of him, let alone a man like Vince who is married to his ex-wife. And three or four lawyers he could recommend have come instantly to mind. But he makes himself wait, to let Vince know he takes this seriously, that it's worthy of a long moment's reflection. He also needs that moment to let a tidal pull of emotion pass by, to forget how they are all related in ways he could not have dreamed of, all of them partners in a long slow dance whose music they could barely hear. He looks across the room at Megan walking slowly back to the table, a steely smile on her face.

He turns back to Vince. "I'll get you some names," he says quietly.

They fly home the next night in the darkened cabin of a small jet, the fields of Pennsylvania black as the sea but broken here and there by metastases of light. They land in Pittsburgh and drive the long hour to the little town, its streets and houses seeming sweetly naive after the controlled chaos of New York, like a child's imagining of how life might be lived, something that cannot last yet does, hidden and exempt. His parents' house smells of dying flowers that Sarah had forgotten to throw away before they left.

13

CHRISTINE AND FELIX HAVE a place in Santa Fe and invite Sarah and Conrad to join them there over a long Labor Day weekend. The house is high on the north side of town in the pine forest near a famously bohemian spa and has been in Christine's family for generations. Her grandfather was an acolyte of Stieglitz, and the adobe walls of the bedrooms are covered with black-and-white photographs in his style, the mundane burnished by the camera to the self-conscious sheen of art. The rooms are small and square and retain the cool of the high desert nights, which blaze with stars like a map of the cosmos.

Conrad had visited Santa Fe with his former spouse, and Sarah likewise with hers, but they've never been here together. The four of them walk the old square and eat in the cantinas, the tourists preparing to leave for the year, casting a final eye over the wares of the locals laid out on blankets in front of the Palace of the Governors. Christine is tanned, her hair burned white, dismissive of the famous spots, preferring the wilderness beyond. She leads them, winded and dizzy from the altitude, up the trails near her house to see the sunset fall on the Sangre de Cristos, on the Jemez range opposite, where Los Alamos glows like a promise of man's mischief.

All this feels familiar to Conrad. It recalls his boyhood days in Mexico, the deserts where he and Walt played. To a young boy it was like living in a western, the heat and the dust and the near mountains looming, the desert infusing the heart with its ancient silences, the patience of stones and cunning desert creatures, the infinite stoicism of land touched with rain only at certain times of year, and then as lightly as a brush on canvas. The utter stillness of the desert nights, like no others, the moon blazing down so hard he could almost hear it, like a mallet on copper. After dinner on the *portal* of the house, the arm of the galaxy hangs above them sharp as a scythe, impossibly close, while Felix plays some Rodrigo. Conrad watches Sarah watching him and cannot muster the slightest jealousy. One couldn't live here and fail to become a saint of one kind or another.

"We might have to give it up," says Christine. "It breaks my heart."

"Oh no, why?" asks Sarah.

"It's too expensive to maintain, and we're never here. It needs a new roof; the cistern is failing. These old houses weren't meant to be left empty for months at time."

"Could you rent it?" Conrad asks.

"I couldn't. My grandfather's ghost would hunt me down."

"Could you move here?"

"With Felix's business, we really need to be in the eastern time zone."

"Don't sell it," pleads Sarah. "It's too beautiful."

"Would it help if you had a co-owner?" Conrad asks on complete impulse, surprising himself. Christine looks at him as though he's proposed sex.

"I suppose it would. But who would that be?"

"That's the first coy thing I've ever heard you say. Any number of people, I would think. But if you'd like, we should talk about it."

"That's very sweet of you, Conrad. Sarah, has he consulted you about this?"

"Not in the least, but it's a wonderful idea."

"Let me talk with Felix about it, when he's sober and not playing guitar."

They look over at him, sitting apart on a low stool, the guitar between his knees, tuning the instrument intently, his white hair glowing in the moonlight. He looks aboriginal, abstracted from the world. Felix is a riddle to them, at ease with himself yet withdrawn, never quite present. Men are usually proud to talk about their work, but Conrad's questions about his are deflected or answered with ambiguities. The women joke that he's a spy, but that kind of work requires a ruthlessness that Felix seems to lack. He has the look of a nomad, someone who sees the temporary in everything and has taught himself detachment. Conrad senses that for Sarah his remove is a mark of romanticism, but Conrad thinks it's bleaker than that, perhaps even a barely managed depression. Christine is the most independent of all the wives they know, and necessarily so; she and Felix seem more like siblings than spouses, nothing like intimacy passes visibly between them. They're partners in a pact different than marriage.

The mornings are glorious, the sky like a solid blue dome. In the afternoons clouds form over the mountains and rain falls in long veils, transparent and still in the distance. They read on the *portal*, drunk on the thin air, the scent of the junipers. They go to the ancient town in the evenings, to restaurants that have been there since Christine was a little girl, and before. Everywhere there is someone singing mournfully in Spanish, the sound of Mexico, where the songs say they long to return, the land under their feet yet forever lost. The name of the place means sacred faith.

It rained suddenly one night, like an ambush, lightning cutting the dark like a jailed man's shiv, rain falling as though to finally cleanse the earth, torrents threatening to beat the old house into the ground as he lay in bed with Sarah asleep beside him, and he felt as if for the first time fearfully connected to the natural world, bereft of memory and human ambition, merely grateful to be alive and surviving the next roar of thunder. He felt he was standing watch in some immemorial way, that what was important and what was not was revealed in those cascades of lightning, and that he would be there in that place at the end.

On the long flight home Conrad begins to regret his overture to Christine about co-ownership of the Santa Fe house. He feels alone in this worry. No one speaks of money. When his parents were alive they regarded him as rich beyond any possible need; they saw no reason not to burn away their own savings. He knows that Sarah has no conception of money; her life has never required her to. It's an abstraction in her world of people and things, like the GPS maps in her car that only become real when the computer's voice tells her where to turn. "Can we afford this?" she would ask, and he'd say either yes or no, not because he thought it was for him to decide, but because she really had no interest. When he said no, which was rarely, she would also say, "You only live once." She has what they call her own money, inherited from her father and her mother's mother; sometimes she'll invoke it when her heart is set on something and he disagrees, but her wants of this kind are rare. They have his pension money, whatever pittance Social Security will eventually pay, and joint savings that amount to a few million. The word itself meant riches when they were young, but no more. Half ownership of a house in Santa Fe sounds like excess to Conrad.

Sarah is all for it. "You only live once," she says.

"Evidently," Conrad says, and leans over in the airplane seat to kiss her nose.

When they land there's a message on his cell from Madeleine, saying she's become engaged to Lloyd Davidson, and to please call.

14

MEG'S MASTECTOMY GOES WELL, and she's able to rejoin Becky and Sarah and Christine for their weekly lunches at the inn. Her breasts have been reconstructed in some mysterious way that Sarah doesn't want to know about, involving implants and flesh from other parts of her body. She's chosen a smaller size than she had previously, but they are high and perfectly proportioned. The other women admire them frankly, leaning across the table for closer inspection.

"Girls, let's not look like a bunch of lesbians," says Meg, crossing her arms demurely.

"Maybe I'll have this done," says Becky, reaching out to touch.

"Very funny. It's quite expensive, and with clothes on it's one thing, but definitely not the same when you're naked. And the little fact that you have to have cancer first doesn't recommend it."

"Has Bill been okay about it?" Sarah asks.

"At first he was horrified of course, wouldn't come near me. But he's made friends with them. The male sex drive brooks many shortcomings."

They grin and sip their wine, visions of the Franklins' lovemaking flashing through their heads. Meg's hair has grown back a coarse gray that she doesn't bother to color. She's twenty pounds lighter and has made this an excuse to buy a new wardrobe, stark whites and blacks, a statement of clarity achieved, a renunciation of frivolity. All excess burned away, her eyes sit shallow and clear in their pools of flesh. Sarah imagines you would find women like her living alone in small stone houses in ancient Alpine towns, rising before anyone else, drinking in the air of cold mornings.

"Enough of that," Meg says, turning to Sarah. "How was Santa Fe? I've always wanted to go there."

"Wonderful. Christine's house is lovely, in the hills. I love the town." She's about to say something about buying a share in the house but checks herself, uncertain whether the general taboo on talk about money extends to such things.

"The food is amazing; I'd forgotten," she continues. "But the most important part of the trip was what we learned when we got back." They look at her. "Madeleine's engaged! To one of her clients. At least that's how Connie describes it."

They squeal and hug her and rain questions on her, as though Madeleine were their own. Sarah explains who Lloyd Davidson is, as best she understands it, that the wedding will be in Maine in the fall of next year.

"You haven't even met him?" asks Becky.

"Nope. But they're coming for Thanksgiving, which is a first even for Madeleine. That will be the official meeting." She hangs finger quotes.

"Do men still ask fathers for permission to marry their daughters?" Becky asks.

"I don't think so," Sarah says. "Fathers don't give their daughters away anymore either."

"Our children are no longer our property," says Meg. "Except when they want us to pay their expenses."

"Poor guy," says Becky. "Conrad's not an easy audience."

"Oh, Connie acts like this is a crisis, but deep down he's thrilled," says Sarah.

"A father's job is never done till his daughter marries," says Meg.

"A mother's job is never done, period," says Becky.

"The good news is that his parents have insisted the wedding be in their home town in Maine, and the incentive is that they'll pay for it."

"Lucky you," Becky says. "The Templetons nearly bankrupted themselves on that blowout they had for their daughter, and that was her second marriage. I never understood that one."

"Guilt," says Meg simply. Now that she's better, Meg's old cynicism has returned. She raises her glass. "Congratulations to Madeleine."

"And to you and yours," says Becky, leering at Meg's new breasts.

"You are such an awful bitch," says Meg with a smile as their glasses ting against each other.

Sarah wanders home after, a little high from the wine and the talk. Conrad is in his office with the door closed. As a result of his visit to New York, the reminder that he exists, the firm has asked that he consult on an airline client's refinancing of some of the aircraft leases that he helped put together almost twenty years earlier. None of the other lawyers who worked on the deals are still with the firm, and those that remain have never done a leveraged lease. There could be no clearer confirmation of Conrad's professional obsolescence than that the form of transaction on which he'd spent most of his career had become a legal relic. He's told that he'll be paid his usual rate of $750 per hour but will have to keep his time down. A European bank will underwrite new, cheaper debt, the old public notes will be retired, and the rent payments, elaborately structured according to computer algorithms that Conrad understands only in concept, will be reduced. The book profits of the airline will appear to rise. The equity investors—banks, all—will have to be notified but have no contractual right to object. An associate at the firm has sent Conrad hundreds of documents, grouped by aircraft tail numbers, on a little plastic flash drive the size of a fingernail. He downloads them to his computer and reads for a few hours, recognizing the section headings like the faces of relatives, knowing what is important and what can be ignored. There's the familiar looming of a deadline, the comforting structure of others' demands, the affirmation of being paid to do hard work.

He writes a long memo to his colleagues outlining the procedural hurdles and tax issues they will face. It's like dropping a stone down a well; no one seems to know or care what he's talking about. He hates e-mail, dislikes the temporal asymmetry of it, the nuances hidden in who's being copied and who isn't, the hackneyed phrases that have become proxies for clear expression, the silences that can mean nothing or everything. He's spent his entire working life in front of a computer screen of one kind or another, starting with those dedicated word processors the size of a small car that the law firms had in the seventies. But it's lost its charm since the advent of what the kids call social media, a meaningless redundancy (what communications medium is *not* social?) if Conrad ever heard one. Now, he'll rant to Sarah, every fool has his say, narcissism is a career rather than a pathology, and every wayward triviality is exalted by the ease with which it can be thrust in the face of millions. He knows this must be the kind of resistance every generation brings to the shiny new obsessions of its children, that his indignation is the crabbed form that dying verities assume. Nothing can stop it, of course, except the boredom of the young, who will find their own blinkered certainty soon enough. Meanwhile his word processing program cannot recognize the subjunctive mood and hectors him to correct it. His daughter's child, he's certain, will not know what it was to write on paper.

His generation had been absolved from history, merely reading about it in the papers, or online. Could they have survived hard times? Even the wars of their parents seem superior to theirs, the clash of great nations, of continents, unlike the post-colonial skirmishes, the petty criminality of terrorism to which the world had been consigned.

He types another e-mail, a request, a suggestion, the timid gestures of his race and time. He sits back before the flickering screen
and waits for a reply. Darkness falls; he hears Sarah downstairs
moving pots and pans, preparing dinner, fixing another drink. She
sends him an e-mail on her phone from a floor away, asking when
he'd like to eat.

15

TO THEIR SURPRISE IT was not Meg who died that year, but her husband, Bill. They knew him less well, but he had always been kindly and decorous, glad to be included, a man with the sandy hair and ruddy complexion of someone who'd grown up being liked, with the loose, easy manner of a former athlete. It was an aneurysm of the kind that had felled Conrad's father and, they learned, Bill's brother years before; insidious, lethally concealed. He'd been scanned annually, but nothing had been detected. He'd walked out the door one morning and hadn't made it to the garage. Meg found him an hour or so later, bright orange leaves from the big elm in their backyard covering his face, looking for all the world as though he'd decided to lie down and take a nap. He was fifty-eight.

Meg's contemplation of her own death had prepared her for her husband's. She was tough in a way that her friends were not. "Tough as a boot," Christine said admiringly. For a middle-aged woman to lose a husband is merely a cliché, and Meg treated it as such. She received sympathy with calm and grace, letting the vicarious bereavement wash over her while she kept her own counsel, content to be the metaphor of other women's fears, broken only in that invisible way that made its low moaning sound in solitude and in the middle of the night.

The memorial service is held in All Souls, its old walls newly repainted a sacramental white, simple as the hope of salvation. Bill Franklin had been active in the local Rotary, so everyone attends; the church is full of people Conrad and Sarah have never met, Meg in the front pew with her grown children and their spouses and one infant grandchild, a girl who cries and cries as though the loss is hers alone. Becky Sternberger is helping usher people into the pews, beautiful in her black suit; she waves, smiling, as radiant as if she were at a wedding, a walking refutation of death's dominion. Sarah sits clutching Conrad's hand as though he too might disappear.

He gazes about the vaulted, peopled space. He barely knew the man, and suspects most of those assembled barely knew him. Why do we come together in this way, he wonders; what passes among us, within us? The answers come to him slowly: we are showing respect to the dead and to his living relatives, showing his children, who live far away, what community means here where their father lived, how many people cared for him. We are showing his wife that we are present for her, that on this day that will forever be the other bookend to her wedding day, we attend to her, to ceremony, as we did then. We are acknowledging our kinship with the bereaved, what we too have lost, what we know we too will lose. We are expressing a wish for ourselves that on that day we will not witness, people will gather and speak of us, remember us, and play music that we liked. And in some unmentionable, inarticulate corner of our hearts, we are saying to the void, *I'm still here; I yet survive.* Does any of it defeat death? Does our presence, do our prayers bear the lost one to some state of rest or joy? We may not believe it. But there is nothing more necessary than that we be here.

The little crew-cut priest leads them in a reading from the Psalms.

. . . Even the darkness is not dark to you, and the night is as bright as the day. Darkness and light are alike to you . . .

Sarah knows this by heart; she's murmuring along, her eyes never leaving the priest.

. . . for you formed my inward parts; you knit me together in my mother's womb . . .

Conrad thinks of his mother, of the day long ago when she died, how suddenly she became beyond reach. Her hair dry and gray.

. . . My frame was not hidden from you when I was made in the secret place, when I was woven together in the depths of the earth . . .

He thinks of Madeleine, in the warm plastic box in the hospital on the day she was born, how her tiny fingers curled so tightly around his thumb.

. . . Your eyes saw my unformed body; all the days ordained for me were written in your book before one of them came to be . . .

He thinks of Megan and Vince, wonders if Vince's operation was successful, wonders if Megan will invite him and Sarah to Vince's memorial service when he dies, if she even has one.

. . . Search me, God, and know my heart; test me and know my anxious thoughts . . .

He thinks of Sarah, dear Sarah, gripping his hand, the slight weight of her next to him in the pew, and wonders what he would say to the people in this place if she were gone.

. . . and lead me in the way everlasting.

The choir is bigger than usual; the best vocalists from other churches in the town have come to join in the ceremony. They sing Morten Lauridsen's *Lux Aeterna*, eternal light in their voices, rebounding off the high windows, the melody pulling at Conrad in a way that puts him on guard. He knows something of the composer, an old man living off the coast of Washington like a hermit, sitting at an upright piano that was hoisted up a bluff and installed in a house made from the trees cut to make room for it, writing down these sounds of heaven on bits of paper. He's never listened to the piece this closely, and part of him recoils from it even as it carries him away; it opens up too much, gently, ruthlessly pulling down this barrier and then that one and then yet another, the phrases heaping up like something dangerous and unstoppable—like death, like life. It goes on and on, and then at last it stops. He glances furtively at the faces around them to see if they're reacting as he is; they are serene, lifted up or tilted down in meditation. He glances at Sarah and she's searching his face, alarmed at the look on it.

There is another reading, the predictable one from Ecclesiastes about there being a time for everything, for gathering stones and for casting them away. At last something not quite true, not quite believable, unlike that searing, knowing music. He breathes easier, the knot in his chest unclenches, he looks out the window at the sky. Then the son of Bill Franklin, perhaps in his thirties, his kinship to the dead man etched in his face, rises to the lectern and speaks of his father, of the example he provided of how to care for one's children and to love one's wife, how his absence is not yet quite believable, how he still expects him to walk in the door at any moment. Saying this, the boy looks up suddenly toward the back of the nave, and Conrad turns involuntarily, along with a dozen others, to look with him, instinctively credulous, hopeful, before they catch themselves and look back down at their hands. There's an embarrassed titter, and the boy says that it's okay, he does it all the time. Meg's head, proud and erect till now, almost defiant, has slowly bowed lower as he's been speaking, and now it drops like the head of a fabric doll.

The priest leads them in the Prayers of the People, the humility of the phrase itself on the page, its democratic sweetness, unsettling Conrad again.

For our brother William, let us pray to our Lord Jesus Christ who said, "I am the Resurrection and the Life." Lord, you consoled Martha and Mary in their distress; draw near to us who mourn for William and dry the tears of those who weep.

"Hear us, Lord," the congregation says aloud, Sarah clutching Conrad's arm. Something is giving way, crumbling.

You wept at the grave of Lazarus, your friend; comfort us in our sorrow.

"Hear us, Lord," they say, the word *friend* piercing some inside part. That Christ had a friend . . .

You raised the dead to life; give to our brother eternal life.

"Hear us, Lord," they say. Each line is like a blow now, and this time the word *brother* tears something away. *I barely knew the man,* Conrad reminds himself.

Comfort us in our sorrows at the death of our brother; let our faith be our consolation, and eternal life our hope.

"Lord, hear our prayer."

He can barely get the last word out; his knees are shaking, and Sarah pulls him down into the pew.

"Are you all right?" she whispers, and he nods and gives her a thin false smile.

The choir rises again; he's almost fearful. A girl, innocent, too young to truly know what she is about to do, sits at the piano by the altar and plays a few quietly lilting bars of a melody that circles itself, like a round. The men in the choir begin to sing.

Sure on this shining night of star-made shadows round,
kindness must watch for me this side of the ground . . .
on this shining night. . . .

The women join and sing the same lines, the harmonies rising and twisting something inside that gives way completely. The voices are formal, uninflected, singing simply of what cannot be said.

The late year lies down the north.
All is healed, all is health.

Tears bubble up, stream down his face. He doesn't know this piece, never knew that it had ever been sung, that it was waiting. Lauridsen on his high bluff overlooking the Pacific, Agee in his city garret, have made this ambush, and he resents them for it. He wants it to stop, and he wants it never to end. The voices rise again.

High summer holds the earth.
Hearts all whole.

This line, its longing, its embrace, childlike and ancient, of a lost time when all is well, is too much. He's thinking of no particular person or place, no memory or loss of his own; in that way that only music can insist upon, he's not thinking at all. He's silent but sobbing now, bent, chest heaving, Sarah reaching an arm around him, worried. The voices repeat the lines in different harmonies, intertwining, dipping fatally into a minor chord then rising into major; hearts all whole. *Dear God*, he thinks.

Sure on this shining night I weep for wonder
wand'ring far alone
Of shadows on the stars.

The music ends; there is nothing to be done. He sits next to Sarah, and they pray.

16

CONRAD TELLS SARAH THAT she looks too thin. She runs four, five times a week along a bicycle path that meanders through woods from the town to another one six miles away. She runs halfway there and back again in the late autumn heat under a canopy of trees that breaks only when the path crosses a road here and there; she looks carefully for cars at these intersections, jogging in place. Sweat streams down her face, down her chest. Sometimes by deep habit she still calls for Box to keep up with her; "C'mon, boy!" she'll say to no one, then laugh at herself and run on. People on bicycles flash past, startling her when they call out from behind her, "On your left!" She dislikes the cyclists, so full of vanity and aggression in their faux Tour de France outfits and pedal clips and helmets, clicking through the gears like cicadas. But it is, after all, a bike path, and there are also children with their moms on bicycles with wicker baskets in front and bells on the handlebars that they ring in hello as they pass, not much faster than she knows she can run.

She listens to her body as she runs, tries to let it speak to her. Her legs are strong; her lungs devour the air. Her hands are loose, swinging at her side. She believes she would know if something like Meg's cancer happened to her; she believes she would feel it immediately. But of course everyone shares that conceit; we're always surprised when the doctors tell us of the metastasis, the blocked artery, the corrupted organ. The only story the body knows to tell its tenant is the story of living every day as before. She finds herself looking forward to the afternoon's first drink, which she knows isn't right; pleasures too much anticipated become something other than pleasure. She runs harder, sweat pouring down like a proof of virtue.

The last great question of any long marriage is who will die first. These days she feels the gnawing of time; she can sense the finitude of the life she shares with Conrad, though she strives to ignore it. His reaction to Bill Franklin's service frightened her, and he couldn't explain it. Usually she can treat this like the other impertinences of adult life that deserve only to be ignored, the slow insult of aging itself, the way the seasons pass abruptly now, like cards flicked out on a table. But in some quiet moments when she is alone like this, running, the thought pierces her. She's heard of couples who took control of the question, lying down together one night and by sheer will—so the stories go—or with the aid of drugs never rising again. She's also seen the couples who live on and on into a befuddled twilight where they cannot remember one another's names or how to open the garage door but cannot imagine life without the comfortable furniture their spouses have become. She's uncertain which she would prefer, surely none of it. The difference in their ages suggests that she will be the one to live on, that she will become the caretaker at the end, but she knows too much about life's great jests to presume it. These thoughts are like the television news, sensational and sinister and ultimately useless. She runs on.

She is childless; she is sere. Her skin has become slightly too big for her, as though her essence had contracted into something denser, undiluted, like the black stars she reads about in the science section of the paper, things so intensely themselves that they swallow space and time. The other women's future is their children, a future that extends beyond their own lives, and that is enough. When their thoughts run this way, that is where they stop. Hers have no such

shelter. What is left to her, what choices? Her body could betray her
at any moment, and what would she have accomplished? A home, a
marriage, yes, but what to show for all the years, all the love lavished?
If Conrad were gone, who would remember her, who would care?
She's often told him that if he goes first she doesn't want to live; this
always makes him angry. A mild panic sweeps over her like a breeze;
she feels faint and breaks stride. The insubstantiality of her life has
infected her, the thousand small choices that have tricked her into
having nothing to show. She thinks of her brother, his hand on hers
in the bus on the way home from the planetarium that day long ago,
his lips on hers in her bedroom that night, the anger and fear in his
face, and she suddenly understands it. He had seen how little there
was to his life, to anyone's, how he had no true home, how quickly
he would be forgotten. These are of course the misbeliefs she sensed
in Conrad too and wanted to correct. When she is gone, who Robert
was will be lost; her sister never knew him as Sarah did. Her legs feel
like lead; her pace slows and slows until she is bent under the ceiling
of green, her hands on her knees, sweat dripping from her chin onto
the asphalt like rain, absorbed in a minute and gone.

The previous weekend they'd gone to a barbeque at the
Sternbergers. They inevitably see their friends over meals; meals are
their true church, their license to gather. The McCaffreys had been
there; the Webbers brought their dogs, two enormous retrievers that
slobbered happily on everyone. The Sternbergers' teenaged children
wandered about the broad yard under the trees, beautiful and distracted, with the tragic look of the bored, while the adults rattled
ice in glasses and stole hugs from one another next to the grill, hip
to hip. Conrad was in a mood, listening to all of them, glancing at
Sarah with a reproving look as he often did in these settings, worried she would drink too much, worried about what intimacy she
might giddily reveal. She doesn't care what people think, or cares
but knows they love her enough to forgive her almost anything. The

talk was about real estate, where they'd all lived, where they might ultimately live.

Later in the car on the way home, Conrad said "We will be dismissed." Sarah recoiled as though he'd hit her.

"What? What do you mean?"

"We act as though we're a big extended family, that we're all going to grow old together. And then you realize that each of these people and their families is really quite separate from us, that they're all making their own choices, that they're planning separate lives that have nothing really to do with us, that we're just weekend entertainment."

"Connie, that's not true. Those people love you."

"No, it is true. It just hit me tonight. If circumstances warrant, we'll be dismissed; we'll become a memory, a story they'll tell other people at some other dinner somewhere else." Sarah understood the logic: once the children are gone, there's no need to stay in the little town, with its good, cheap schools, its green fields for the children to run on, its safe narrow streets. Once the children are gone, better to revisit the thrill of city life, or of foreign countries. Leave it behind; live again, as you did in your youth.

She stared at him in the flickering light cast from passing living rooms and porches. "I can't believe you're jealous because our friends have lives of their own," she said.

"It's not jealousy. Of course I know they have their own lives. But I'd somehow begun thinking of all of them as people who would always be part of ours. And that's just not necessarily true."

"Connie, that's life! Their kids are still in school; they have decisions still ahead of them. I'm amazed I'm the one telling you this and not the other way around," she said, beginning to laugh. He glanced at her, took a hand off the wheel, and placed it on her knee.

"Of course it is," he said. "I'd just forgotten for a while. We came here from a big city where no one knew anyone else, and we suddenly made all these new friends and thought we'd entered a different world. But it's really the same world, only with more dinners and shorter buildings."

"I think that's an exaggeration," she said. "Those people love us and always will. Some of them may leave, but that doesn't mean anything. We moved away from Madeleine. Do you love her less because she's in New York and we're here? You're just feeling melancholy tonight, and I don't know why. Was it Bill's funeral?"

"That was two weeks ago."

"You've been quiet ever since."

"It's just the cavalier way everyone was talking about moving away. As though it would mean nothing."

"They were just dreaming out loud. They're younger than we are."

"That's the point," he said. "I thought we all had the same dream."

"Connie, please. Sometimes you're so unrealistic."

"We enter the world alone, and we depart it alone."

"Now you are being truly silly," she said, and looked away and out the window at the darkened houses.

17

HE WORKS IN THE mornings, answering e-mails, marking up documents, but the firm calls less and less, not enough to keep him busy all day, so he's begun to read in the afternoons, tentatively at first, as though it were something forbidden, an admission of dereliction. He sits in the garden under a huge magnolia tree whose shade is deep as a confessional, or in the small library on rainy days, imagining his mother sitting in that very place with her own books about her, before Sarah took her place and changed the cabinetry, stripped the floors, replaced her books with their own. Against one wall of the library sits his mother's upright piano, on which he'd practiced scales as a boy. Those lessons are all forgotten; he never learned to read music, but when he lifts the fallboard, the keys tempt him like the fingers of a beautiful, complicated woman.

He browses the books on the shelves, titles from his college days, from his thirties and forties, books he's carried from place to place and put back up like familiar wallpaper, each title transporting him to the place and time where he first read it. Pynchon and Updike and Roth, oh my. The lyricism of those old books, the glimpses into an adult life that could otherwise only be imagined. The sex, forbidden and adulterous, luminous; the utterances of a survivor of an alien war, completely astonishing and completely real. The revelations of domesticity, the inconsequential writ large on God's great sky. But mostly he loved the language, dense as the prose of a legal document, demanding to be as carefully read. Closing the book and rising from a bench in Gramercy Park, walking its shaded oval with the musical prose still ringing in his head—there were no better times. Later it would seem a bit precious, but in those days those books had instructed him in what was possible, what might be known, what might be forgiven.

He reads some of the old books again and is startled by how different they seem, how the protagonists now seem absurdly young, how passages he remembers fondly seem insignificant, while the paragraphs that stun, that make him gape, bring tears to his eyes, seem entirely new, though he must have read them then, and they've been waiting on these pages for decades.

The books are in no order, Sarah's mingled randomly with his. He tells himself that someday he'll separate them into fiction and nonfiction and alphabetize them by author. Sarah's books include some fiction, mostly by women, about life in small towns, but most are nonfiction—what she calls "true" stories—about conversations with angels, survivals of suffering, redemptions of the fallen, first-person reports from heaven. There are cookbooks on the cuisine of every continent, coffee-table books on Princess Diana, on Sargent's watercolors, on the art scene in New York in the seventies, on Dior's salon in Paris. He shifts some titles around, stops.

On his computer one morning appears a formal e-mail to all of the firm's lawyers, announcing an agreement to merge with another New York firm. He knows the firm and lawyers in it, well-respected in the tepid way of his own, slightly larger, with many more foreign offices. The e-mail goes on to detail the advantages of this merger, the big jump in head count, the synergies that will emerge, the gaps in each firm's practice that will be filled by the other. He's unconvinced, but has no say. The announcement reads like something produced by a public relations firm, smells of hucksterism, desperation, and decline.

The first snow that year falls in airborne bales that blanket the land overnight. It's on this day that he's to be sworn in to the Pennsylvania bar. He's been procrastinating about this, but knows it must be done. A member of the bar has to sponsor new applicants, so he calls on John Webber, the only Pennsylvania lawyer he knows, to make the drive to the state courthouse in Pittsburgh for the ceremony. John is in his early fifties, balding and affable, a litigator with an interest in politics. He has the voice for it, the deep baritone of a stage actor, which he uses to great effect on the telephone.

"Conrad, my man, it's snowing like a banshee out there, have you looked?" It's dark outside, six in the morning, so he hadn't.

"I'd better drive," John declares. "We don't want to get stuck in that old car of yours." Sarah, her bathrobe drawn about her, pleads with him not to go. "It's too dangerous, Connie. They can admit you some other day." But he wants it over with.

They ride in John's big black SUV with tires like a semi's. They're both dressed in suits and wing tips under overcoats and boots. When John picked Conrad up, he came around and opened the passenger door for him, making him wonder how a man like John viewed him, whether he saw him as old, someone to be indulged, for whom allowances must be made. Conrad has learned to count the differences between older men's ages and his own like a miser with his shekels; he can't pass a stranger on the street without guessing his age, in an unspoken competition he knows he can only lose, the only question being how far along in losing one is.

They're silent for most of the drive, sipping coffee from insulated mugs. Visibility is terrible, the highway reduced to two blurred tracks of black in the snow, the shoulders invisible, the white torrent rushing at the windshield and then up over it. There are few other cars; the road hasn't been salted. Conrad is nervous at the conditions but doesn't want to show it, acting as though he does this every day. How stupid if we were killed driving to a swearing-in to the bar, he thinks.

John drives carefully, slowly, twenty-five, thirty miles an hour, while the radio mutters news of distant wars, the coming elections. Conrad knows from Sarah that John and his wife, Agatha, are conservative Republicans and part-time Baptists to boot; he makes no comment on the headlines.

To pass the time John tells a long story about one of his clients, a married man who had fallen in love with, of all people, a prostitute he'd hired on a business trip. The man had no intention of falling in love—what man ever does, really?—but he had, and unlike most men in this position, he saw clearly that it could not possibly end well, that all he cared for—his successful business, his family—would be destroyed if he persisted in the relationship. Still, he could not stop seeing the woman; she had given his life a meaning that he had forgotten. Sure enough, she eventually tired of his endlessly unfulfilled promises to get a divorce, demanded money under threat of revealing all to his wife, and the man was confronted with the choice of either paying her or neutralizing her threat by confessing to his wife and risking what that might mean. It was at this point that the man had come to John, who had previously handled contract litigation for the man's business.

"They call us counselors," John says. "That was one time I had to stop being a lawyer and become a counselor."

"What did you tell him?"

"I told him to do both—pay the woman and tell his wife."

"Why pay the woman if he's going to confess to his wife?"

"Because it would be a kind of penance, even if his wife forgave him, and it would put the woman back on the commercial terms their relationship had started with. Telling his wife was the only way to neutralize the past. It was a way of being true to both women."

"Did he do it?"

"Yes."

"And did it work?"

John barks a laugh and slaps the wheel. "No, his wife divorced him, and the woman kept after him for more money. But I still think it was good advice. Hell, it's not just about the outcome, is it?"

Conrad looks at him, thinking that, yes, it damn well is just about the outcome, but he says nothing.

The drive takes twice as long as usual, but eventually they reach the tunnel through the mountain leading to downtown and are for a moment sheltered, then emerge again into the blowing whiteness and cross the bridge, the gray rivers stretching away on either side. Entering the city is like coming into a great room, the buildings its walls crowding the rivers, the sky unable to penetrate it. The snow is lighter inside, swirling and tamed, the streets already plowed.

The courthouse has been refurbished at great expense to the taxpayers, its limestone bulwarks blasted clean of a century of mill soot, the industrial murals restored to earth-toned vividness, the marble floors glistening. Commuters hurry by outside, never entering this monumental space, the hallways vaulted like the transept of a cathedral, mimicking the grandeur of the continent where the men who built it had been born, their work done before the idea of separating church and state could be made clear to them.

They wait on wooden benches with a dozen others in the hallway while oral arguments are concluded for the day, then file quietly into the courtroom, grand and vast as a theater, where the seven Supreme Court justices sit waiting in their robes on a raised dais. All the other applicants are younger than Conrad, most just out of law school, eager and awed. Names are called, and the sponsors introduce the applicants in order of their year of graduation from law school, the most recent ones first. *If it please the Court . . .* they all begin, and when John in his turn finishes his rather windy introduction, citing Conrad's memberships in the bars of the great states of New York and California, his partnership in the renowned firm of Mason & Gannett, his decades of experience in the thorny realms of finance, he rises last of all and, at the prompting of the chief justice, raises his right hand and vows to defend the Constitution of the Commonwealth of Pennsylvania and to conduct himself in a manner befitting an officer of its Supreme Court. And despite himself he feels a surge of pride and of comradeship with all these strangers. It means nothing, this small ceremony, and yet it means he's not quite finished, not yet dismissed. They will send him a certificate, and he will hang it on the wall of his and Sarah's bedroom.

The drive home takes not nearly so long, and before they part Conrad buys John a drink in the tavern in the little town, and thanks him. A fire is burning in the hearth by the bar; snow has drifted up to the windowsills. They feel like survivors, like friends, and in that small shared pride they order martinis with blue cheese–stuffed olives and toast one another. Later, warmed still further, they call their wives to join them for dinner, and they do, kicking snow from their boots as they enter. And it's sometime during the dessert course that Conrad feels Agatha Webber's long legs leaning into his under the table, and from nowhere comes into his head an old Joni Mitchell song that Megan loved and sang to him at the door of her apartment one snowy night in Greenwich Village long ago, a song about being renewed and disabled by love and its edifying fire, about coming in from the cold.

18

THAT WINTER THEY DRAW closer to the Webbers and their children, a daughter in college in New England and a son in the local high school, each named after saints. With the specific gravity of certain friendships, the two couples keep to themselves for a season, rarely mixing with the others. Sometimes Sarah is explicit about this, confessing that she prefers that a dinner or an outing include just the four of them. Conrad feels the same but would never say such a thing.

Night in the snow at the end of the year, the dinner cooking. The Webbers bring their son along; he's grown tall and shy and skinny, a dark down on his jaw. The final recital of his years of study with a local pianist is approaching, and Sarah asks him to play. As they enter the library Conrad finds himself oddly embarrassed; the books on the shelves around them are a diagram of a thousand longings and past passions, clear as newsprint. The boy sits at his mother's piano and plays some Debussy, some Chopin, his unblemished young heart finding its easy way onto the keys. The music itself is an unutterable intimacy, and the adults avert their eyes from one another. Conrad purses his lips as though to hold something in. The boy's hands move over the keys and evoke the grownups' own childhoods, the great continuity of care of which they are only the most recent vessels. The chords rise one last time like a tide, and then his hands lift in unison, and he primly stands, and they applaud.

In the short winter afternoons Agatha teaches Sarah how to knit, and they sit together in the sunroom making scarves and socks. She sometimes brings one of the Webbers' big retrievers, who watches them intently, as though the yarn may be edible like the other things the humans handle.

Drawn as Conrad is to her, he can't quite decipher Agatha; there's a deep, carefully shuttered reserve to which no one is admitted except perhaps John, though Conrad doubts it. There is none of the convivial silliness that Sarah and Christine share, the spirituality that Meg confides, Becky's carefree sensuality. Taller than most men and blonde and unconsciously imposing, Agatha is a serious woman, younger than Sarah, barely fifty, carefully composed in her dress and manner, almost masculine in her care with words, her decorousness, as though from a different era. She'd gone to business school and was once an advertising executive, but gave it up when the children were born, almost too late.

"John always wanted kids," she explains. "I put it off as long as I could, then got pregnant primarily for him. I couldn't believe I'd be a good mother, didn't understand this dementia women get into over their babies. Then I had one, and I understood. I never went back to work. I couldn't leave them."

"I'm sure I would have done the same," says Sarah. "But what about now? Stephen's almost grown; you could go back now."

"No one wants me now. An older woman who's been out of the workforce for twenty years? Forget it. You have to keep your hand in or get out. I chose to get out. That door has closed."

"Do you miss it?

"Working? Sometimes, I suppose," she sighs. "I miss the camaraderie of it. I miss certain people; I miss getting paid to do things. I think that's why men work the way they do; it confirms their sense of worth. They don't have childbearing to fall back on. I hope I'm not offending you."

Sarah keeps her eyes on her stitches, which are tight and fine. "Not in the least," she says. "I have Conrad's daughter, and I know what you mean. I'm lucky I never really had to work. And I've had practice in living a totally adult life that you mothers never had, if I may say so. I don't know how you go back to just the two of you after twenty years of raising kids."

Agatha falls silent. "I'll let you know," she says finally.

Madeleine comes for Thanksgiving as promised, with Lloyd Davidson at her side. He is diffident and suave, like a gambler who knows he holds a winning hand; his face shines with cultivated blandness, reflecting everything back. What strikes Conrad first is that he's shorter than his daughter, dressed like a college kid in loose shirttails and jeans. He's slender as a boy, but his hair is thinning, making him look older than he is, the age Conrad was when Megan and he divorced, when his world was disintegrating instead of coming together as this young man's must be. Looking at him, his arm casually circling Madeleine's waist as they sip wine in the kitchen, Conrad perceives the real difference between jealousy, which he doesn't feel, and envy, which he does.

There is no moment when he's alone with Lloyd, no talk of the marriage to come, much less any asking of permission or blessing. Instead they talk of business and deals, Lloyd's specialty in alternative energy and subsidized housing, the tax-benefitted transactions du jour. None of the people Conrad did deals with at GE Capital are familiar to the younger man; after a few minutes of fruitlessly trading names, they fall silent and smile at each other while the women sip their chardonnay. There is nothing about him that reminds Conrad of himself at that age, no hint of the obsequiousness he would have shown to the father of the woman he would marry, the wish he felt then, strong as fever, to be thought well of. He notes that Madeleine has done something to her hair; it takes him a moment to realize she's begun to color it, covering up the gray that he'd been so proud of when he was her age. It had made him more credible back when he was what they called the youngest guy in the room.

At Madeleine's insistence, the four of them go to a movie, something she'd wanted to see but never had time for in the city. It's about a couple who meet by chance at ten-year intervals in different European cities, always in love, always separated by their respective fates. They are childless, beautiful, untethered to everyday life. They walk cobbled streets and talk like screenwriters; it all seems unreal to Conrad. The subject is in part the passage of time, the implacable toll of decades, but the nature of film, which makes a joke of time, undercuts the point.

"Was this true?" Sarah asks him as the final credits roll.

"Not a bit of it," Conrad tells her. Madeleine, on the other hand, is beaming; it has confirmed something for her, her hand knitted into Lloyd's as they walk out to the car.

Thanksgiving evening, candles and silver glowing on Sarah's table. Conrad says grace, something they never do normally, giving thanks for the presence of loved ones, the nourishment prepared for them, asking that it be blessed to their bodies, and their bodies to God's service. It's a couplet he learned somewhere long ago, from his mother, perhaps, and they are each left wondering, glasses raised, what God's service might mean. Then he thanks the younger couple for coming, and the peas are passed and the turkey carved, and in the morning they're gone.

19

MADELEINE CALLS CONRAD A few weeks later with a request: to go skiing, just the two of them one more time before she gets married. After her mother and Conrad divorced, he'd taken his daughter to Aspen and Snowmass and put her in ski school at age six or seven, later to Telluride and Park City, and by the time she was in college, she was leaving him behind on the steeper runs, straight down, barely carving. He'd learned to ski late, in his thirties in California, and knew he'd never be as good. It was one thing he'd given her, he thought, this casual familiarity with mountains and snow, the joy of yielding to the fall line.

So in March they go back to Telluride, where he'd recommended Walt take his doomed ski party so many years before. Sarah doesn't ski and is happy for him to go without her, pleased for him that Madeleine has made what she considers a great gesture. Conrad tells her that he doubts it means much more than a vacation he will pay for.

They meet in Denver and board a tiny jet that flies them down the chute between mountains to the town's short airstrip atop a plateau, stay in a hotel high on the mountain, and in the evenings take the big gondola into town, up over the peak, the immense San Juan range sprawling like an alien castle in the distance, down into the box canyon that encloses the town, twinkling in the ocher light of dusk. The last steep descent is like flying in a dream, silent and slow and with the eyes of a god, everything laid open, the streets, the modest houses dark against the snow; man's meek grid of order cupped in the palm of nature.

They alight as though from heaven and walk to dinner. Cabernet and venison, the self-congratulatory bonhomie of the diners after a day on the sunny altar of the mountain. The sky had the opaque blue of Colorado winters, like a great inverted bowl, the snow unblemished in the early morning, virginal. He'd caught an edge, skis flying, and fallen hard following Madeleine down a black diamond run he would never have attempted alone; she stopped and looked back up from far below, knees cocked, hair pulled back, edges dug in expertly to hold her to the plunging slope, and waited for him to collect himself, retrieve his skis, click back into them, brush the snow from his jacket, and lean back into the run quickly enough that she could see that he was all right. She watched him pass, then followed. His shoulder still throbbed.

"I think I'll let you do the blacks tomorrow," he says as she wolfs down the thick red meat.

"I thought you did fine."

"No, I did not do fine. You did fine. I'm too old for that stuff. I'll break something."

"Okay, we'll do blues."

"I don't want to hold you back. You can do the blacks, and I'll meet you at the bottom."

"I came to ski with you, Dad," she says. He can only smile back at her, this grown woman, her face glowing with the day's weather, strong and certain. All the tables at which they've sat together like this, all past. She's been long gone from his life and is leaving again; this is another goodbye. Most of what they share passes in silence; she gives no hint of wondering what he really thinks of her fiancé, seems to know that in the end it won't matter. He silently wishes her happiness and the courage to accept it.

That night in bed in their adjoining rooms, they feel the mountain beneath them, its great gravity holding them like a lover, the slant of the earth and more snow coming, the silence and white like a fortress all around.

The wedding comes before he's ready, the fall fierce with color like a fanfare. Camden in autumn, the bay a sheet of glass, steeples and sailboats white as love's hope, the riot of color on the hills. Neither Sarah nor Conrad have ever been here; it's as though they've suddenly found themselves in another country. Lloyd's family has put them up in an old hotel overlooking the bay, the scent of past centuries in the rooms clashing with the flat-screen TVs and op art on the walls. The town is full of tourists, but the wedding guests are removed; the ceremony and reception are to be in a house that the Davidsons have owned for generations, down a road that follows the bay shore out of town. Megan has come with Vince, who looks thinner, a constantly startled look on his face. The four of them sit at the bar in the hotel and raise a toast.

"I must say I never thought I'd see this day," Vince says, stirring his martini, which has arrived in a delicately small cocktail glass. He regards it suspiciously. "Where are we, Utah?" he sniffs. No one mentions his heart operation, which evidently went well, nor his ex-wife's rapacious children, against whom Conrad had dutifully recommended several sources of legal defense. They all see one another so infrequently, and the threads of their stories have grown so long that the elements of casual conversation—who owes whom thanks for what; which problems should be inquired after—have become hard to keep straight.

"Don't blame Madeleine," says Megan, who alone among them is avoiding alcohol. "She could have gotten married several times over. She was waiting for the right guy."

"I don't think so," says Vince. "About the several times over, I mean. Most men are scared of her. I don't know how anyone meets anyone anymore."

"They meet online now," Conrad offers.

"It's that or at work," says Vince. "They don't have time for anything else. It's nuts. Even when I was an intern, we went out in big groups and had a good time. Everyone's too worried about making money these days."

Megan rolls her eyes. "*These days* are two words that people over forty should never use," she says. Vince ignores her, turns to Conrad.

"What do you think Lloyd makes?"

He considers how to answer this; he's certainly thought about it often enough.

"I'm guessing around two-fifty, salary; twice that all-in."

"So more than Madeleine, right?" says Vince, gesturing to the bartender for a refill.

"A bit more, I think."

"That's good."

Megan, who has been chatting with Sarah about how wrongly they've packed, turns on him.

"What are you saying? That Lloyd should make more than Madeleine? Are you crazy?"

He holds up a hand to her, the knuckles sprouting curly white hairs. "I just think," he says, enunciating each syllable, "that things usually go better in a marriage when the man makes more than the woman. That's all I'll say."

"That's all you'd better say," says Megan, and turns away. Vince winks at Conrad, asks the bartender to make it a double this time since, he tells the man, they are all apparently in Utah. "Must be the Puritan thing," he mutters.

There's a reception the next day, hosted by the groom's parents. Lloyd, like his fiancée, is an only child, though Conrad can't decide if this bodes good or ill. Lloyd's parents are his age, and as he takes Adelaide Davidson's hand, he's sure he's met her somewhere before, her slightly faded beauty a window to what she was like at age fifty, or thirty, resonating like a secret memory. He feels himself blush, wondering for a startled moment if she was one of those women he knew for a night or two in New York back when. Her husband, Bob, is a big booming ringmaster of a host, self-made in the boatbuilding business and looking like a vessel himself, guiding people this way and that through his big white colonial house. It's hard for Conrad to see how skinny little Lloyd resulted from these two, unless in reaction or by adoption, though he can see the boy's mother around his eyes, in the deliberate way he lifts his wine glass to his lips. There's a blithe calm in him that Conrad never knew at that age; it must come from wealth, or further back. Madeleine, beside her man, is radiant, greeting friends from law school and New York, impervious to doubt.

"We're so grateful that you've let us host this," says Adelaide Davidson, keeping hold of Conrad's hand.

"I'm the grateful one," he says, and they both laugh. "Your town and your home are beautiful." Her look is penetrating, as though she, too, is searching her memory for their prior meeting, for the feel of her hand in his. Conrad chuckles to himself; in some parallel universe they must have had quite a life.

The wedding day dawns cloudy and damp but clears to warm sunshine in the afternoon. They walk the town, the small parks along the water. Behind the Davidsons' big brick house the green lawn sweeps down to a point fingering the bay, where a hundred white chairs sit facing across the water toward the harbor, its spires and bare masts like a forest in winter. A huge tent has been erected on the stone veranda, and long tables plated with silver and crystal, bouquets of pink roses. Conrad can't imagine Madeleine having much to do with all of this, but she's older now, and mellowing. The crowd is divided cleanly in age between the impudent youth of the bride and groom and the late middle age of their parents. Though it's past Labor Day, Conrad is dressed in a beige three-button suit, one he hasn't worn in years, but which he thought would look festive. Most of the men are in navy blue, and he feels insufficiently nautical.

The hour arrives, and the crowd gathers in the rows of chairs, Sarah and Vince seated in front with the parents of the groom. Megan and Conrad wait together for the bride to emerge from the house, and when she does, in a simple white sheath and the pearls they'd given her when she turned sixteen, Megan, Conrad's strong, feminist ex-wife, begins to weep. Their daughter, clear-eyed, laughs at her mother's tears and kisses each of them on the cheek, and they link arms and walk slowly, as though reluctantly, up the aisle through fallen leaves toward the young man who waits there with a smile and a tall gray priest. To Conrad's relief there is no music, nothing but the breeze and the lapping of the water on the rocks below, no arbor or altar, just the bay and the indigo sky and the distant harbor, nothing but the sighs of the people in the chairs and the tightness of his daughter's hand on his arm to declare that another phase of life is ending in splendor and ceremony, as if it were something they had earned.

20

BECKY STERNBERGER INVITES SARAH and Meg Franklin and Christine McCaffrey to go with her on alternate Thursdays to work in a soup kitchen in Pittsburgh run by the Episcopal archdiocese. This will replace their weekly lunches, she explains, but the drive will provide even more time to talk, and they'll be doing something worthwhile when they get there. Only Meg declines; she's been constantly fatigued since Bill's death, thin and pale, and all of them worry that it's something more than grief.

All of the women's children are gone now, to college or the military. As she drives, Becky talks about her eldest daughter, Kristin, who is flying a fighter over Afghanistan, hard and deadly as any man. Becky tells the story of when she was a young mother and her daughter watched as Becky killed a raccoon that had invaded the family's vegetable garden, with a shovel. After the final blow had been delivered, Kristin, then four, contemplated the carcass for a moment and then said in a calm, steely voice, "Fuck you, mister." It became her family mantra, recited often as she grew into a beautiful young woman who liked to hunt turkey and deer with her father and didn't wash often. They all imagine her firing off Sidewinder missiles with the same salutation.

These stories end with laughter, then a sigh. Sarah feels less an outsider now that there is no more talk of schools and soccer, proms and advanced placement exams, but she misses the children as their mothers do, misses most of all watching them as brothers and sisters to one another who could not know what that would mean all their lives. She loved how they would sit patiently at the tables where they ate and drank and laughed, and listen to their elders with utter, uncomprehending boredom. They were like sea creatures glimpsing life on land. *Not for me*, they thought. *Never for me*. And now they were gone into that life they could never imagine, that would elude their imagining even as they moved through it.

In the basement of the church are long tables with warming trays laid out, food steaming in huge vats. Their job is to ladle it out as the people file by with paper plates. The priest who runs things calls the bedraggled souls who come every week "clients," which sounds absurdly clinical to Sarah. She and the other volunteers put on aprons and hairnets and thin plastic gloves that don't quite fit and stand waiting while the doors are opened. Her friends are scattered around the big fluorescently lit room among the other workers; she's lost track of them. Most of the people who come are Black, though some are white and exceptionally dirty, like they've been sleeping in the street, their clothes torn. Some smile and thank her; others keep their heads down or simply stare at her in anger, as though she were insulting them. Her station offers "comfort food": creamed corn and chicken and string beans, the fragrance of the food mingling with the smell of the bodies that pass before her; she smiles at each of them as she raises the big metal spoons to their plates. They've been instructed not to say much, but she wants to. The steam blurs her eyes. *There but for the grace of God*, she thinks over and over, her chest tight.

On the drive home the women say little. Sarah watches the suburbs scroll by, the shopping centers and office buildings, the green order of farms, the unthinking normalcy of it all. Why had she been so lucky and those people in the church so unlucky? Why was she deserving of the grace of God and not them? Was it only bad luck or something more, some obscure moral failing or sheer dependency, as some of their male friends said? No, no one would choose that sort of need if you could avoid it, if it wasn't stamped upon you like a curse, like an illness that you've done everything to prevent, but it finds you still, like Meg's cancer or Bill's aneurysm, changing everything, ruining all your plans despite your worthiness and good intentions.

Sarah visits Meg later that afternoon, walking all the way to the Franklins' house on the outskirts of the little town. There are paths through the woods for part of the walk, but in some sections she must walk along the roadway, watching for cars. She's in her running shoes so she can do her daily jog on the way home.

Meg is in the sitting room of their tidy house, her legs drawn up on an ottoman, sun draped across her shoulders. She looks like she's been asleep, her eyes sunken, her face pale. A book is open in her lap, several pages dog-eared. She smiles at Sarah but doesn't get up as she leans to hug her. Meg offers tea from a small black metal pot, and Sarah tells her of the day, the trip to the city, of the people lining up for food.

"We were doing so little for them, it seemed so unfair," she says. "I don't know if I could do it again."

"You can't pity those people," Meg replies. "That's the last thing they want."

"It really wasn't pity I was feeling. I was angry."

"At what, for heaven's sake?"

"At the way the world works, I suppose, for failing so many people."

Meg sighs. "Aren't you the one who also swears at insects?"

"Flying ones, yes. I'm afraid they're going to sting me," Sarah says, playing along, the petulant little girl to Meg's wise grandma. "And spiders. I particularly hate spiders."

"So you get angry at them."

"Damn right, the bastard-ass bastards."

"What makes you think they understand English?"

"I don't care if they do or not. I just want them away from me."

"You've got to become more accepting of things as they are." Meg's face is pinched, her head back against the chair. She looks immensely tired, and Sarah searches for something funny to say.

"I've been reading this book," Meg says, lifting it and letting it drop. "About letting go."

"Oh, Meg."

"No, it's good; it's a wonderful book. It's helped me a lot. We all live lives of excessive attachment to others. The greater our attachment, the greater our vulnerability to loss. We lose someone we love, and we experience it as a loss of ourselves. The Buddhists know that attachment is one of life's great illusions, a failure of vision. I know you hate these ideas, Darling."

Sarah waits for a moment before answering, as she's seen Conrad do. "I don't hate them; I just don't agree with them," she says finally. "We're social beings. What are we, what are families, what are friendships, if we're not attached to other people? It seems absurd to say that attachment is an illusion."

Meg is smiling now, reaching for her hand. "It's attachment to what we represent to one another that's the illusion. I love you because you're pretty and you treat everyone kindly and you remind me of my mother. You love Conrad because he treats you kindly and reminds you of your father, or your brother. Sorry," she says, seeing the shock on Sarah's face, "that's just an example. I'm sure you love Conrad for all sorts of reasons. But the fact is that what we see in others is not what they are. That, too, is an illusion."

"I think I know who Conrad is. I don't have any illusions about him."

"But your attachment to him is a liability, Darling; please see that. I'm not saying you should be less devoted to him or less in love with him, but remind yourself that what we see in one another is transient. Beneath it is something eternal and divine. We have to let go of our attachment to appearances and personalities to see it. You should read this."

Sarah examines the cover of the book, sips her tea.

"I'll give it to you when I'm done," says Meg, leaning back again, closing her eyes. "Meanwhile, don't worry so much about the people in the breadline. They're all divine, just like you."

21

GOLF IS A GAME Conrad never felt comfortable with: a suburban game, wasteful of land and water and time, an old man's game, yet impossible to master with the tools old men can muster. He played it as a teenager in the suburbs of Pittsburgh, only wanted to be average at it, but it's eluded him; he avoids it now, plays only once or twice a year. So when Felix McCaffrey asks if he would join him in a round, his first instinct is to say no. Then he considers the length of the autumn days and the clubs sitting idle in the garage, and he relents.

They play on a course just outside of town, someone's farm converted to fairways and bunkers, hilly and short off the tee. Leaves litter the ground, making their balls even harder to find. It's still hot enough in the afternoon to make them sweat as they carry their bags, line up their shots, compliment one another on the occasional good stroke, remain silent at the balls that slice hopelessly into the woods or travel just a few feet through the grass. They would laugh if it wasn't such a beautiful day and it didn't seem important to do better at something so simple in principle.

Golf reveals character, Conrad has read, and Felix's game is completely consistent with his: laconic, terse, his swing elegant but underpowered, possibly because his takeaway is too slow and he pauses overlong at the top of his backswing. Conrad on the other hand swings too fast and hard, usually lifting his head and topping the ball in his eagerness to see what's going to happen. Even the landscape is metaphor, burnt and serene, its green strength collapsing by almost perceptible degrees. They talk the way men talk, their eyes roaming the horizon, circumspect, presuming nothing.

"The Santa Fe house will need a new roof soon," Felix says. "I hope we can count on you for half."

"Of course, that's what we agreed."

"I hate to ask. And my lawyer friend says he'll have the retitling papers over to you next week. Sorry it's taken so long."

"No rush," Conrad says, then holds still as Felix hovers over a putt. The ball goes long; he hasn't read the break, that the whole green, though flat as a pan, is tilted back toward the creek that borders it. He's still away and putts again, and this time the ball drops with a sound like money in the bank.

"Double bogey," announces Felix, shaking his head.

"I stopped counting some holes back." This is the only way he can stand to play the game, by not keeping score, which he realizes is a character flaw, a denial, like not playing the game at all. He reads the break again, overcompensates for the slope and leaves it short.

"How did I let you talk me into this?" he mutters.

"You need to get out more," says Felix, and Conrad glances at him from under the brim of his cap to see if he's serious. Conrad wonders if there's a point to this outing, if Felix wanted to say anything more than that he would be needing Conrad to ante up his share of the cost of a new roof for the house in Santa Fe. He reminds himself that there should really be no point, that companionship and the long reach of the afternoon should be enough, but the habituated need for process and outcomes still itches. Felix still works, still jets off to New York almost every week, full of purpose; he knows Conrad is at the very end of his career. They speak of none of this, talk instead about the lack of good restaurants in the little town, the volatility of the stock market, their wives.

"I honestly don't know what Christine ever saw in me," says Felix as he contemplates the next drive. The tee is elevated, overlooking the steeples of the town and the homes scattered among the ancient trees. The fairway is far below, stretching into shadow, and starts a hundred yards out. "We were such kids."

Conrad doesn't answer. Felix is Sarah's age, still a young man as far as he's concerned. He tries to imagine Felix and Christine as new recruits at Goldman Sachs, working together on deadlines, flirting over late dinners downtown. "If we had to rely on personal merit, none of us would be married, would we?" he says finally. "So much of life is about chance meetings and luck. Sarah and I might never have met if I hadn't gone to a certain dinner a long time ago." Saying it makes him feel old, the driver heavy in his hands. Felix hits and then Conrad, both their drives straight and long for a change, landing within a few yards of one another in the broad dark below. The sun drops behind a distant hill, and Conrad feels his phone buzzing in his pocket. He ignores it and they stride down the hill in silence, their clubs clicking in their bags with each step like the ticking of clocks.

Conrad's second shot slices badly and stops too close to a low fence to play. He kicks the ball out a few feet, knowing that Felix won't care even if he sees. His phone buzzes again, and this time he takes it out and looks at it. Sarah. He puts the phone back in his pocket and hits the best iron of the day, perhaps of his life, a high looping draw that hits the green's far edge and stops as though painted with glue. Felix overshoots, chips back to within a yard of the pin. As Conrad waits next to his ball in the gathering dusk for Felix to hole out, absorbing the peace of idleness and comradeship that he imagines golf was meant to impart, his phone rings again, and this time he takes it out and walks off the green and stands with his back to Felix and answers it.

"Connie, I've been calling," says Sarah, and he knows something's wrong.

"What is it?"

"It's Vince. Megan called, and Vince has passed away."

The jet descends through rain to the runway at LaGuardia. Sarah grips his hand hard until the wheels touch down. The face of his ex-wife, which would be transformed if it could split open into a smile, is haggard and strained as they walk out of the long concourse to meet her. This face, in which he watched tiny blood vessels erupt like explosions on a distant planet on the day their daughter was born, is the face of an old woman. Her hair is wild and white, the hair of a witch in a child's book. He's never seen defeat in her eyes, but he sees it now, and something else, something like apology; for their trouble in coming, for the way she looks, for not being better prepared for this horrible trick time has played. Sarah drops her bag and runs to her and holds her while Conrad stands by in his customary way, waiting. Then Megan turns and looks him frankly in the face but holds him away from her, her hand tight on his arm.

"Thank you," she says formally. "Thank you for coming." Then she turns and they follow as she hurries away through the crowds, as though Vince were waiting for them.

They drive a long way east on Long Island, Megan at the wheel, Sarah in back. It's disorienting for Conrad to be traveling away from Manhattan rather than toward it after getting off a plane. Madeleine has already taken the train out from the city and is waiting for them. They talk of Vince's last few days, his tired, patched heart's final rebellion, his confusion.

"I don't think he knew what was happening," Megan says, tears starting down her cheeks again.

"Megan, let me drive," Conrad says.

"No, no. I'm perfectly all right. I do this all day; I'm used to it."

"You drive all day?"

"Cry all day," she says, then laughs in spite of herself. Sarah offers a Kleenex from the back seat. Megan dabs at her face and they all stare out the windshield, the wipers beating at the rain.

"He'd had enough," she says after a few minutes. Another long pause. "He'd spent his whole life in hospitals. He didn't want to die in one."

"Where *did* he want to die?" Conrad asks, hoping she'll take this as cleverly rhetorical, the obvious answer being nowhere, never.

Her glance is sharp. "On a golf course."

"Really? I didn't know he played."

"He played terribly. But he loved it. I even took it up for him."

"I can't imagine. You're such city kids."

"Yeah, well . . ." and her voice trails off because, Conrad is sure, the tense of the sentence has torn at her, and calling them kids is too intimate. He reminds himself that this is ground they don't yet know how to walk, and he must be more careful.

They're silent the rest of the way to the house, one he's never seen even in pictures. It's a simple two-story Cape Cod in a white-fence town on the south shore, old money and modest about it. Megan and Vince moved there from Brooklyn after his first operation, from which, she claims, he never quite recovered. It had been Vince's mother's house, a fact that had caused Megan to resist the move for years. Conrad wonders: Why do we all end up back in our mothers' houses?

He's shocked when they enter, as though plunged into cold water, to see how far his life has diverged from Megan's, how each marriage puts on its own clothing, distinct as a fingerprint. It's like a hoarder's house. The rooms are in thorough chaos, filled with books and newspapers, old magazines stacked high in the chairs. Dust fills the air. It smells of recent cooking and a hint of mold. He tries to calm himself against a wave of claustrophobia, quells an impulse to run around opening windows and drapes. Madeleine yells hi from the kitchen and comes out wiping her hands on her skirt.

Megan ritually apologizes for the mess, and the three of them go upstairs while Sarah waits. Megan wants someone to review Vince's testamentary papers, something Conrad told her she, who was a fine trusts and estates lawyer in her day, could do herself.

"I can't do it right now," she says. "I'm not thinking straight. Besides, he told you something about all this that he didn't tell me."

He knows this isn't right, that Sarah and he are there just to attend the service, that their daughter could do this as well or better than him, that this is some obscure melancholic gesture on Megan's part. "If you mean that night in Brooklyn, he didn't tell me anything. I just referred him to some lawyers."

She points to the chair behind Vince's desk, sweeps a space clear of clutter, and places a manila file before him. Madeleine sits on a stuffed leather sofa by the door, watching her mother carefully. "I'm going to go see after Sarah," Megan says, and is gone.

Conrad sits at the desk and looks at Madeleine, who shrugs and pulls out her phone. He glances around the musty old room. The disorder of the rest of the house may have started here where it is densest, and with Vince, who is finally free of it. Medical diplomas hang crookedly on the walls; loose papers are crammed into the spaces above the books that line the room. The musky scent of disintegrating paper mixes with something else, cigar or pipe smoke. The dark desktop is covered with rings bleached into the wood by decades of sweating drinks. He feels like a thief, or an adulterer who will surely be discovered and thrown out the front door in a heap, the mustachioed cuckold shaking his fist behind him. Ah, Vince, he mutters to himself, why did you have to go first?

He peruses the file and finds what he expects, reading none of it as he believes Megan is trusting him not to do: last will and testament recently executed, revocable inter vivos trust, health-care directive, a list of trust assets. Vince's attorney in the city will have all this, and only needs to be told that his client is dead to set things in motion. At the bottom of the short pile is a separation agreement on yellowed on-ionskin, signed in the seventies, when Conrad was still in law school and had not yet met the woman who was to become his wife and the mother of his child and later the great love of the man in whose chair he sits. Attached to the post-nup is a letter from a partner in one of the New York firms he'd recommended to Vince, assuring his client in rather technical terms that his concerns about his exposure to the claims of his ex-wife's latter-born children were largely unfounded, and providing a number of citations to court cases in support of this view. Conrad can't imagine Vince having the patience to read it.

He returns to the list of assets, mostly securities and real estate, which to his surprise total over twenty million dollars in fair market value, more than twice what he and Sarah have. He surveys the shabby room again with a twinge of shame; they've lived so simply. The list is something Megan should see and may not have seen, but he can't bring himself to be the one to show it to her. He's relieved to see the big number, and hopes that Vince was as good as his word and has left most of it to his widow. He looks up at Madeleine, who's bored, distracted, scrolling through messages on her phone.

Widow. What a strange diminishing word to attach to Megan, who had seemed indomitable when she was his wife and whose widowhood he'd once assumed would mean his own death. For a shameful moment he feels a twinge of pride at having outlasted his old nemesis-turned-friend. But as they walk back downstairs to join the two women talking in the kitchen, a powerful anxiety rises up, with Sarah at its center. She will have none of Megan's quietly tearful aplomb in dealing with his death, and there will be no one like him, a man who knows all of her adult life, joined in parenthood, to come and sort through papers for her, to sit with a glass of wine and talk about first times as he is about to do, to remind her that life long preceded him and will persist long after him. She has said that she doesn't want to live when he's gone, and he's afraid she means it. He wants to hurry to her side, hold her, comfort her in advance, but the last thing he can show to Megan now is the mutual solace of a whole couple. Instead he touches the back of Sarah's neck as he passes and finds a place among the women and lifts the glass they've poured for him. *Please don't let her be a widow,* he thinks. *Let her go first.*

22

SARAH WANTS TO CELEBRATE her fifty-ninth birthday in Santa
Fe, so they go, trying to feel as though the McCaffreys' house is theirs,
shopping for new furniture for one of the bedrooms, cooking in the
unfamiliar kitchen, eating under the stars on the *portal*.

Conrad lies in the sun in the utter stillness of autumn in the mountains and watches a bee curry pollen from a Russian sage. Above, as
against a screen, a thrush pursues a moth through the transparent
blue of the sky, the ancient avarice of life for life.

They hike in the desert to the north of Santa Fe, through a narrow
canyon where millennia are spelled out in the rock strata as clearly
as a child's story: here there were forests, here fires, here seas and
creatures lost to the earth. They hold hands and climb the wall of
the canyon, helping each other up. He's surprised at Sarah's strength,
how the altitude doesn't seem to affect her as it does him; it must be
her running. Or perhaps that the difference in their ages is beginning
to manifest itself, is slowly dividing them. From the top of the canyon
wall they scan the horizon of mountains in which Santa Fe is cradled,
distant thunderstorms flinging lightning into the Jemez range, shafts
of sun painting the Sangres an impossible green. Breathless and smiling in the thin clear air, they turn to one another, Sarah lifting her
face to be kissed. And suddenly time stops, and they're both aware of
it, the presence of the moment, and of the next, and they cling to one

another, holding still, dreaming that the current might not find them again, that a century from now they might be here, unchanged, part of the rock, the sky, fleeting and eternal as lightning.

The Webbers divorced that fall. All the wives were shocked; they had seemed so serenely married, and were good Baptists as well, though they recalled that Agatha had converted for John's sake from something less strenuous. Their son had just left for college; they'd waited for that. Sarah remembered her conversation with Agatha about children leaving home and what that might mean to a couple. Conrad remembered the conversation in the car on that snowy morning on the way to his swearing-in, about John's unfaithful client. But neither of them had seen this coming. It was evident from the way the deed was carried out that it had been long planned. There was nothing tentative about it, no couples therapy, no trial period of separation; one week they were living together in their stately Georgian on Main Street, and the next they were both gone to separate refuges, each taking one of the dogs, he to Pittsburgh, she to her parents' home in Ohio, the house dark and up for sale. It was like a sudden death.

Rumors circulated that Agatha had taken a lover, or that John had, that Agatha had received a job offer that John had opposed, that their daughter, about to graduate from college, had declared herself gay. They'd said nothing, even in goodbye, so that their disappearance seemed a rebuke, a disavowal of what Sarah had thought was a bond almost as close as family. It shook her.

"It's like an elopement in reverse!" she cried, her hands pressed to her ears.

"Don't take it personally. You never know what's going on in someone else's marriage," Conrad said as though it was comforting. "And I'll bet they come around again after they sort things out."

But he felt much the same, as though he'd been taken in by a particularly convincing and prolonged con. He'd felt a professional kinship with John Webber, considered him utterly reliable, a man he would have turned to in a crisis. Agatha was harder to know, something in her always held back, her grace and beauty and intelligence haunting rather than inviting, recalling the loves of his nervous youth, when everything was in flux, when women ceded no advantage to men, and lovers thought themselves equals. There are some women who seem to inhabit more than one face, more than one body, who come in composite elements, potent and universal, with a kind of beauty that silences reason. Agatha was, for Conrad, one of these. Once when she had leaned over him in the kitchen, peering over his shoulder at a meal he was preparing for her and John, he felt her long body beside his like a deep curvature in space, pulling at him. And once, when they went to the Webbers' house after a summer's hiatus in their nearly weekly dinners, she and Conrad had hugged, his arms slipping under hers with instinctive, unearned ease, whispering greetings in one another's ears. It meant nothing and everything. She was so much younger, too young, even if there were no Sarah or John. He wondered who would have her now.

He remembered the winter night when the Webbers' son had played piano for them, and he had felt they were a kind of family. He remembered the summer night when all their friends had suddenly fallen into conversation about living elsewhere, as though the life they were living together was just a rest stop on their way to other lives; the feeling he'd had then that he was a fool to place expectations of fidelity on anyone but his wife, or to think that a life full of friendships ultimately led anywhere but back to feral solitude. John and Agatha, like the rest of them, owed him nothing. They were pursuing what they understood to be happiness, or at least some kind of peace. For most people that would trump everything.

It did seem like a death. He was appalled by the economics of what the Webbers were doing: the payments to lawyers, the division of assets, the waste being laid to a lifetime of careful gathering. The remaining couples in their circle became reluctant to meet, as though some dark communicable disease had been loosed among them. Sarah went into a kind of angry mourning. Her daily run became even longer; there was an extra drink at night. Conrad complained again that she was getting too thin, too tiny, that when he held her in bed he felt like a child molester.

After a time they begin again to issue and accept invitations to dinner. Felix and Christine are the first to come, on a late autumn evening just after the annual suspension of daylight savings time, when the days seem to have jettisoned several hours and the year seems spent. Sarah greets them at the door, hugs and kisses each of them while Conrad waits to do the same. Felix looks tired; he's just come from New York where he spent the week in conference rooms, his nights in an astonishingly expensive boutique hotel.

"What has happened to hotels all of a sudden?" he asks as Conrad hands him his scotch. "They all look like the set of a science fiction movie."

"The kids like it, I guess," Conrad says. "Besides, it's much cheaper to decorate that way."

"It's like you never left the airport. The world is becoming an airport."

"I'm sure it feels that way to you, poor thing," says Sarah, leading Felix toward the kitchen. It's become their custom to swap spouses for cooking purposes, and tonight's chore is hers and Felix's. Christine asks for red wine and leans against Conrad, happy to watch, taller than him in her heels, her clothes like art, just those beads and that scarf, her makeup understated; she looks curated, though this kind of care is how they flatter each other.

Sarah and Felix are making a curried chicken in a big ceramic tagine that Christine had given her for her birthday. "I meant to take this to Santa Fe," she says to Felix as he arrays the spices, "but it's too heavy."

"By the way, we fixed the roof," Felix announces, and they all toast. "It cost less than I expected. I'll send you the bill, Conrad."

"Don't bother, just tell me what we owe." He hasn't mentioned the financial troubles at Mason & Gannett, the threat of bankruptcy that has spilled into the press, but Conrad presumes everyone is following the story and is too polite to ask, or thinks the Burrells beyond the reach of such folly.

"When are we all going to Santa Fe again?" Sarah asks. "I miss it so much."

"Weren't we just there?" Conrad asks.

"I meant all of us together," says Sarah. "It's been almost two years, and I miss those nights on the *portal* listening to Felix play his guitar in the moonlight."

"Where *is* your guitar?" Conrad asks.

"Home, where it belongs," says Felix, dicing an onion in an intricate cross-hatched way that Conrad has seen on TV cooking shows.

"Oh, you should have brought it," Sarah says, real disappointment in her voice.

"*Concierto de Aranjuez,*" Conrad intones in a booming accented baritone, trying to sound like an announcer on Mexican television introducing a wrestling match.

"I'll go get it," offers Christine.

"Don't bother, really," says Felix, stirring the tagine as he sips his drink. "I'm cooking."

"Would you stop cooking and start playing if we got it?" asks Christine.

"You can't reach it; it's on that high shelf in our bedroom."

"I can reach it," Conrad says. "Give me the keys and I'll go get it."

Christine gives him a salacious look. "I'm not having you in our bedroom by yourself," she says. "We'll both go. You kids finish up with dinner, and we'll be right back."

And before Sarah can grasp what's happening, her husband and her friend are out the back door laughing, and for the first time in her life she's alone with Felix McCaffrey and can think of nothing to say. His blue eyes are fixed on the steaming pot. "That's a dangerous pair," he says in a tone they always use when pretending to be jealous. The notion of Conrad as dangerous makes her want to laugh, but she feels suddenly weak, searches for her drink, backs away from the stove and sits on a stool, gazing at him like a pupil. The scent of curry crowds the room. When he looks up she looks away, the silence lengthening.

"Are you all right, dear?" he asks finally, and she thinks she hears in his voice a different question, an opening. "You seem down tonight."

"I'm fine; I've just been upset about the Webbers."

"Ah, the Webbers. That's all Christine has talked about too."

"It's so sad."

"We really have no way of knowing whether it's sad or not, do we?"

"Any time a marriage ends it's sad."

"I don't know about that. Some marriages aren't meant to last. Some aren't meant to begin." He looks at her, the spoon hovering, his face a portrait of knowing melancholy. *This is the moment it will happen or not*, she thinks. *There may never be another time. He either feels as I do or never has.*

She rises, reaches for his drink, her fingers brushing his arm. She could turn it into nothing, she could pat him on the back like a sibling, she could sink against his shoulder like a lover. It's all there before her, utterly clear.

"Thanks, dear, I could use another," he says in a voice that doesn't sound quite his own, his calling her that too much like a husband, and before she can draw back her hand he's caught it in his, and draws it to his mouth, and kisses it as though they did this sort of thing every day, as though it were nothing but the brusque endearment of spouses. She turns from him like a mechanical doll and walks toward the bar, and is struck by a thought so much like one of Conrad's that she thinks he must be telepathically eavesdropping: that the downside of this situation far exceeds the upside; that even if Felix feels as she does, there is nothing to be done; that to express it in the way she did when she was young—as she had expressed herself to Conrad on that Manhattan street long ago—would ruin everything, whereas their silence was a kind of loving in itself, like the mute devotion of oblates. She longs so strongly for the reassurance that reciprocity in love has provided all her life, and for the chance to indulge that love in the ways that the young can't bring themselves to forego, but she sees that this time, and perhaps for the rest of her life, that longing would be fulfilled by being denied. Anything else would diminish herself, or Conrad, or the life they lived, or the dream of love itself, the dream of another life that Felix evokes in her. It's simple greed to want anything beyond what she has, the greed of an infant seeking more of what it already knows. She's more willing than ever before to take on the risk of love, but the need to follow it to its end has fallen away.

She fills his glass with ice and his favorite scotch and brings it back to him. "Almost finished; where are those two?" he says and takes the glass from her and kisses her again, as though to make it seem less special, this time on the cheek, and they turn from each other and back to their tasks just as Christine and Conrad come through the back door, loud and happy, lugging the guitar case. The cold has electrified them.

"You should see what a mess their bedroom is. I thought we were bad," Conrad says, searching their faces, reading them.

"You now know my complete repertoire of lingerie," Christine says, stripping off her coat. Sarah squeals and hugs her as though they haven't seen one another in days.

Conrad refills their glasses. "Your husband is very neat, though."

"I'm never there, so it's easy," says Felix. He watches as Conrad takes the guitar into the living room and puts it carefully next to the fireplace. "Not there, Connie. Let it warm up slowly. Over here."

Sarah serves them at the old mahogany table, praying a quick grace to herself before lifting her glass, glancing from face to face. Felix has brightened in a way they haven't seen in months, as though something has been lifted from him, something resolved.

23

MADELEINE CALLS ONE SNOWY Sunday afternoon to tell them she's pregnant. The baby, sex as yet unknown, will be born in the fall. She's excited, even triumphant, but Conrad can hear worry in her voice for the tiny inscrutable being inside her, and for her life, forever changed. He listens, swamped suddenly by memories of her infancy, of her mother, furiously brave, looking up at him as she was being born. He'd imagined this call many times, wondered when it would come, and like so many other predictable turning points—her marriage, his own—its arrival seems less momentous than he'd dreamed.

He offers to put Sarah on the line so she can hear the news.

"No, you tell her," she says. "You should tell her." And this puzzles him, as he would have thought that she would want to manage the presentation of this milestone in her life, but she may fear that Sarah's childlessness is a wound that this news would reopen. He knows better but doesn't argue. Instead they talk logistics: whether this will mean she and Lloyd will have to move out of their apartment, how much maternity leave she'll be permitted by her firm, how often she'll visit the doctor. But all the while he's thinking of how his life had been utterly changed by having a child, how frightened he'd been the night Megan told him in her matter-of-fact way and let him know by her inflection that there was to be no debate about it. The look on her face implacable as stone, as though her pregnancy was an armor she'd put on, a state that instantly rendered him a tourist in the teeming city of her life. And of course the fear gave way eventually to awe and stolid duty and ultimately love and pride, but it was a journey that had consumed decades, and would never end. He'd learned that loving a child is the purest love, the most unselfish and impossible to fake. Their few childless friends in town, successful and worldly and kind, would always seem slightly fraudulent to him, like beribboned generals who'd never been to war. He knew that till a son or daughter comes along and rips your heart open, you could not truly know what you were capable of or how awful failure could be. None of this could he say to Madeleine, his self-possessed and competent daughter. None of it could be shared, though to him it seemed the true sum of what he knew of love, and all that was left for her to learn.

Sarah is thrilled when he tells her, this new life another opportunity to share the joy that still brims in her. She begins immediately to plan trips and clothes and furniture, the architecture of domestic comfort that she long ago mastered.

A week later a sickness fells him. He calls it a cold, but it's something worse, his breathing oddly labored, as though he were diving at great depth and his regulator had failed. He shuffles about the house like the old man he knows he's soon to be, and it's easy for him to imagine how the great decline happens, how the aches and pains and slow failures could accumulate in no time into lethal fatigue. Sores break out on his lips and, ashamed, he stays in bed most of the day, energy gone, humorless. "Your immune system is compromised," Sarah informs him. "It's stress. What are you worried about?" He doesn't know, exactly. Madeleine, the baby, the infinitely branching futures that this new life implies, final proof, though none is needed, that the world will go on without him. Sarah offers hibiscus tea and zinc lozenges, which he sucks sourly, not even attempting to read, merely watching the light shift across the bedroom, allowing himself to feel time tick, its great rolling weight. She wants to take him to the doctor, but he refuses. The black slab of the television hangs lifeless above the dresser; on its two hundred channels there is nothing to watch. Outside it's snowing again, snow on snow, endless gray. He pulls a pillow over his head, burrowing into darkness. There were childhood days like this, afternoons of paralyzing ennui when to move at all seemed impossible, and the idea of play was a frivolous dream. In adult life he's had the occasional fantasy of grave illness, something nonlethal but sufficiently debilitating that he'd be allowed to abdicate his pretense of ambition and be not so much cared for as simply left alone. As work has receded like a tide, Sarah worries that he's become bored, and he's quick to say that he's never been bored in his life, but this is untrue; boredom is inside him like a childhood virus, ready to reemerge.

Finally it's his body that rebels and drives him from bed and back outside, some cellular resistance to the indifference with which he greets each morning. No one is around; Sarah has gone to the grocery. The cold is like a slap across the face; he wishes for a beach on which to lie down again, but his feet keep moving against his will and he's trotting down the street, then running, breathing hard, the air lacerating his lungs. Past the church, past the pharmacy, he dodges the sheets of ice on the sidewalks like a girl playing hopscotch. Black naked trees inert as stones, the sky unforgiving. Past the entrance to the college, past the Webbers' home, grand and empty, mournful as a mausoleum, his pace quickening now, the pain in his lungs gone, the smell of fires in the silent houses, sweat beginning to run down his arms inside the heavy parka, ears numb, a manic smile parting his chapped lips. A friendly black dog paces him for a while, then falls away. Down to the bike path, to the meandering river, frozen over now, its banks heaped with snow where the plow trucks have dumped it. Small tight flocks of birds, black as chips of coal, cut the air. Beneath the ice, the brown trapped water still running. He thinks of his father, his bones in this cold earth, his mother's ashes on her hill in California. He's far from home now, feet growing cold. *This is a stupid thing to do*, he thinks. He makes himself stop, turn, begin to walk home.

Darkness has fallen by the time he crosses their threshold and calls out to Sarah, but by then he's imagined a trip to Colorado with his grandson (he imagines a boy) and rehearsed how he will teach him to ski, and how, one sunstruck day, the boy will whip past him at the precipice of a run and plunge down the steep fall line ahead of him, poles trailing carelessly, knees and skis locked together, his laugh drifting back to him through the cold air. The boy is nameless, but he is thin and tall and unafraid.

24

HE'S NEVER LIVED IN any house long enough to witness its decline, the subtle failings of paint and joint whose gradually perceptible accumulation mirror the aging of a body. He'd left his parents' home in its Pittsburgh suburb before it had stood for even ten years; the homes of his adulthood had been apartments in cities, his for a clutch of seasons and then left behind. When he had inherited his parents' place in the little town, they'd gutted it and turned it into what was essentially a new house; it was only now, almost twenty years into that chance stewardship, that he's begun to notice the cracks forming in the plaster, the scuffed paint and wallpaper that they'd stopped worrying about, the old flooring that they'd so carefully preserved beginning to splinter again. The furniture they filled the place with has become almost invisible to him, but when he looks at it as a stranger would, he sees that it's fraying at the edges, stained, faded. It's an idea they had long ago about how a home might look, frozen in place while they lived on and changed. He wanders the yard, noting that the west wall needs a new coat of paint, that the gravel paths have begun to show the dirt beneath. He's seized by a sudden fantasy of pretending that they'd just came upon the place and gutting it again, of starting it all anew, but another part of him wants not to care, wants to put all that, all these accumulated *things*, behind him.

He walks through the back door into the kitchen. Sarah is on a short stepladder removing things from one of the cupboards.

"Pantry moths," she says. "We get these every year, and I never know where they come from. Bastards."

"They ride in with the groceries," he says. "Can I help?"

"No, I'm just going to throw out everything that's open and start over."

"Not everything, surely."

"It's the only way to be sure," she says, raining boxes and rolled-up bags of snacks down into a black garbage bag. Something in him recoils at this—the waste, the profligacy of their lives.

Meg never leaves her house, and Sarah visits her twice a week, seeing finally that Meg is determined not to have life resume for her, that her cancer and her husband's death are like a singular message she has received and accepted. It frightens Sarah, but there is a part of her that can't help but admire Meg's stubbornness about this; it's like a religious faith that has to be respected. They sit by the fire and often read together in silence, the turning of pages like a secret conversation between them, the sighing of a great calm sea.

"You're the only one who still comes," says Meg after an hour has passed.

Sarah doesn't look up, deep in the dream of the novel she is reading, about a marriage that slowly crumbles over a span of thirty years. "Everyone loves you, Meg," she says a little too automatically.

"Yes, but you're the only one who comes."

Sarah puts down the book. "Well, if you must know, dear, I think you scare them. You scare me. You stay cooped up in the house this way, and everyone thinks you're still in mourning. They stay away out of respect."

"I am still in mourning. I'll always be in mourning."

"Meg, really. You must stop."

"No, I mustn't. We're too casual in our relations with people when they're alive, and too quick to forget them once they're dead."

Sarah smiles slyly. "Weren't you the one lecturing me a while back about the fallacy of excessive attachment?"

"Very good, dear," Meg says, rising to go into the kitchen. "I'll make a hard-ass out of you yet." They laugh, and Sarah watches her as she comes back with tea and pours it for each of them. The contentment this evokes in Sarah is so deep that she feels her throat catch.

"The truth is," Meg is saying, "my being alone isn't about Bill being gone. It's about me. I have my sons; they'll live on. But I know when I'm beaten. Don't get upset; I'm not suicidal or anything, but I've had it with the world, or it's had it with me. I know this is heresy, that you're supposed to rebound from a spouse's death and get all busy again and go on with life, and that cancer victims are supposed to be brave and cheery and resilient and fight to the end and all that, but really, what a patronizing set of expectations. It seems to me that refusal to participate ought to be an equally permissible choice in these circumstances. In any event, that's my choice. When I say I'll always be in mourning, I mean my life has been permanently changed, and I won't pretend otherwise. Same with the cancer. I just don't want to put myself out there anymore. What I need now is quiet and solitude, and that ought to be okay. I don't miss people much, never have, and don't take this personally, but if you stopped coming over, I probably wouldn't miss you either."

"Well, thanks . . ."

"No, really. I love you and always will. But I really have learned to let go, maybe a little too well for most people's comfort. Bill and all of you wonderful friends are inside of me and always will be. You did your work as friends, and I did mine, and we don't need to do it anymore. You're here." She presses her fingertips to the space where her breasts used to be. "I don't need you anywhere else."

Sarah draws a deep breath. "Of course you have the right to be alone and live your life the way you want. I just don't believe that's healthy for you. Look at all the studies that say social people live longer."

Meg snorts. "Don't get me started on living longer. We're all in denial. I'm ready, Sarah, I really am. I won't do anything to hasten the process, I promise, but this idea that we must postpone death for as long as possible is just another form of animal attachment. The day you die is just as good as any other. It has to be. I learned that the afternoon I found Bill in the backyard."

Sarah wants to hold her but believes that she's just been told not to. "I should go," she says, rising.

"Sweetie, please don't think I don't want to see you. You don't have to go. I love these afternoons with you."

"No, it's just that it's late. I need to make dinner." She grabs her coat from the sofa where she'd tossed it and struggles into her boots. At the front door she turns.

"I love you," she says with unintended finality.

Meg blows her a kiss from where she sits, unmoving, next to the fire in the darkening room.

"I don't know what to do for her," she says to Christine later. "I think I'm helping, and then she says something that makes me think I'm just bothering her."

"Take her at her word. She loves you, she appreciates your company, but she wants to be alone. It's the most plausible theory. Not everyone responds to human contact the way you do."

"She keeps talking about death."

"Maybe she needs a dog."

"She has cats."

"Oh. That's no help."

"She has no faith to fall back on."

"Neither do most of us. We're all great churchgoers but not-so-great theologians."

"I thought you were a good Catholic girl."

"Ha. I wish I were. I'm really more of a pantheist. At the end we're creatures of nature, and nature works in mysterious ways. Let me ask you: What do you think Conrad thinks about all this?"

"I've always assumed he believed as I did. He goes to church with me; he prays. I never saw a man so undone as he was at Bill Franklin's funeral."

"Maybe he was crying for someone other than Bill."

"I thought of that," Sarah said, staring at her friend across the kitchen counter, Christine's strength and careless beauty and the smells of cooking and the winter light slanting through the French doors and her own breath forming words and her own heart beating, all denying that anything but more life waited at the end of it all.

"Let's go to the city," says Christine. "It's our turn at the soup kitchen."

"Meg won't go. And Becky and Stu are in Florida."

"Just you and me then. Next Tuesday?"

25

HE HAD REACHED THAT age when life becomes almost tangibly finite; he could reduce it to numbers like an actuary: the times he might again go skiing, or to a Caribbean beach, or sit down to his mother's piano and work out a few bars, or make love to his wife, or read a novel; all these, once common as rain, endless in their repetition across the years, could now be numbered. Work had dwindled to nothing, everyone at the firm too preoccupied with professional survival to start anything new, much less to think of that guy Burrell in his little town on the edge of nowhere who knows something about transportation finance. He worries about falling out of the stream of things, of becoming not so much obsolete as uninformed, detached from the iterative knowledge of the day-to-day, the parade of media, the negotiations of love and sex, the strivings of work. If all that is in the past, what's left? An old man, a relic, someone to be pitied or, worse, forgotten. A nonparticipant. The great Other. This is the hardest thing for him; age is the body's way of grieving for the past.

He longs for spring, but it's still far off. Sarah suggests going to Santa Fe, but the thought of travel is daunting, and it would be no warmer there. Besides, Christine and Felix are hosting a Valentine's Day party that weekend, with a theme that requires that everyone dress as though for their high school prom. Sarah is gleeful at the prospect, leafing through the dresses in her wardrobe like a philatelist paging his albums, coordinating outfits with the other women. For the men this is easy, as long as they still own a tuxedo that fits.

The evening of the party is preternaturally clear, the moon a huge plate of mottled light at the apex of a dome of stars, encircled by a glowing ring of ice ten diameters wide, almost touching the horizon. In what universe could all this come into being accidentally? he wonders. This one, perhaps, yet its beauty is so extravagant that it seems contrived. He's driven for several blocks before he notices the Mercedes' lights aren't on, so bright is the snow in the moonlight. They've taken the dress code seriously; Sarah is dressed in purple tulle that billows up out of her coat around her neck but leaves her cleavage exposed, with high heels she's dyed to match and, for good measure, a sequined toreador jacket that her mother bequeathed to her and she's not worn since. She's shedding silver sequins on the black floor of the car. Despite her effort at irony, to Conrad she looks faultlessly stylish rather than dated, calm in her beauty, aware that she has once again failed at understatement but sure she can make people feel at ease regardless. He's oiled his hair and combed it straight back in attempted mimicry of an adolescent punk, but his tux is one only a middle-aged man could afford and in fact is only two decades old, bought to wear to his first Christmas dinner at Mason & Gannett, after his divorce, before he'd met Sarah. He fingers the satin of the lapels as if to retrieve something from those times, some lost linkage of then to now. Nothing comes; the present has swallowed it all.

The McCaffreys' house sits on a quiet cul-de-sac just outside of town, and when it was built in the seventies had been considered stridently modern, almost an insult to the benign, retrospective styles of the homes around it. Conrad's parents had talked about it in the sort of tones they would have used had a prostitute shown up at the bar of the local pub. Felix and Christine have made it new, with great vertical sheets of glass and square pillars of blond stone, and tonight it's lit up like a casino, the naked windows framing the throng already gathered inside, their animal surges of motion and color like gaudy schools of tropical fish in a crowded aquarium.

They enter to shouts of greeting, the women squealing and clutching and feasting on one another's outfits. The men shake hands or hug, sometimes merging the two by shaking first, then folding into a hug with the other arm. All their friends are there, and a half-dozen other couples they don't know. Even Meg Franklin is there, dressed in her offhand way, surrounded by women; her widowhood has made her queenly. People are still streaming in from the cold night, knocking snow off their patent leather slippers. Everyone looks grand and smells of aftershave and mingled perfumes. The rooms are reverberating with the high manic chatter of anthrophiles who've been confined to their homes for too long. Some of the men have gone full out for comedy, in tight sky-blue tuxedos and wildly ruffled shirts against whose buttons their big guts strain, but the women with this inclination have only succeeded in making themselves look sultrier, in sheaths slit to the thigh, bare shoulders, slutty makeup that suits some of them surprisingly well. Down the long stone hallway the hosts are trapped in the kitchen behind a wall of tuxes and gowns. Servers in crisp white high-collared tunics circulate with drinks and canapés.

Conrad orders a Gibson and wanders into the living room, remembering how much he loves this house, which shouts money and style, the colossal stone chimney wall rising two floors, the fireplace a blazing tunnel that connects adjacent rooms. The mid-century furniture looks less lived-in than curated, like an exhibit at the MoMA. He puts a hand on the soaring stone wall above the burning hearth and takes in its monstrous heft. He can't help but think of the money behind this, how it's done. Felix must be paid much more than he was at his age, Christine's family must be truly wealthy, or both. But then why bring him and Sarah into the house in Santa Fe? They've always been generous beyond reason, beyond anyone's willingness to repay,

picking up checks at restaurants, hosting weekends at expensive resorts to celebrate an anniversary or a birthday, taking groups to con-
certs in the city, buying all their friends small, exquisite, expensive
presents at Christmas. After a time they'd all become accustomed to
this, accepting this largesse as another facet of their lucky lives, this
good fortune that they happened to know the McCaffreys, who must
be rich. But what if they had no more than anyone else, or less? No
one speaks of these things. What if they've simply made a decision to
spend it, to give it all away, to hold nothing back, to have nothing at
the end? Conrad could never do this, but he's sure some people do.
Felix in particular, approaching from across the beautiful room in
what looks like a smoking jacket, his white hair hanging before his
steel-blue eyes, a brown drink in hand, has an air of weary acceptance
that borders on the nihilistic. Women pluck at his arm, reach up to
kiss him. He smiles benignly and brushes past, comes up to Conrad.

"Has anyone offered you a drink?" he asks, looking with dismay at
his friend's empty hands.

"Several people. I told one of them I'd like a martini."

"Ah. I heard the shaker going when I left the kitchen. We're out of
Belvedere, so I hope you don't mind Tito's. Where's Sarah?"

"I've no idea. She was engulfed the moment we arrived. You know,
the theme of this party is a total failure. This is much more elegant
than any prom I ever attended. And the women are much more
beautiful."

"We work with what we have," he says, smiling. "Listen, we may
not have a chance later, so come with me for a moment." He opens a
sliding glass door onto a deck overlooking the moonstruck yard, cold
washing over them like a wave. A waiter hands Conrad a drink just
before they step out.

"I've got something going on at work that I could use your help
with," Felix says in what strikes Conrad as an excessively conspiratorial tone. He raises an eyebrow receptively, sips his drink. "I'm

advising a client on an acquisition, a merger really. Both are finance companies; I can't tell you who they are until you sign a nondisclosure agreement, but it turns out that the target company has an aircraft-leasing subsidiary, and nobody on my client's legal team knows a damn thing about aircraft leasing. They're pretending they do, but even I can tell they don't. Luckily, however, I know someone who does." He smiles his thin smile.

Conrad is surprised at how these few words have altered his mood so suddenly, how his drink, so cold that a thin film of ice has formed on it, tastes like moonlight, how the burbling crowd inside suddenly seems glamorous, full of people worth knowing better. It can't be the drink, he's just begun to sip it, so it must be what Felix is saying: that he's needed, that someone believes he's unusually good at something.

"Come with me to New York next week. Monday or Tuesday if you can. I'll e-mail you an NDA tomorrow. I can make you a subcontractor, an advisor to the advisor. I need you to listen to the target's presentation of the finance sub's business model to see if it makes sense and then do some due diligence on their lease portfolio. I'll give you an associate to do all the grunt work and draft the report."

Conrad has already downed half of his martini and is feeling expansive, wonderfully urbane. "I won't need an associate, but I will need an indemnity."

Felix pauses. "We'll indemnify you. Or pass through the indemnity we're getting from the client."

"That'll work, assuming it covers every crazy thing I might do."

"I doubt you're remotely capable of doing anything crazy, but I'll send you the indemnity tomorrow, and you tell me what it says. The meetings are in Midtown; we're staying at the Carlyle. This will be great, Connie; I really appreciate it. And we might have some fun." His smile has broadened to show his teeth, something Felix never does. All this sudden comradery makes Conrad giddy. They toast, and he can see the grooved calluses on Felix's fingertips as he brings his drink to his mouth. Then they plunge back into the bright, noisy room like boys diving off a dock in summer.

Sarah is in the dining room, deep in conversation with two couples, her hands flying in emphasis, radiant, a magnet. Conrad walks up next to her and puts a hand to the small of her back, filled with pride and the beginnings of lust, so casually beautiful is she in her extravagant gown, her short hair carefully feathered in a way that recalls the day they married. Watching her talk, watching the delight in the eyes of the group listening to her, it comes to him that her love is her way of attacking the world, of protecting herself from it. His martini is gone; he asks for another and surveys the women: his wife and all the wives of their friends, each beautiful in her own way, unconsciously regal, instinctively loving. *They are all angels.* He says it aloud but unheard in the noise of the crowd. They are proof of heaven. He could have loved them all, he thinks. With enough time and lives, he could have loved them all. His gratitude that they exist vies with the mute frustration of a child who realizes that all the toys in the world are not his. Becky Sternberger comes up quietly, not wanting to interrupt what Sarah is saying, kisses him wordlessly and stands next to him, running her fingers up and down the bones of his spine as if by reflex, the way a mother touches a child, caressing, almost compulsive in her intimacy, giving comfort constantly because one never knows how much will be enough, and for a woman like her it's easy to give. He leans back into her fingers as they move.

Later, much too late, Sarah and Conrad drive home through moonlight thick as milk, and he tells her about his conversation with Felix.

"How wonderful!" she says, reaching through the dark of the car to hug him, making the car swerve. "Is Felix your best friend?" She's mostly drunk, vibrating with the energy of being with so many people, not yet on the edge of the collapse that will come.

"I don't know what that means, darling. I don't think in those terms. Friendship isn't a competition."

"But you must know who you feel closest to. If you had to talk to someone about something terribly personal, would you rather talk to Felix or to Stu?"

"I'd have to think about it. But regardless, Felix could never be my best friend."

"Why not?" She sounds hurt, as though this diminishes her as well.

"Because you are."

They're almost home, but he snakes his right hand up under her dress and finds the spot where her nylons end, then moves higher. In the garage he leaves the engine running while they paw each other in the dark like kids.

26

THE STORY HE TELLS himself is this: he's left for New York long before Sarah rises into the unknowing day. She never sleeps well without him, and in the dark of predawn she'd broken into a sweat that drenched the sheets and drove her into the bathroom to towel off. She'd had a disturbing dream about being lost in a great, vertiginously hilly city, separated from her luggage, dressed inappropriately, late for a plane, the usual nightmare. She believes in dreams as harbingers or messages, perhaps from the dead, perhaps from loved ones far away, perhaps from her own mute soul, but she almost never remembers them. Her thoughts flit over those she loves as she strips the bed and gets dressed and thinks about the dream, seeking a connection. The part about being late for a plane must be about Conrad's trip. The sense of being lost was of course about one's life slipping out of control, as any life could in a minute, she knows, even one that seems safe and filled with purpose.

And it is with great purpose that she prepares for the drive to the city, picking clothes that are not too showy but respectfully smart, as though she were going to a fancy department store rather than the basement of a church. The priest calls it the "undercroft," which sounds oddly sexual to Sarah. She snaps her purse shut against the thought, against the thought of the drawn faces of the hungry poor, and hurries downstairs, already late; she's supposed to pick Christine up in ten minutes, and she must eat or she will pass out standing over all that aromatic food. It occurs to her that she might still be hung over from the night before. She makes her coffee and fries an egg, no time for toast today, and eats it from the pan, glad that Conrad's not there to see it. She tosses the pan in the sink and drinks the last of the coffee and hurries upstairs to brush her teeth and check her makeup and returns to the kitchen and there it is: a spider, an unseemly large spider, tropically huge, squatting in front of the stove past which she must walk to get to the garage. She jumps back a step by reflex and hears herself let out a little yip of fear and shock; the thing is so big she can see the fur on its legs, which are arched like brown bows. Spiders have always terrified her; Robert used to tease her about it, catching them in jars and leaving them for her to find in the most unlikely places around the house in Gladwyne. Once she'd found one where he'd left it under the sink in her bathroom, and in a perfect mix of horror and rage she'd taken the jar outside and thrown it across the broad front lawn, farther than she'd ever thrown anything, and into the street, where the jar had shattered like a bomb. Now the thing rotates to face her, the tips of its limbs tapping on the floor with a mechanistic precision, adjusting, adjusting, then defiantly still. She knows the cold has driven it inside, but why is it so big? Why didn't the winter kill it? She looks around for something to hit it with, telling herself that if she were quick enough she might step on it, it's not really that big, but the thought of it under the soles of her flats makes her gag and she takes another step back and begins searching through her purse for her cell phone to call Christine, but she can't find it and realizes she's left it upstairs and turns toward the stairs, then back, praying the thing will have disappeared, but there it is in the exact same spot, unmoving, unavoidable. She advances cautiously on it; she can't let this thing prevent her from doing what she needs to do, but it arches its legs as though suddenly electrified, proving in an instant that it sees her and is ready for her, and she backs away again, a soft whimper rising in her throat. She takes one shoe off and throws it at the thing but misses, and the shoe bounces off the oven door and almost gets the thing on the rebound. She blinks because it doesn't move at all; it's as still as though painted on the floor, some strange kind of primitive decoration. Then to her horror it raises its two front legs and points them at her, the tips of the furry limbs waving slightly. She hears her cell phone trilling upstairs and half-turns to go get it but looks back, almost fearing that the thing will follow her. And it's suddenly gone, as though evaporated, or as though it never was. She stares at the spot, expecting it to return, to flit back into existence like a light switched on in a darkened room, but there is only the stretch of oak floor in front of the stove and her black shoe next to the spot where the thing had sat defying her. Conrad will later find the spider, quite dead, in this very spot. It could have been the spider, he will tell himself, but it could have been anything—a bird hitting the window, or something harsh he'd said to her before he left. But her hands are trembling as she smooths her hair and hurries upstairs for her phone, very late now, Christine calling, wondering where she is. She takes several deep breaths and decides she won't call back; she'll just go. But she's shaking so much that she stops at the refrigerator door and opens the freezer and pulls out the bottle of vodka and takes just a sip to calm herself. It burns, the vapors mingling oddly with the taste of coffee still on her tongue. Another sip, then another.

The hardest part is retrieving her shoe from in front of the stove, but she does it, and carries it outside into the cold and shakes it and looks carefully inside of it before putting it back on. A brittle crust of refrozen snow covers the path to the garage, and she walks on her toes, leaving prints like the hooves of a deer. Her SUV is like a big block of ice covered in road grime, and the driver's side door creaks and snaps when she opens it. The engine starts reluctantly, shuddering. She backs the big car out of the garage, being careful as always not to scrape the frame of the garage door; Conrad would kill her.

Everything seems in high relief, and she has the sense of observing herself from above, her every movement burnished with intense significance. It occurs to her that this must be what they mean by being in the moment, in a state of lucid mindfulness, but she's always found self-consciousness distasteful and hopes the feeling will pass quickly.

The streets are not yet plowed, and she moves through them slowly. Christine is waiting on her front porch with a covered mug of coffee in her gloved hand, her neck wrapped in thick bands of a knitted scarf, her breath streaming into the gray air. She hops in, and Sarah is surprised at how old she looks, her makeup thick and contrived as a mask. Sarah kisses her and adjusts the rearview mirror in order to see if she, too, looks this bad, and is not reassured.

"I'm so sorry I'm late, but there was a spider in the kitchen."

"Oh God. Did you kill it? Damn it's cold. Isn't winter supposed to be over?"

"No, it finally disappeared."

"They're more afraid of you than you are of them."

"That doesn't seem possible," says Sarah. She picks her way down the dim streets toward the interstate. A light snow is falling, and she turns on the wipers. Christine shivers and sips her coffee, not as interested in the spider as Sarah thinks she should be.

"Did Connie get off all right?"

"Before I was up. When did Felix leave?"

"Sunday."

"They make him travel on a Sunday?"

"Oh sure, 'the deal' never rests." She scratches finger quotes around the words.

"I'm so glad they're working together," says Sarah, slipping off her gloves for a better grip on the wheel.

"I am too; I think in an odd way they're suited to each other."

"Why odd? Connie loves Felix."

This makes Christine laugh out loud, an almost guttural laugh that reminds Sarah of Lauren Bacall. "Oh, sweetie, I doubt that. You love Felix," she says, and Sarah, startled, glances quickly at her, "but Connie doesn't have to love him. In fact, it would be better in these situations if he didn't."

"Can't people love each other and still be professional?" Sarah asks, hearing how silly this sounds.

"Not in M and A, darling," says Christine, looking out at the sky. "I am so sick of winter."

"I'm just grateful Connie has something to do. I worry about him being bored."

"Connie seems entirely capable of entertaining himself," says Christine absently, examining herself in her compact. She gives a little helpless shrug and snaps it shut.

"But he's used to being so busy," Sarah says. "Men decline so quickly when they're not engaged."

"That seems a bit harsh. Connie's a young man."

"You and I know that," Sarah says. "But I don't think Connie knows it. He's really quite vain and can't stand the idea of getting older. He can't even utter the word *retirement*." She turns down the long street that leads out of town.

"If he wants to stay busy, he can," Christine says. "Don't think Felix hired him out of charity, or because he loves him," she smirks. "He did a lot of checking, and Conrad is the guy he needs."

"Well, whatever, I'm grateful to him," says Sarah.

The trees of the town yield to the naked white of farmland, through which the highway cuts like a thick black scar. As Sarah accelerates down the on-ramp, she feels the rear wheels flinch sideways before the tires bite, and she lets off the pedal. The interstate is wet with melted snow but clear. She clings to the left lane where it's easier to tell where the shoulder begins, and stays just at the limit, but cars fly past her on the right.

"Idiots," says Christine.

"I wish I could go faster. We'll be late."

"Don't worry about it. They're grateful that we just show up."

"You think? Sometimes I think this is more for ourselves than for anyone else."

"I'm sure it is," says Christine. "Two other women would take our place if we didn't appear, but that doesn't mean it isn't something we should do."

"You just show up," agrees Sarah. "No matter what." She hears the forced vehemence in her own voice, still seeing herself from afar, two coddled women in an expensive car driving fifty miles in bad weather to ladle food onto the plates of people who could not imagine their lives and would probably want no part of them if they could. She glances out at the tawdry malls scrolling past, the blighted forgotten neighborhoods that once were grand, then middle-class, now crumbling under the weight of a century's dust. A great fatigue sweeps over her; she's tired of it all, tired of this place, this sad old state, this life with all its small errands and squandered affections. Then she catches herself thinking it, realizing it's blasphemy, and flings a twinge of guilt skyward in a bid for forgiveness, but it's already out; she's felt it. She stares at the cars ahead of her in the murk, waiting for the feeling to pass, and it does; to comfort herself, she reaches out to Christine and takes her hand, which closes on hers reflexively, warm and dry. Her throat still burns from the vodka.

They are comfortable in their silence together. Sarah has always thought it evidence of true friendship when nothing needs be said to fill the holes in time. She steals another look at Christine to see if she was wrong in her first assessment of her appearance, but no. She looks bad today, as though roused from insufficient sleep or just recovered from a long illness, her eyes rimmed in gray, bloodshot, little fissures radiating from the corners of her mouth. Sarah wants to hug her, but she returns her eyes to the road. The cloud cover presses down like a great dark hand, pitiless and inert. A semi rips past and sprays the windshield with brown slush, and for a second, then another, Sarah is blind at the wheel, trusting that she should do nothing sudden. "Jesus," Christine says as the wipers flail; Sarah flicks the stem by the wheel, and water shoots up at the glass.

The windshield has just begun to clear when something enters her field of vision from the left, something big and white and moving fast.

AFTER

1

A CONFERENCE ROOM IN Manhattan. Conrad is leaning forward with his chin in his hand, at home in the halls of an old Wall Street law firm with a floor devoted entirely to conference rooms, a kitchen to serve them, wine if one wishes (no one ever does), thick carpets, paneled walls, everything to make what goes on there seem momentous, though he knows it's only about money when you come right down to it. He's the oldest guy in the same room where he'd once been the youngest, there because he's a repository of lost knowledge instead of just smart like the rest of them. Too comfortable, he will later think, a little too smug, just waiting for a chance to justify what his client and friend, Felix McCaffrey, is paying him to be there.

Kids like his daughter are running things, overachievers a few years out of law school, none of them old enough to have learned what he knows about deals, or life. Conrad glances at Felix at the head of the long table, simply dressed, almost rumpled, professorial. He's making a commercial point to a boy in a Brioni suit, his pencil raised for emphasis, and at that moment, when his world seems to have composed itself for another brief aria in a familiar key, his phone buzzes, and he removes himself to the dim paneled hallway, and a woman with a very formal tone to her voice tells him that it is her sorry duty to inform him that there's been an accident, that a truck has struck his wife's car, and his wife has been killed. "Ms. Burrell did not survive," is precisely what she says, the *z*-sound in the feminist honorific like a saw on a small bone. And grasping this only slowly, he's at first angry and indignant, and demands her name (Lieutenant Denise Klapak) and her position (Bridgeville Police Department) while he tries desperately to think of how to prove her wrong, and hearing apology but no uncertainty in the voice on the phone, slides like a drunkard down the wall to the door of the men's room and into the quiet inside and leans against a marble wall, whose black-veined patterns will appear in his dreams for years afterward, the shadow of the physical world on stubborn memory, and he stands there in his polished black shoes and shakes with a kind of frightened rage.

Christine had survived the crash. He hadn't thought to ask about her, was vague about why she was even in the car with Sarah, but Felix's phone had rung a moment after his, and when he returns to the conference room not knowing what he might say other than that he had to go, Felix is standing with his phone in his outstretched hand as though it were poisonous, anguish and hope smeared on his face, staring at him, and he comes quickly around the huge table and pushes Conrad out into the hall, and the two of them don't stop until in a great rush they've fled down to the street like thieves and stand there leaning against the wall of the big building clutching each other. Smokers haunting the entry stare at them and move away. The cold of the city plucks at their thin, expensive suits. They pull apart and search each other's faces, and Conrad sees that Felix's wife is still alive, and Felix sees what Conrad has been told, and the anguish in his eyes changes minutely. They say nothing, but fall together again like trees whose roots have been burned away.

They retrieve their things and without a word leave the roomful of lawyers gaping after them. On the short flight home, suspended above the earth and isolated from it as if in a dream, Conrad prays continuously to his neglected God, begins to convince himself that it was still possible that a mistake had been made, that the person in the demolished car was not his wife, that he had not heard the woman on the phone correctly, that when they land the impossible will be proved impossible as it has always been. They sit mute in the low din of the engines, not daring to look at one other, holding hands like schoolchildren on a bus going home in the dark.

He waits for the rush of apology from the police, the confession of error from the doctors, but none comes. They instead go about the business of making him agree that Sarah is gone. There is surprisingly little to do, he learns, when one's wife is killed: identify her body, which he refuses to do, arguing that if they have her ID that's all they need, when actually the thought of seeing her is so terrifying that his legs lock up, and after a few tries they give up. They ask him to sign a few papers which, with a cursory lawyer's eye, he sees mean nothing, so he signs them. The driver of the van was killed too, so there is no one left to blame. The van is owned by an automotive tool supply company, and of course he thinks of suing them out of sheer vengeance, but knows that would involve putting a price on Sarah's life.

Felix had reminded him that Sarah and Christine had been on their way to do some volunteer work in a soup kitchen in Pittsburgh. Christine's right leg had been crushed by the mass of the dashboard when it folded inward like a sprung trap. The surgeons had waited until Felix arrived and could sign the releases before convincing him to allow them to amputate the shattered limb at the knee. She was concussed and unconscious and had lost a large volume of blood, but she would live, they tell him, unless she wished not to.

Sarah's body is somewhere in the same building where they sit. Conrad wants to run, to hide, but he stays with Felix for most of the night, sitting silently in the dull waiting room awash in fluorescent light, feeling nothing but bitter envy as he watches the younger man wring his hands, watches him struggle with hope and yearning and fear for his wife, things that are no longer his to feel, but which he still feels like a phantom limb.

Felix keeps telling him to go, and eventually he calls a cab and rides home through a dawn like any other, rosy light at the horizon. The driver, a talkative Black man, is surprised when he gives him the address; it's far enough away that the fare will be more than he makes in a week. He sits in the dark of the back seat, ignoring the man's attempts at conversation, grateful that he assumes that Conrad has been visiting some ailing relative at the hospital, and doesn't know what a blighted, diminished creature Conrad has become, that he believes himself and his passenger to be of the same human stuff. But finally, in the little town, on their street, their house looms up like an accusation, and he knows the driver sees it, that he's that most pitiable, alien thing, a man alone, coming home to an empty house.

He leaves the lights off as he moves through the rooms, wanting to see nothing, to make none of it real. He avoids the master bedroom and lies instead, fully clothed, on the couch in his office, making as little sound as possible, as though he can hide from this unmentionable thing if he's quiet enough, as though his presence, once expressed, will harden the world into one where the inconceivable would remain real, the way ice forms in frigid water when disturbed. So he lies quite still and presses the forefinger of his right hand to his sternum, above where the heart lies, for some time, and stares at the ceiling, and sees in the streetlight through the windows that his fingernail has turned white where it presses against the bone. He looks at his hand, that convenient companion and window to the body, wrinkled and pale and somehow shrunken and not like his hand, the bones beneath glowing darkly like an animal's bones, and he sees clearly that this is the hand of a dead man, that all the remote unknowable inertness and alienness of the dead is in his hand, in his body, already.

It's still dark when he rises from the couch and walks down the long hallway to the bedroom and strips off his clothes and leaves them in a heap on the floor and pulls back the covers on the bed with arms as heavy as if they were shoveling earth, and crawls into the scented fissure of the sheets and waits for them to warm.

So the night of the first day passes, the animal brain refusing to empty though he tries over and over to empty it of everything he remembers, there in the lasting dark of their bed.

He's unable to avoid imagining the particulars of Sarah's death, the way he imagined the final moments of the passengers in Walt's doomed jet those many winters ago. He could ask Christine, but he didn't have the courage to visit her in the hospital, or to see Felix. She's been moved to some sort of rehab center nearer to home, where she's been outfitted with a prosthesis. The village paper printed a picture of her in bed, bravely smiling, with the glossy thing attached in the foreground. *Local Woman Starts Long Road to Recovery.* He stared at the photo, seeing for what seemed the first time how her smile resembled Sarah's, how her hair is the same color. Perhaps all women's smiles are the same; he can't remember. There was a vertiginous moment when he thought it might be a picture of Sarah, that after all it was Christine who had died. Then things snapped back into focus, and a furtive guilt rose up; he would trade anyone's life for hers.

He e-mails their estates lawyer in New York, a sleek Black woman, wife of one of his former partners, her body like a scythe but with the softest of voices, to tell her the news. She recites the well-practiced words of sympathy, then business: half of Sarah's money will come to Conrad, half of the rest is to be donated to a veterans' foundation that she and her sister created long ago, and a recent codicil, one he didn't know about, calls for the remainder to be donated to the Episcopal archdiocese of Pittsburgh, for the specific purpose of supporting a soup kitchen called "First, Supper." Like a child, he feels betrayed that she didn't tell him about this. Like a child, he thinks about the money, three or four million, what he could do with it: buy a fast car, tear down the house and build something scandalously modern like the McCaffreys', get an apartment in New York, somewhere rich like Murray Hill, where Sarah used to live. And with that thought his avarice dies, love wilting lust.

The memorial service falls on an imperially beautiful Thursday afternoon in April, the dogwoods in bloom, the sky cloudless. The world runs on such ironies, he's learned. He ties his tie in the mirror of their bathroom, averting his eyes from the other sink, once cluttered with her drugs and potions. Her clothes still hang in the closet; he can't approach them, their silkiness, their lingering smells bring him to tears, but Becky Sternberger said that she'll be by to pick them up on Tuesday; she's rented a truck and wants him out of the house.

He goes to All Souls early to avoid being seen and sits in the front pew. The place is empty, serene, the walls recently repainted a robin's-egg blue, the altar simple and spare, sun flooding the tall windows. It seems unlikely that anything will happen here. Father Rick arrives in his street clothes, hurries up.

"Conrad, so good to see you," he says, grabbing the widower's hand in both of his. "This will be a wonderful service." Conrad gives him a tight smile, like a croupier who knows the odds. The priest is full of businesslike bustle, ordering altar boys around, checking the program for typos. Conrad had insisted that there not be a photo on the front, there being no way that a single picture could fail to lie about his wife.

Someone has sent a huge bouquet of flowers, roses and hydrangeas, which a pimply boy in a bad suit hauls to the front of the nave and sets carefully on a silver stand in the chancel. Conrad looks around, walks up to the arrangement, inspects the card. Of course: Felix and Christine. Then he turns to see the boy bringing another bouquet up the aisle, this one full of lilies. "There's a lot more of 'em comin'," the boy says, sweating, as he looks around the transept. "Yer not the minister, are ya?" he asks. "We're gonna need more room."

"No, I'm not the minister," Conrad says, steadying himself against the back of the pew. "I'm just here for the service."

"Well, a lot of people liked whoever died," says the kid. "We ran out of roses."

The kid hurries back up the aisle and Conrad sits down again and faces forward, his eyes on the cross, while the flowers arrive in huge sheaves one after another, a river of flowers, a comedy of flowers, so many that he has to laugh, and in laughing for the first time in what must be weeks, his throat catches, and he's crying instead, tears blinding him, running off his chin as he wipes them away quickly with his hands. He doesn't have a handkerchief, something he never failed to carry when he wore a suit every day. He straightens himself; something about the missing pocket square disturbs him, suggests he may be forgetting how to dress, that one day he might run around in rags or start wearing white belts like his father did toward the end. What he fears more than death is the thought of his own decay, the way his muscles have started to go, his arms spindly things now that rattle around inside his suit sleeves, his belt cinched an extra notch, wrinkling the waistband. He shoots the French cuffs of his white shirt and waits for his vision to clear, tastes salt in his throat.

He hears people enter behind him, but doesn't turn, instead bows his head as he imagines their stares, pictures himself alone in the front pew, stark as the crucifix, a figure of pathos. The organ starts, and he jerks involuntarily; he hadn't expected music this soon. He's gone over the selections with Father Rick in a pro forma way, accepting everything he suggested. "Ave Maria," because she loved the piece, loved Mary, deification of the motherhood that had eluded her. Something by Gluck that he's not familiar with. "Blessed Assurance," which he'd resisted at first for its triteness, but which Rick knows from experience everyone likes to sing, and he remembers Sarah belting it out when it came up on Sundays. He thought of Lauridsen, of course, but knew that would destroy him. Sarah didn't like it the way he did anyway; he's succumbed to the universal shadow play of the bereaved, evaluating the world as though the departed were watching.

He closes his eyes, concentrating on his breathing, and is startled when he feels someone settle into the pew next to him. Meg Franklin grabs his arm and folds hers into it and leans over to kiss his cheek. She looks wrecked and patched together but somehow regal in her long strand of pearls, her eyes insinuating, as though they share a secret, which he realizes they now do. He feels a presence from the other side, and looks up to see Felix guiding Christine ahead of him into the pew, her new leg pink and shiny and dangling under her, her makeup not quite covering her bruises, her crutches in his hand, both of them in jet black but for a scarf of defiantly hot pink that Christine has knotted around her throat. She lowers herself heavily next to Conrad and takes his hand, and he's bracketed suddenly between these two injured women who he knows can't help but try in their loving sum to fill the void that has opened up around him. What he feels is not so much comfort as a sudden fierce pride.

Father Rick enters in his white surplice, they all rise as the choir files in singing the last stanza of "Amazing Grace," and he's startled that there are other voices almost drowning out the choir, almost shouting the wonderfully presumptuous line *When we've been there ten thousand years*—and he turns for a moment and sees that the nave is full of people in their dark clothes, crowding the entrance, filling the sunny balcony, singing. Megan is behind him with Madeleine, showing in a navy maternity smock, and Sarah's sister, Fran, startlingly thin, her thick gray mane tied back, her face like stone, and Paul Stinson, tanned and balding and openly weeping, to whom he'd written a perfunctory letter with no expectation he would come, and Becky and Stu, smiling reassuringly at him, and Agatha and John

Webber standing together again, their hands almost touching as they rest on the pew in front of them, and dozens more he doesn't know, strangers who knew his wife, or had only met her once or twice, but who have come to honor the small beautiful woman who had shown them the same naked, unmediated love that he had known. Shame hits him like a fist as he realizes what a small part of her he had really possessed, what a small part of her was uniquely his to mourn. He's one of many. He has to sit back down before they do, his legs have given way, and he sits like the stump of a felled tree in a teeming forest.

2

THE TWO REMAINING WOMEN in his life stand together on the periphery of the crowd after the service, New Yorkers out of place in the wilds of Pennsylvania, befuddled by the gregariousness of the Midwesterners. Madeleine hugs him tearfully and rushes off to the airport, pleading work and obstetric appointments, but first makes him touch her swollen abdomen. He does it shyly, reluctantly; he's never touched her in her life except to comfort her, and here is the reverse. Megan lingers another day, invites him for coffee at the inn, laughs when he suggests she save money and stay at the house.

"You don't know what you're saying yet, do you?" she says. "What would that look like?"

"I really don't care what it looks like. You're family, and there are four bedrooms, for God's sake."

She ignores the mention of family. "Well, I do care. These are pious people around these parts, and I won't contribute to the local gossip," she says, affecting a Southern drawl. From anyone else it would be too flip, but she looks more undone than him, her eyes rimmed in red, her face bare and blotchy, her white hair wild, like a haggard prairie woman, devoid of vanity, her plainness a dare. She's always been one step ahead of him, always seen around corners he didn't know existed.

"Listen," she's saying. "I'm not going to try to give you advice, but you need to take care of yourself. You don't think you need to, but you do. This is a dangerous time for you."

"Dangerous how?" he asks, gazing out the window to show her how casually he takes everything she says. "Here we are having coffee, not a car wreck in sight. What could go wrong?"

"You're mad at the world and mad at yourself. How could you not be? I was the same way, and I had years to prepare for it. You've had nothing." She holds her cup of coffee before her like an offering, her fingers knobby and cracked.

"You don't seriously think I'm suicidal or anything."

"No, but you're neglectful of yourself. You don't think you need to pay attention anymore, since the person you paid most of your attention to is gone. You think you're finished, that you have no more stories in you."

"Is that how you felt?" he asks her.

"Yes, absolutely."

"And now what do you think, Megan? Do you think you have another story in you?"

He means it kindly, but she hesitates; his saying her name has thrown her off. Her hand comes to her mouth. "I don't know yet. I don't think I'll ever be in love again, if that's what you mean."

He smiles at her. "That's pretty much what I mean."

"You're such a romantic. You really need to get a hobby."

"I'm working on it." He pauses. "So what happens to us now?"

Her eyes narrow, gauging his meaning. "Well, for starters, I'm not staying in your house."

"I got that. I don't mean you and me personally. I mean people like us. Widows and widowers."

"We go on," she says. It sounds too glib even to her, and her lips purse with the need to amend it, but she stops herself.

"I don't think I can live here anymore," he says. "There's too much history here."

"I know, I felt the same."

"Maybe we should move to New York," he says because it occurs to him; he feels entitled to be ridiculous. "Be near Madeleine and our grandkid, get out of these little towns we've ended up in."

"Connie . . ." she sighs with an eye roll in which he recognizes the girl he courted in the hallways of their long-forgotten law firm.

"Buy a co-op in the Village. With both our money we might be able to afford it."

"Connie, this isn't going to happen; just put it out of your mind."

He won't beg, but the idea has such sudden logic that he can't let go. "How many people in your life have you known as long as you've known me? How many people do I know as well as I know you?"

She puts down her cup, which till now has been a little barrier between them. "Connie, this is grief talking. It will pass. There is a way in which I do love you: you're the father of our child. But we've been living separate lives for decades now. You don't really know me anymore, and I don't know you. What we think we know about each other is from when we were thirty. We were different people then, you know that."

He nods, relieved to be absolved so quickly; he's unaccustomed to owing nothing to the woman he's with. Still he adds, "Weren't you the one who said that people don't change, they just become more themselves?"

"I never said that. What a very clever, wrong thing to say."

"So. No New York?"

"No New York, Connie. At least not with me. That's done."

The next day she's gone.

He lies in bed in the pale mornings listening to the house warm. With a trick of the clock the days are suddenly longer, dark retreating past dinner. In the evenings he drifts down the streets of the town in the dusk like a blown leaf; behind the closed doors, children tell their parents about the Walking Man.

Sarah's silver laptop computer sits on a counter in the kitchen, plugged in, humming, still connected invisibly to the world. It's another box of her belongings that he can't bear to open. The things in it, all those little glassy electrics, are liars in their bland persistence, like her clothes and her jewelry. To look at her e-mail would be too much like listening for her voice, which he still does, forgetfully. The notion has occurred to him that she must have known what was going to happen, must have hidden somewhere a final message, a comfort, but he can't bear to look for it for fear it will not be there. The bag of broken things they'd given him included her cell phone, yet he catches himself checking his for a text from her. It was her way to think only of the present and future, not the past, and it occurs to him that she's moved on not to a different place, but to a place yet to be, that he's not so much left behind as trapped in her past.

In the lengthening afternoons he sits in the bare study and coaxes melodies from the piano, cheap triads with the left hand, fingers of the right stumbling like a drunk on broken pavement, stopping where the melody outruns the few chords he knows, backing up, running at it again, trying the blacks. He's forgotten everything about it except the touch, the phrasing, which fool him into thinking he could be better.

He asks Becky Sternberger, whose kids all play, if she knows a piano teacher.

"We had an Amish girl," she says. "She was wonderful for the kids. Don't know if she teaches adults."

"Amish?"

"Not real Amish. Raised Amish. She escaped, or something. Roberta Moss."

He calls Ms. Moss, and she arrives at his door on the appointed day looking like a nun: no makeup, black sweater, black hose, black flats, white cotton blouse, hair the color of chocolate in blunt-cut wings at the sides of her jaw, eyes the color of her hair, carefully expressionless. He doesn't know if this is how escaped Amish dress or whether she's showing sympathy for his bereavement. She looks him up and down, noting the T-shirt, and offers her hand, warm and soft. She's young enough to be his daughter, twenty-eight or thirty, respectful of the old man who's lost his wife, wary. She could be pretty if she tried, but it's clear in an instant that she never will.

They sit in two chairs in the study, the piano like a witness beside them.

"What are your goals for the piano, Mr. Burrell?" she asks, her voice a level contralto much older than she is.

He shrugs like a truant. "I'd just like to be able to play better. I play mostly by ear now, and it's too limited. I'd like to be able to read music."

She waves a hand in dismissal. "You're a smart man, Mr. Burrell. Reading music should be no problem for you. It's just like learning a language, but with fewer words and declensions. Piece of cake for someone like you."

Like him. Meaning someone as vastly old as he is? He wonders what she's heard about him, how much she knows. "Don't be so sure. And please call me Conrad. Or Connie."

She ignores this, smiles. "The playing better is just a matter of practice, truly it is. I teach kids, so I usually don't get to talk like this about it, but there's nothing mystical about playing the piano. It's just a little theory, learning to read, and then a lot of work."

He frowns. "Well, I don't know. I hate work. You don't have an easy way?"

"Nope." She giggles. He's glad to make her laugh; now she sounds her age. "Why don't you play something for me just to let me see where you are?"

He was afraid of this but is prepared.

"Please," she says, standing and gesturing at the piano as though he might not know where to find it. He sits on the bench and opens the fallboard and removes the red felt runner that protects the keys and folds it and hands it to her. She giggles again, puts it on top of the sound cabinet.

He plays "Yesterday," the Lennon and McCartney ballad from when he was a boy, plays it slowly and simply, which is all he can do, chords in shifting triplets with the left hand, single notes with the right, but with a grown-up's hesitant phrasing, the unheard words informing the notes, moody as a dark bar at midnight, where he doubts Roberta Moss has ever been. She's at his shoulder, still as a post, the wool of her sweater smelling faintly of rain. He stumbles on the key change in the bridge, stops.

"See, here's where I fall apart," he says.

"You're cheating, you know," she says. "The right hand should be triads, not single notes like that."

"Well, of course. I don't know what I'm doing. I made it up completely by ear," he says proudly.

"I'm not criticizing; you're very good for someone who's had no lessons."

"I had them once, but I was, like, ten." He hopes the "like" will sound young.

She sits on the bench next to him. "I couldn't do what you just did," she says, her fingers resting on the keys. "I need sheet music. But once you have sheet music you have a map; you can never get lost." She plays a few bars of a Chopin nocturne, technically perfect, lifeless in a way that he assumes is deliberate.

"That's what I want," he says. "To never get lost."

Her brows arch, and she smiles as though at a clever, difficult child. "I can come once a week at this time, if you want. I'll give you some practice sheets to start with. I'm very strict with adults; if you don't do your practice, I'll know in a minute, and we'll just stop the session and try another time."

"Not like a psychiatrist? I don't get fifty minutes no matter what?"

"No, you don't," she says, rising. "I am definitely not a psychiatrist."

"May I call you Roberta?" he asks. "Or do you prefer Miss Moss?"

Her brow knits in pretend thought. "Let's start with Roberta, and once you get to know me, you may prefer Miss Moss. Is that agreeable to you?"

"Very."

"Good," she says, heading for the front door. "Let me get some things out of the car."

3

FELIX CALLS OFTEN TO check on him, at first with the pretense of discussing the deal they'd worked on so briefly, but he can't talk about it; he would remember the conference room with his phone buzzing in his pocket and his mind would freeze.

"Do you need anything?" Felix would ask.

"Nothing, I'm fine. Unless you have a time machine."

He wouldn't play along. "And if I had one, would you go backward or forward? I of all people know what you're going through, Connie. I'm here for you. We both are."

"I know that. I just don't think there's anything you can do."

"Want to play a quick nine this Friday? Get out of the house?"

"I've forgotten how."

"We all loved her, Connie."

"I know."

"I loved her."

"I know," he says, not sure what he knows.

"Remember how lucky we all were to have known her."

"Luck sort of turned there at the end, though."

Long pause. "Do you remember how to eat?"

"What?"

"If you won't play golf with me, would you come for dinner on Friday?"

He wants to see their house more than he wants to see them. They remind him of Sarah's death, but their beautiful house reminds him of a time before Sarah, before he knew what it was to earn enough to have a house like that, when he was just someone's guest, just passing through.

He arrives in time for cocktails, feeling foolish in his jeans, wishing he'd kept a dress shirt. Felix hugs him, his stubble scraping against Conrad's face as he kisses him like a Tuscan duke, looking better than ever: long silver hair and bright pink shirt and creased khakis. Christine hobbles out of the gleaming kitchen on her plastic leg, smiling, pressing her head to Conrad's chest. She's put on her lost weight and then some, the toll of forced indolence. Her smile is apologetic; perhaps it always will be. He's fascinated by the mechanics of her prosthesis, and over drinks asks her questions about how it's mounted and cleaned. If they can talk about Sarah, he can talk about this.

"Does it hurt?" he asks.

"Not the wound, but the device itself hurts like hell. I can't wait to take it off at night."

"Take it off now."

She laughs and looks at him as though he's asked her to bed. "I'd have to use the crutches then. I prefer the pain."

They sit on the deck in the waning sun like survivors, gently rocking the ice in their drinks, aware of their persistence in the world, basking in its random beneficence. Fireflies fleck the dusk with slips of light. Conrad's chest aches where Christine's face had pressed; the intimacy of their knowledge of his hell makes it more hellish. There are details he wants to ask after, things only she could know, but he knows it would be cruel and probably pointless, like confessing love to someone else's wife. He hopes that being near her will inoculate him against the wish that it had been him and not her in the seat next to Sarah that day.

"I think I need to get out of town for a while," he says finally.

"Some exotic travel," Felix says. He speaks like this now, diffidently, in fragments, as though not to intrude too much. Like Conrad he's learned that nothing can be assumed. His head is tilted down out of the setting sun, and Conrad sees that he will be bound forever to this man, to this couple, the way he's bound to Megan, by a turn in life that can't be outlived.

"I've never traveled alone," he muses. "Except on business."

"That's not real travel," says Felix.

"Where would you most like to go?" asks Christine.

"I'd start slow, maybe just spend some time in Santa Fe."

"The house is sitting there empty; you should go," she says. "The weather should be beautiful."

"It just seems like the sort of environment to be in right now."

"The austerity of it," says Felix.

"Yes, that, and the expansiveness. The size of the sky. The skies are too small here."

"No horizon," Felix agrees.

"And the stars. You can't see the stars here. Too many trees. Too much light." They all look up together, into the trees returned to full leaf, canopies closing in a green density that had seemed impossible only a few weeks earlier.

"Maybe not alone, though." It's Felix who says it. "Maybe we'll join you."

Conrad looks at him. "That's not necessary."

"Not necessary, no."

"Christine shouldn't be traveling, I'm sure."

"I'm fine to travel," she says, rising on her new leg as though to prove it. "Dinner's ready."

Felix rises to follow her. "I'm in New York this week. But we could come later."

They sit at the long glass table, Christine at the head, the men on either side. The food is delicate, perfect, the wine carefully decanted. The moment comes that he's been dreading, when they raise their glasses and look deliberately into one another's eyes, but to his relief no one speaks; there is only silence, red wine shimmering in their lifted hands.

That night he dreams of her, or rather, in the dream he *is* Sarah, looking out through a windshield at a snowy highway speeding toward him, his hands before him on the wheel, and suddenly from nowhere there is an impact, unimaginably powerful yet strangely familiar, foretold fractionally before it happens by each cell of his body, which is flung sideways like a doll. The smell of alcohol from somewhere. The world goes silent, and she feels neither fear nor anger; someone has made a mistake, that's all, and mistakes can always be corrected. Time dilates, like the slow motion in those movies Sarah watched with her brother long ago, a white pillow flying out of the steering wheel to fill the space where she had been, her mind racing, not to the past, as the stories said, but to the future, to those she loves, to Meg, to Christine somewhere outside her field of vision, to Felix, finally to Conrad leaning down to her, holding her face in his hands, to the way the folded napkins lay in the sunlight on the table at home, waiting for them all to come together around it again, to the bed upstairs, waiting for their bodies. There is time to think all this, and then to imagine God observing her thoughts. There is even time to think that she will have an eternity to think these things, to watch over him and be glad she has escaped living without him, like a child who realizes her parent isn't as angry as she thought and will let her go to bed without further punishment. Then there are more concussions, far off; she hopes no one will be hurt, and then despite all this, despite her slow surprised realization that she must resist it, a growing, grinding dark.

And he awakens suddenly into another dark, his heart racing, his fists hanging in the air as though gripping a wheel, her hands wearing his like gloves, her love swirling inside him like a river that's broken its banks, bearing him up.

He goes then, the long flight to Dallas, the short one to Santa Fe, one among the throng in the airports, on the crowded planes, studying them as he hadn't before, their lives a curiosity, opaque with purpose. Suddenly everyone looks like a wife or husband; it's stamped on their faces as clearly as their race. He moves among them, invisible. To pass the time he thinks of all the women in his past, how he would have been a different man with each of them; his life, like his profession, has been one long sequence of reactions. He has no clearer sense of himself than when he was a nervous kid abroad in the city, all hope and evanescence, all work and sex and duty. He tries to recall the feel of another woman's flesh, what it had been like to make love to someone other than Sarah, and cannot. There are fragments, indelible images, often of the most inconsequential encounters, but nothing coheres into memory, into a story that he might tell himself there in his seat above the clouds. *Do you have another story in you?*

The tiny airport in the desert with its cool red-tiled floors, its faux-adobe walls. A cowboy airport. The long taxi ride into the hills on the far side of the town, up the long, dusty driveway to another empty house. It smells of desert, burnt and dry, dead moths on the floors, dust on the sills as he opens the windows and the tall doors onto the *portal* drowned in late sunlight, the long, steep valley of pines stretching down to the desert basin. There is less of her here, more of the world, perhaps more of himself, that meek thing that emerges only into empty rooms. He throws his bag on the better bed, makes himself a drink and sits out in the lengthening shadows, waiting for the night, for the stars. And soon they come, so bright they seem vengeful, the constellations like garish tattoos.

He waits patiently through the long days, the starlit nights, and still not a morning arrives when the first tendrils of thought don't probe for the wound, when he's able to rise without glancing at the space he still leaves beside him in the sheets, the untouched pillow. The space feels sacred; no one could fill it. He knows this now; the only thing that changes is that it frightens him less.

There is no piano, but he dutifully studies the books Roberta Moss has given him, practices on imaginary keys on the edge of the dining table, on the screen of his tablet computer. He looks around the small living room for where a keyboard might fit.

He goes into town for dinners, sits at the bars in the expensive places on Canyon Road and chats with the bartenders. No one knows him; no one cares. The food is better here than at home, the clientele just flown in from New York and Dallas and LA, knowing, jaded, proud of their cleverness in being here, dressed in someone's imaginings of the Southwest. He studies them, the women with their faces like shields held before them as they move through the rooms, the cautious men in their wake, their eyes roving, appraising. The wives are in better shape than the men; they have time to take care of themselves, whereas the husbands' appeal is their money. For these couples are all married, their bond evident in the certainty in their faces, the bland familiarity with which they arrange themselves at the tables and address everyone but their spouses. Sarah would have chided him for staring at people like this. Being with a woman chang- es a man, makes him defensive, as there is something to defend. The women glance at him as they pass, sizing him up instantly: an older man at the bar, alone, underdressed but not a bum, well-manicured, perhaps an alcoholic or gay or both. Because: alone. The singular, shouting fact, a story there, an unusual story, inexplicable to the naked eye, of some rupture, some anomaly or evasion. They want to know it, and they don't want to know, their eyes flicking quickly away after the first penetrating glance; something feral in them knows all the odds, sticks with the safest bets.

Mail is forwarded to the house, letters of sympathy, store-bought cards with florid script, religious imagery. He stacks them by the computer and reads several a day while he sits in the sun, skipping the printed ones, looking for handwriting, the press of human choice. Those most affected say nothing: Paul Stinson, Sarah's sister, Frances, Madeleine, Megan. Their friends from town struggle to find words; the women have written the messages, of course, these tenders of hearts, observers of form. *Her smile is ours forever,* Becky says simply in a trembling, jagged hand that looks electrified. Meg calls Sarah a *warrior of love,* which seems right to him; in his dreams she appears armored, like Ingres's *Joan of Arc.* Agatha Webber sends her favorite Sarah quotes, written in florid calligraphy on a stack of thick cream three-by-five cards, one to a card:

> *There are no "shoulds."*
> *You can't lead a dead horse in the water.*
> *I'm a black-and-white person.*
> *Meaner than a two-fisted billy goat.*
> *Are you happy?*

He stops, puts the cards aside, picks them up again. He remembers that she said these things, but none of them seem like her without her voice to carry them. They are more about Agatha than Sarah, smell of Agatha's perfume. He holds the cards to his mouth, breathing in the scent of a woman not his wife, and tries to remember both of them. Memory is a liar by omission, he thinks.

The days take on the languid indeterminacy of a childhood summer, passing swiftly, mornings into night like the beating of a wing. He wants to lose himself in them, like a swimmer seeking the point in a wave that will carry him forward thoughtlessly. He avoids

the computer and his books, tries not to think, to emulate the emptiness of the skies, the desert. Storms cross the distant mesas like vast
gray ships that he watches like a harbormaster who knows nothing
will be needed of him.

Felix and Christine call to say they're coming, and he pretends
he's pleased. He's trying to learn acceptance, so he accepts this. They
arrive at the house and take the smaller bedroom without comment,
join him on the *portal* in the evening. They sense the quiet he's been
living in and say little. They've brought with them a package con-
taining sheet music and a long message of instruction from Roberta
Moss, which she'd left on his porch at home. Scales to play, a few
études with her annotations, a message in pencil on the last: "I don't
believe you're practicing, so come home soon. We miss you here in
town. -R."

He sits next to Felix under the stars and listens to him play his
guitar, listens with Sarah's heart, inside him since the night of the
dream, her love of these people, of this man, her smile pushing out
through his lips. In great swaths the long dusk pours out to them; a
low wall separates them from the valley that runs down to the desert,
the desert ends at the distant mountains, the mountains end at the
sky. And beyond that there is no end.

4

HE LOOKS FORWARD TO the piano lessons. He's never quite well enough prepared, but Roberta Moss is patient with him, sits on the bench next to him, and has the habit, formed with her school-age students, of touching his fingers to guide them to where they should fall on the keys. She's immensely kind and has begun to wear perfume, the weight of her next to him like Sarah's when they sat together in the pews at church.

On an October day when the little town is drowned in fallen leaves, the year putting on its final show, his granddaughter is born. The news arrives in a text, along with a photo of Madeleine in a hospital bed, disheveled hair over tired eyes, Lloyd leaning in from off-frame, kissing her cheek, and a small loaf of humanity held tight in her arms, a purple thing with dark animal eyes wearing an outraged expression and a little cap that Sarah had knitted the previous winter as soon as she had heard Madeleine was pregnant. Helen Sarah Davidson, the message says.

"Congratulations," he says to Megan when she calls.

"Congratulations to you, Gramps."

"When should we go?"

"Not for a while. Let them get settled."

"Is there any way we can warn them?"

"About what?" she asks.

"Not to make the mistakes we made."

"No, of course not. And I don't think we made that many."

"Just the big ones."

"You're forgiven," she says.

"Thanks, you too."

"It's not about us anymore, Connie."

Flying in over the deathless city, golden in the waning sun, like a great scaled beast hugging the edge of the continent. Among the thousand repetitions that have composed his life, arrival in New York by air is like a sacrament, familiar as daybreak, always new. He looks down on all that incandescent desperation and feels an echo of the half-blind seeking that had been the engine of his youth. He can see the landmarks of that passage, the streets he'd walked, the towers where he'd worked, the lost homes of those years. The long glide path out over the ocean and back, the long ride in through the gray tunneled boroughs, under the rivers the color of slag. Into the city again.

The baby is in Megan's arms when Madeleine lets him into the small bedroom. Night has fallen; the room is lit only by a clock that glows with the face of a smiling moon. She smiles and silently rises and puts the child in his arms just as she had handed their daughter to him night after night long ago, the motion still ingrained in their bones. She touches his arm and walks out without a word. The universal infant face, blank, anonymous; the eyes tracking his. "Hi, Helen," he says. He strokes the warm little head, soft with down, kisses the place where the skin covers the dime-sized hole in the skull; the whole world there, nothing lost, everything possible.

"I wish . . ." he begins.

"I know, Dad," says Madeleine, her hand on his back.

He walks to the window with the baby and stands looking east over the rooftops and water tanks of the Upper West Side toward the blank expanse of Central Park. "See?" he says to the child, holding her higher against him before the glass. "See?" he says in a whisper to Sarah.

They eat a vegetarian dinner in the apartment's cramped rooms, Megan helping out in the sliver of kitchen while Conrad opens a bottle of champagne and chats with Lloyd. There is talk of the pros and cons of raising a child in the city, the expense, the schools, the terrors of a suburban commute, the metropolitan privileges that Madeleine had known as a little girl. Later the grandparents are told it's late and they excuse themselves and make their way to the street, into the dim clamor of the midnight avenues. Memory billows in the soft air perfumed with ozone, rains down from the streetlamps, laps at the curbs.

"Share a cab?" he asks.

"I'm staying with friends in the Village."

"I'm at Gramercy Park."

"Let's go, then," she says.

There is time to talk in the back of the cab, but not enough, so they say little, looking out at the familiar streets whipping by, their hands resting a foot apart on the battered seat. He gets out where Lexington ends, hands Megan some cash and kisses her on the cheek and says goodbye, and instead of going into the hotel, which had been a dump when he lived around the corner but has turned into a chic, shiny place full of people his daughter's age, he walks the half-block south to the park and crosses the empty street to the tall iron fence that surrounds it, walks the sidewalk that encircles it, past the darkened townhouses that shelter unknowable lives, under the old caged trees, once, twice, once again, growing cold in his thin coat, looking in, unable to enter, not wanting to leave.

5

SUMMER AGAIN. THE AIR lies heavy and impenetrable as the lead blanket one wears at the dentist's. Holly Battle, his real estate agent ("Let Holly Battle for YOU!"), fusses around the house, placing flowers, moving the few items of furniture that remain, poking her nose down the stairwell to the basement, sniffing. Weathered, orange-haired, she specializes in homes in the little town, has seen hundreds of them bought and sold, the births and divorces and emptied playrooms and aged in-laws, the unforeseeable sudden changes like his, the tides of families washing in and out as decades passed and desires changed and permanence proved temporary.

To her the house is still the Williamsons', a family that hasn't lived in it since Vietnam. Conrad had offered the house to all their friends first, thinking someone might want a place bigger or smaller than what they had, knowing how much it had been admired when Sarah drew them all together in its rooms. They thank him when they say no, worried they'll offend, that he'll see that they think it would be a kind of trespass, an unnamable brand of infidelity. He understands.

Holly and he have agreed on a price, but she wants to lower it again, noting that if the summer passes and the school year begins, everyone will be frozen in place and it will be next spring before an offer comes.

"Okay, but not a dollar under six hundred," he says.

"Five ninety-five, please," she says. "Makes all the difference, and it means nothing to you."

Her tactlessness is her charm, passing as it does for hardheaded practicality. He doesn't tell her that not only does he not care about the five thousand, but doesn't care about the next hundred thousand, so little does it figure in the scheme of things now, so much does he want to be rid of the place in which he once loved so much.

It's a cicada year, the trees vibrating with their black bodies, the shriek of their song unrelenting even at night. He keeps the windows open now, something Sarah would never have permitted, and when he can't sleep, he walks the town, peering into the bars from doorways, seeing no one he knows. The broad sidewalks in the moonlight, chairs atop tables, the stoplight marking time at the town's one intersection. In a year he'll be seventy, certifiably old, one of those unmoored men one sees occasionally, belonging nowhere or anywhere, about whom one wonders briefly, their story soon to end, so different from one's own.

One of the last battles of a long life, he's found, is to resist delusion. The delusion of immortality, for starters, but also the delusion of a constant, continuous self passing through a welcoming world. At some imperceptible point he had not only shed that old self but moved from that old world into one where the dream of love that had saved him so many times before began to feel delusional.

Roberta Moss arrives each Thursday on the dot, and he's always unprepared. She always wears black, like a nun, or like a sweet female version of death without the scythe. Their ritual is that first he confesses his unpreparedness, then she scolds him for a while, then they play. He goes first and plays what he was supposed to have prepared, usually a simplified piece of Bach, which he butchers but forces his way through while small moans escape her throat. Sometimes she can't help herself and repositions his hands under hers, and they play together like that for a few bars, mechanical as dolls, the picture of joint duty. Her palms are warm and dry on his wrinkled knuckles. Then he asks her to play something for him and watches her consider whether he deserves this, and having concluded that he doesn't but hoping that her example might inspire him, she agrees to play just one piece of her choosing, which tends to be Chopin or Liszt. He's fascinated by her playing, always precise but deliberately passionless, as much like a machine as she can make it. He wonders if this is a teaching persona, if there is a different Roberta Moss who, at home with her post-Amish boyfriend, rips through Rachmaninoff with her head thrown back and the chords chasing each other in a fever. He's come to understand that there will never be a time when they finish their session and she turns to him with her customary closing argument that his progress will be directly proportional to the time he puts into practice and he interrupts her by kissing her hard on her thin lips. He accepts this impossibility the way he's come to accept Sarah's death, as a brute fact unworthy of reflection. Her hair is fine and the deep brown of mahogany, her perfume almost undetectable so that he has to lean her way a little to catch the scent of juniper.

One day, however, when he's done what he thinks is a particularly good job on a bit of watered-down Schumann, and it's her turn to play just before she leaves, he asks her if she knows any Satie.

"I know one or two pieces," she says. "I know the first movement of *Gymnopédies*, which everybody knows."

"*Lent et douloureux.*"

"Yes, that's the one. I don't know the other two."

"Slow and painful," Conrad says.

"Is that what it means? My professor always said that was how to play it, but I didn't know that was the title."

"That's what it means," he says, and is reminded yet again that she's younger than his daughter.

Her hands find their place above the keys and come down on the alternating major sevenths, those first few wistful bars. She plays more slowly than he would have expected of her, slower than he's used to hearing the piece played, almost languid, almost halting, as though one hand had forgotten the other for the instant before the next phrase. She plays with her usual directness, her lack of inflection, but it suits this piece, which is one simple thought laid bare. He thinks of Sarah's face, and of Megan's, of afternoons before Roberta Moss was born. She looks at him and stops.

"I think that's enough for today, don't you?"

"Can I take you out to dinner?" he hears himself asking with complete nonchalance.

She blinks, but only once, as though she's seen this coming a long way off.

"That's very flattering, Mr. Burrell," she says evenly. "But I'll have to say no. I never date my students."

His heart is suddenly in his throat. He feels himself flush. "Who said it was a date? I'm too old to date. I'm just taking you to dinner."

"I'll have to say no. Thank you, though."

"We'd be in public," he explains.

"That's exactly what worries me," she says. "Not that I wouldn't be glad to be seen with you, but, you know. I have a lot of clients in town."

"Well then, come here for dinner. I'm not a bad cook."

"No, Mr. Burrell."

"You haven't called me that in months."

"Perhaps we'll start again."

"One more piece, then?"

"What?" she says, truly confused now.

"Play something else for me now, before you go."

Her face is asymmetrical, one eye smaller than the other, the corners of her mouth curling differently. It makes her look quizzical, sardonic. She looks down at her hands as though to consult them, looks up again.

"One more," she says. "Then I really have to go."

And what she plays is *Clair de Lune*, played in a way he heard once long ago, before everything changed, when we were all still alive, immortal for yet a little while. She's playing it the way she never plays, the way she would for a lover, every note naked and believed in, as though each was a word in the heart's own tongue. He searches for the place and time, and it comes to him that it was on a winter's night in this very room, at this piano, that he was sitting in a chair in what is now an empty corner, and Sarah and he and John and Agatha Webber listened to their son play this piece, with its timid beginnings and soft spill of chords, and they all pretended not to weep. But they wept, he knew, because it's a piece a child can play in one way and only an adult can play in another, and because the boy had played it the way an adult would, but was still a perfect creature as yet un-touched by time, and because they knew, even then, that the moment would never be repeated. Agatha raising her glass to her lips, tipping it slightly toward him before she drinks, her look lingering a fraction, her eyes brimming, the snow behind the dark windows.

Roberta Moss finishes the last phrase, her fingers lifting slowly from the keys, her foot next to his on the sustain pedal, making the chord linger. They sit for a moment, side by side on the small bench. Then she kisses him lightly on the cheek and rises and leaves without a word.

6

AFTER HIS DIVORCE, he had gone through a period of wild disorientation not unlike what he was feeling now. He spent a lot of time crying at the slightest provocation, and finally resorted to therapy in an attempt to recover his equilibrium. In one of his therapy sessions he was presented with the idea that the problems in his marriage to Megan stemmed from some deep insecurity planted in him by his mother, or by some other important woman in his past. He was unwilling to blame his mother for anything as soul-destroying as his failure to keep his family together, so he thought the problem must have originated in one of his earlier relationships, of which he had had a few. As he had no job at the time, he decided to set out and visit as many of his old girlfriends as he could find and try to pinpoint where he had lost his belief in his essential lovability.

This quixotic enterprise, daunting in prospect, was surprisingly easy to execute, at least up to a point. The women of his past were, once listed on a yellow legal pad, a surprisingly diverse and far-flung group, and he had managed to remain friendly with most of them. He wrote to each of them and told them fairly frankly of his intentions, and most were willing to see him, preferably in daylight and in a public place, but willing, nonetheless. He planned his itinerary, bought plane tickets, even made some restaurant reservations for two in the cities he planned to visit.

But he never went. Somehow the process of preparing for the trips, the searching for current addresses, the reveries about all those lost loves, the writing and receiving of letters (such was the practice in those quaint days) from those mostly considerate, bright, open women was enough to make the trip unnecessary. There was nothing more to be learned by actually sitting in the same room with them and seeing how they each had aged. There was no need to rehash the past. They knew the past. They had discussed it ad nauseam as it was happening. There was no point in revisiting them in person, unless for some seamy ulterior motive, like getting laid for old times' sake, and that was exactly the kind of divided motive that had gotten him into trouble with most of them in the first place.

He was reminded of his list of old girlfriends when the thought of trying to find Agatha Webber first occurred to him. He believed that the world can be divided into those who, when confronted with crisis, look instinctively to their pasts, and those who open themselves to what might happen next. He knew himself to be decidedly in the first camp, distrustful of fate and inclined to believe that salvation must have been missed on some old road not taken, in some past opportunity foregone but perhaps recoverable, rather than in the messy business of new narratives, new people, new places. He decides to call Becky Sternberger and ask her what she knows.

"I heard she moved in with her parents in Columbus," she says. Then, inevitably: "Why?"

"I thought I'd try to get in touch with her, see how she's doing," he mumbles, as if checking up on recently divorced women were a normal activity of a married man, which is what he still believes himself to be.

After a long pause, during which he can almost hear Becky's fine brain sorting through a number of undignified scenarios, she says, "Connie, can I offer some advice?"

"Sure," he says, not wanting it.

"Go slow. Agatha's not easy."

This was Agatha's reputation among the women: pretty but prick-ly, standoffish, a bit too full of herself, defensive and regretful about having given up her career for her family, which was the sacrifice that most of the women were proudest of. To be dissatisfied was, in their circle, to be ungrateful, the one great sin of the privileged.

He looks up John Webber in Martindale's online, and finds he's become in-house counsel for a brokerage firm in Philadelphia. He considers calling John on some lawyerly pretext and casually asking after his ex-wife, but they haven't spoken since he left town and Conrad is sure he'll see through it. He was always proprietary about Agatha, and Conrad has no reason to think divorce will have changed that. Men are funny that way.

He puts the whole idea aside for a while. Holly Battle calls to tell him there have been no offers on the house, suggests another price reduction, which he rejects. And it's fall again, the foliage blaringly bright, almost unseemly, the sidewalks knee-deep in color till the town vacuum truck comes to suck it away. The streets are quiet, the kids back in school, their parents hard at work in their offices, making the next month's nut. Ahead lie the dreaded holidays, the second round of them since Sarah died, and worse this time because last year he was still numb and everyone stayed away, whereas now friends and relatives will assume he's healed enough to rejoin these nostalgic festivals like a normal person, which he's not, and believes he never will be.

Mornings are still hardest, gray light through the curtains on the old floorboards, the world reassembling itself out of the detritus of the night's dreams, the comrade pain in his side more generalized now, still below the threshold of alarm. His first thought is still of her, of the empty space behind his back in bed; the mind flies there, like a bird to its nest.

There are things of hers he still keeps, some scarves and blouses haunted with her scent, a pair of sexy taupe heels that stir him still. Her slim computer, silver as a rocket, sits on a shelf in the library now emptied of books, glinting with purpose. He means to wipe it of memory the way he wishes he could purge his own, and give it to the library for some even poorer soul to use to connect himself to the world. He's picked it up a hundred times and put it back, sometimes even getting as far as opening its slick lid and staring for a moment at the square, flat keys—chiclets, he thinks they're called, like something you would chew—where her small, thin fingers rested and flew, rested and flew.

He fixes himself his first coffee and grabs the thing down from its perch, opens it quickly as though this were a familiar thing to do, and punches the "on" button with its punctured circle-symbol. On. A robot chord sounds, and he's warned immediately that only a 5 percent battery charge remains, so he rummages around for the thin white cord, plugs it in, closes the lid because he feels some unguarded fist of grief rising up, stares off into the garden till his mind goes blank, opens it again.

A password is required, and he remembers some of the ones she used, as the whole concept of preventing access to things had seemed so bizarre to her that she had asked him to make them up for her. *BoxDog1. LovemyMeg. Eyeh8computerz. 2BON2BT1TQ. RUhappy? ACKS3SS.* None of them work. He's warned that he'll be locked out after five more tries. In frustration he starts randomly to type his name and bingo—"ConnieB" was her password.

The home screen is bright blue, the color of a Santa Fe sky. Her e-mail folder opens automatically, which panics him, and he fumbles to close it, his eyes drawn like stars to a black hole by the list of dates and names and subjects from before the event horizon. Meg, Becky, Madeleine, even Megan; *Lunch Thurs* and *Food Warning* and *Book Club* and *Drinks 2Nite?* and *Soup Kitchen Nxt Wk.* There's one addressed to Agatha called *Answer to Your Question*, and he hesitates, as it's something he's promised himself he would never descend to, this retrospective voyeurism that seems somehow adulterous and would undo in a moment what little progress he's made toward forgetting. He finally finds the right button with the cursor and the e-mail file is sucked back down into nothingness, and he's looking for the system file where there should be a helpful "reset" button with which to lobotomize this stubborn silver piece of her, when he sees, down there next to the Trash file for which it was no doubt intended, a Word file named "Dreaming."

And he means to move it the last fraction of an inch over into the wastebasket icon, but instead his finger twitches twice and it springs open, filling the screen the way he never allows anything to do, and again he's racing the cursor to the upper right where the red X sits like a fat red bug, but it's already too late, because he's reading: *I dream of him in daylight, when I'm running, when no one knows where I am. How do you find your way home from a place so beautiful? How do you say no to yourself so many times that it becomes a habit?*

There is no cure for this. There is nowhere to go with it. Meg says she tries to live in the moment, and I know that's the only place where my love for him can live—in the moments when we're together in the midst of our lives with others.

Stop now, he says almost aloud. *Stop.*

I have that much, and it has to be enough. It's better than having not known that he existed, better than thinking that life had given me all that it could and there was never any more. Now I know. There was more. I just missed it by a bit. At least I was in the same place at the same time. I have an hour with him here and there. Some women never get even that much. And it might go all wrong if there was more to it than that. So it has to be enough.

He closes the file, his heart pounding, moves it a fraction on the bright blue screen. "Dreaming." Opens it again, scans down and down.

Maybe there was a prior life with him. Maybe there will be a later one. Meg believes these things, but I'm not sure I do. I believe in God, but I think this one life may be all we are given. This heaven, the only heaven. We are at the same table, and I get to touch his calloused fingers when I hand him a drink.

And up to that point he's telling himself that this dream his dead wife had might have been about him, might represent a yearning for some hidden corner of their relationship that she had yet hoped to open up and make her own. But then he knows beyond doubt that it was not his fingers that electrified her when she had passed that drink, because his are smooth as an accountant's, and that he had no place in this dream except as the sanctuary from which to dream it, which is something we all need if we are to dream at all.

There is more, another paragraph or two, but he closes the file and shuts down the computer and unplugs it from the wall and puts it back up on the shelf where he'd found it and decides there is no good reason to give it away, no one who needs it any more than him. For here at last he sees an exit from his cul-de-sac of loss, his guilt at not having died with Sarah, or before her. If he can forgive her for dreaming of a life with Felix, which he cannot help but do, then maybe he can forgive her for dying, and move on.

Sometimes these days he's caught up in the finitude of it all, and his hand goes involuntarily to his mouth, and his breath is caught away, and he sees to the core of things for just a moment, and a dry, spastic sob comes to his lips. And he sees himself and those he loves for what they are and for the self-deception that allows them all to live and to forgive one another for all they've done and left undone in the day that's now gone, and then he'll push all that down where it came from and turn the page.

7

A FEW MORE DISCREET inquiries and he's exhausted the local female intelligence network with respect to the probable whereabouts of Agatha Webber, assuming that's still her name. Meg is quite certain that Agatha's sojourn with her parents in Columbus was only temporary and that she lit out for the West Coast some time ago. Christine is at first too loyal to Sarah's memory even to discuss the matter when they meet for lunch at the inn one rainy autumn afternoon. Felix is in London, trying to hire a younger version of Conrad as in-house counsel so that he can stop paying the few grand per month that Conrad still bills for his occasional and increasingly dated legal wisdom.

"It's a bit soon, don't you think?" she says, squinting at him over her wine glass. This is of course what all the women think, secure in the conjugal eternity of their lives, even Christine, who has come closest to having it all taken away. She's become sinewy, her arms muscled from months on the crutches, and it becomes her; even her limp becomes her, the way it would a war hero. "Not that I'd begrudge you whatever you think you need to do. We all knew you liked her."

"It's not like I'm stalking her," he says. "She's just one of the few single women I know relatively well who's remotely my age. We've both lost a spouse . . ."

"She rather jettisoned hers, I think . . ."

". . . and it's almost two years since Sarah died. It just seemed a harmless, natural thing to get back in touch with her."

"Connie, you don't have to justify anything to me, of all people. I just don't want you to get hurt."

"Why does everyone think so badly of Agatha? She never seemed the hurtful type to me."

"Women see more than men. Men are blinded by beauty."

"I wouldn't call Agatha a beauty," he says with trumped-up nonchalance, but in fact he's sure she is, though he can barely recall what she looks like, except that she was very tall and very blonde. He's scrolled through hundreds of photos on his phone and found only one or two of her, from that year when the Webbers and he and Sarah were inseparable. Her face is averted, unwilling to be caught unprepared, her ash-blond hair falling forward around her pointed chin. He's no longer sure of what drew the four of them together, and thinks now that it was accidental, simply easy, the absence of mutual expectation, the similarity of certain tastes in food or movies, the social dialect some couples speak and not others. But he does remember how the air shaped itself around her when she passed, how some unnamable gravity dragged him toward her in whatever room they stood in, passing off their smiles and touches as gestures of courtesy, the rote flattery of friends.

He's keenly aware that some of the disapproval that radiates from the women with whom he's discussed his proposed foray back into a social life has to do with his age, or more accurately the difference between his age and Agatha's. She's almost twenty years younger, not prohibitive by European standards, but Americans meet their spouses in school, lumped together in cohorts, see the proximity of their ages as a proof of their rightness for each other, and sense venality in an older man attracted to a decades-younger woman. Another hitch in all this, of course, is that Agatha Webber may want nothing to do with him. Offsetting the advantage of prior familiarity and briefly intimated mutual attraction is the fact that they each will remind the other of a lost life, and he knows that's never a comfortable foundation for anything.

"Meg was closest to her of any of us," says Christine. "Except of course Sarah. And she lost a spouse too. You should ask her."

"I did. She doesn't know much."

"All right. I'll ask John for you," she says, as though this is what he's been working up to all along.

"You don't have to do that."

"No, but I will. I'll just call him and ask for her address and say I want to send her a book or something."

"Will he believe that?"

"Does it matter?"

A couple of weeks pass before he hears back from Christine, in a simple e-mail with the subject line *Her Address*. It's an office building in Phoenix, care of a company called Afriquatic Inc., and an e-mail address, amitchell@afriquatic.com. So she has changed her name back, or forward. And Phoenix? What, he wonders, would take Agatha Webber, née Mitchell, to Phoenix?

He believes that for most of one's life, family or love or work or simple habit determines where you put your body. You live where your parents live, or where you go to school, or where your lover lives, or where you come into adulthood, or where you have a job. But late in life, all that falls away, and you're left with the looming question of where in all the world, in all your remaining corporeality, you belong.

For Conrad it's partly a question of where solitude would be tolerable, or even comfortable, and most people have no experience with it. Even in those brief spans of time when he technically lived alone— during college and law school and after starting to work, and in those backwaters of transient solitude that followed his divorce—his life was filled with people he saw daily and knew intimately: fellow students, his professors, coworkers, mentors, friends. At Mason & Gannett they routinely worked fifteen-hour days, took their meals in groups after hours on the firm's dole. That, he knew, was not really living alone in any meaningful sense, even though he returned at night to a space where no one else lived.

Then love or marriage or parenthood or friendships or all of them, if he's lucky, absolve a man from solitude for most of his life, if he's lucky. The places he lives have little to do with where he might be if he were alone; the question hadn't begun to present itself in Conrad's life. And even when marriages end as his had, or loved ones died as his had, or children grow up and disappear into their own lives as his had, there were always those few friends who would be there, and by being there would fix you to a place, like this little town that Sarah insisted was her true home.

But sometimes, he now knew, solitude happens, and there is no one to prevent it. Sarah was his tether to the world, the keeper of the skein of their friendships. With her gone, his instinct is to go away too, to leave behind their house and town and all the thousand reminders of her and of their life together, and find a place that was solely his. A quiet place, he thought. Probably not a seaside, where people tend to go in crowds when temporarily leaving behind their real lives. It wouldn't be a tourist town, where you're constantly distinguishing between locals and transients. He'd want to be among people who belonged to where they were. The deep woods, maybe, or in a working mountain town, or a combination of the two. Colorado had its places like this, away from the ski resorts, along rivers and streams where nobody bothers to raft.

But when all else was forgotten, when the symbolisms of birthplace and heritage and career and prestige were put aside, what beckoned to him was the desert, the hot, dry land, with mountains in the distance. The heat of the Mexican plains had imprinted something in him when he lived there as a child with his brother and their parents, all dead now; the scorched mountains rising in the west, the starry chaos of the night skies. He wanted finally to be in a desert hemmed by hills, like the high desert around Santa Fe, their dusty little house among the pines.

He'd ask Agatha to meet him there.

8

"HOW'S PHOENIX?"

A round of e-mails has established the time for a call. It's early evening Conrad's time, the wan sun of these shortening days already sinking behind the neighbors' gabled roof, mid-afternoon in Arizona where, he dimly recalls, they don't observe daylight saving time like the rest of the country.

"It's nice," she says. "Hotter than hell, but the mountains are pretty, and there's no winter."

"A dry heat," he offers, trying to remember if she appreciates his droll sense of humor or if it was something else that he'd fantasized her liking about him. In their e-mails they left unclear what the point of this conversation would be, what possible reason they had to talk after almost two years since laying eyes on one another. The phone is slick in his hand, and he puts one foot up on his desk to remind himself how blasé he should be. He suddenly feels like what the local women implied he'd become: a smarmy old man with delusions of romance.

"I actually live in Scottsdale," she says.

"Of course you do."

"My office is in Phoenix."

"What does Afriquatic do?" he asks, staring at her e-mail address and grateful for the business small talk, willing suddenly to let it be their entire agenda if in exchange he can avoid making a fool of himself.

"We make antimicrobial water filtration systems. They're portable and solar powered, so Africa is a principal target market." Her voice has shifted down a register, the way it must at work.

"And let me guess, you're their PR person."

"I'm the VP of communications, yes," she says, to let him know that her title is nothing to be trifled with, that he's still just a blip on her screen, far off, barely registering. He backs off even further.

"Do you get to go to Africa a lot?" he asks like a schoolboy.

"More than I'd like to. It's not fun duty. I've been several times this year, just got back from Nairobi, hope that's it for a while."

"Because of the poverty?"

"No," she says, "because of the death." And he's silent. "The poverty isn't like ours. It's part of the fabric there; it's just a different way of living. But there are too many people dying for no good reason, diseases we beat last century, the lack of simple things like clean water to drink."

"Hence Afriquatic," he says.

"Hence," she says.

"How did you find the job?"

"It found me," she says. "A guy I knew from a long time ago became CEO, and he reached out to me." And his heart sinks, because she's used that awful corporate-speak so naturally, and because he's visualizing this CEO, tanned and slick-haired and urbane, probably rich as Croesus, who "reached out" to Agatha just as he has, but did it long before he had the sense or courage or widowhood to do it, from some part of her past, before John Webber, that he has no part in. And he realizes he doesn't have time for all this, all the feints and gestures, the sidling up to the point of things.

"So is his interest in you just business?" he asks, knowing it's rude, not caring. Long silence, wherein Agatha weighs whether to be hurt or insulted or amused.

"No, it's not, Connie. I'm living with him." She says this apologetically, because of course she knows why he wanted this call, but there's also disappointment in her voice, as though she'd hoped he would have more sense than this, that he'd let things play out longer. "But he's a lot older than me, so I'm not sure it literally has a future."

Finally her voice has lost its professional edge, has lapsed into the softness he knew late at night at parties when they'd all been drinking and boundaries began to blur.

"Even older than me?" he asks like a pauper cadging alms.

"Even older than you, Connie, yes," she says with an embarrassed laugh.

"Isn't this sort of thing frowned upon in business life these days?" he asks, knowing this is a fruitless path, that making her uncomfortable is exactly what he shouldn't do.

"We struggle with it every day," she says, the "we" piercing his heart. "But luckily it's a privately held company, so we're not as constrained as we might be."

Constrained. He knows this woman, has known a hundred like her over his working life, these pretty, sharp, determined women who have learned the vocabulary of consensus and solicitude, walk the knife-edge of gender, contain their sexuality for the benefit of their poor male colleagues, suppress their rage and wrap it in gratitude, and will eventually run all their companies because their patience and perseverance so far exceeds that of the men who expect their due and don't comprehend theirs. Sex is at the heart of it, as it is at the heart of everything, yet their goal, it seems to him, is to be neutered the way men are, to be treated just as heartlessly, to render their lives just exactly as pointless as their own. He knows this woman and he loves her; he married her long ago.

–

She comes to Santa Fe anyway, because in the end he asks her to, and he doesn't ask what reasons she's given to her CEO, who may be wiser than him in addition to older, beyond the petty jealousies that would torment him if his live-in girlfriend disappeared for a few days. Perhaps they have one of those understandings one sometimes hears about but never seem to work. He meets her at the town's little airport and sees that he'd suppressed how heartbreakingly pretty she is, and how much younger than him. Perhaps she's trying to impress him, her white pants just tight enough to show off her ass and long legs but not seem provocative, her blouse a sweet knock-off Lilly Pulitzer to put the old man at ease, her face brown from the desert sun like an Apache queen, her hair, shockingly, no longer blond, but a uniform matte black, cut with a calculated raggedness that says, *See how little I care?*

He's blocked out a week to make sure the McCaffreys don't show up unannounced; they're gently disapproving in the way of parents whose son is determined to do something stupid and brave, like join the Marines or take up parkour. He drives the long way through town to let Agatha, who's never been here, see the shops around the square, the Palace of the Governors, more a hacienda than a palace, the ancient churches. She stares out the window obligingly. The tourist season is past, the streets reclaimed by the locals, the town gearing up for the annual burning of Zozobra, Old Man Gloom, a horrific giant wooden boogeyman into whose frame are stuffed pieces of paper where all the cares the people cared in the past year, and wish not to care about anymore, are written down and then go up in flames. He loves Santa Fe for its sweet literalism, its dismissing the past in which it wallows by pretending you can burn it away.

They chatter aimlessly as the rental car climbs out of town and into the eastern hills where scrub gives way to tall pine and the houses are hidden back from the road. He has no idea what her presence means, or just what to do about it other than try not to turn it into something tawdry. He asks about her change of hair color and gets the usual story about needing a fresh start. He brings her up to date on the families they know in common: the Sternbergers' fighter-pilot daughter now back from the wars and looking for work, Meg Franklin's withdrawal into her own dark strength, sure to outlive them all, the McCaffreys' recent announcement that they plan to put their beautiful house up for sale next year and live, as they put it, more simply. He doesn't know if this last is an admission of financial crisis or just philosophy; friends never speak of such things. Agatha's children are "both great," she tells him, her son majoring in math and her daughter now out of college and, having declared herself gay, planning to bring her new partner around at Christmas for Mom and Dad to meet in their separate homes, worlds and lives apart. He briefly imagines that difficult itinerary, the one on the planes and the one in the heart.

As was his plan, they arrive at the house just at sundown, the Jemez range aflame, the hills around Los Alamos, farther north, shadowed by thunderheads. "It's like a Maxfield Parrish!" she yells, her arms outstretched to it all. "Or a Bierstadt!" he yells back, and smiles and shrugs as though it's all old hat to him, and carries her bag to the bedroom that he's carefully made up to be hers, the sheets freshly washed and ironed under an antique Navajo quilt, a crucifix above the small bed, Stieglitz on the walls. She follows, glances into the empty closet and back at him, smiles at this elaborate attempt to assume nothing. They are, after all, old friends, and he's trying to adopt that barely remembered guise, where all you need to know about a woman is what she likes to drink and how her kids are doing, and telling her she's beautiful is just another way of acknowledging how lucky you both are. Instead he's laughing nervously at things he knows aren't funny as he shows her around the old house and leads her out onto the *portal* just as the last elbow of sun slips behind a band of cloud above the mountains. "I see why you love it," she says, and he remembers what she likes to drink and goes to get it.

Never once have they been alone together. He feels a certain sadness in what they're doing, even though they're doing nothing that anyone but a monk would identify as wrong. It's the sadness of impermanence, of screwing around with the past, and he's worried that she's already regretting it, as he is. But he still uses the moment when he hands her the wine glass to pull her to him, and she steps into it, taller than he is, and he stands on his toes like a boy to kiss her forehead, held up like a flag of surrender, and then her delicately cleft nose with its deep-brown freckles, and then her lips, the way they used to kiss in front of their spouses, dead-on, but brief, chaste, closed-mouthed. He has no idea how to do this, and they step apart again, laughing, holding hands, grateful to have the gaudy show on the horizon to look at.

Dinner at a favorite place in town, a converted adobe home, Milanese food prepared by a tiny bob-haired girl chef from Chicago, a maître d' from New Jersey who's built like a linebacker and who's known for refusing to seat people who arrive wearing fragrance. He's warned Agatha, so they're scentless but for whatever rebel phero-mones he's sure are bubbling from their pores, seated at a table in a corner away from the bar. She's realized she was overdressed for this raffish little town and has changed into jeans and a white cotton button-down that may once have belonged to her ex, back when he was as sure of the future as Conrad was.

"I never knew how to talk to you about Sarah," she's saying over a plate of burrata and blood-red tomatoes. "I'm sorry I wasn't in better touch then."

"You had your own problems."

"Not like yours," she says, so softly he can barely hear, her face aglow with candlelight.

"What would you have said?"

"Just that I was sorry. And that we all loved her."

"I knew that. Both those things."

"But you should have heard it from me."

"You came to the service. That was enough."

"I feel like I abandoned you."

"You had no obligation to me, Agatha."

"But I did, didn't I? We always had a connection; I knew that. And I just ran away."

He puts his fork down. "I'm going to say this, so we can get it out of the way. I always thought you and I would have been perfect together if we'd met twenty years earlier. I really can't say why, but you never can say why. You're lovely, yes, but you also seemed to be someone I already knew." She starts to speak, but he raises a hand. "Every man has an ideal woman buried in his subconscious, and she's often different from the one he thinks he wants or who he's married to. And when we got to know you and John, I knew you were that woman, and it was appalling, because it meant that even though I was enormously lucky and happily married, I hadn't been as lucky as I might have been, and there was nothing I could do about it. Nothing constructive, anyway, except to enjoy being together as couples and families and respect the luck we had."

She reaches across the white linen and takes his hand. With that shirt, it's seems to Conrad as though John Webber were at the table with them. "I felt the same, if it's any consolation. I came mainly to tell you that."

He smiles benignly, feeling old, no longer in her league if he ever had been. Her hand in his is carefully inert, like the hundred times they've held hands over dinner tables to hear grace said, links in a wider circle that included their spouses and friends and children, and sat quietly with their heads bowed as they said their thanks to Jesus Christ with all his attention focused on her fingers curled around his, until the "amen" was pronounced and they released one another back into the fallen world with a final squeeze that surely meant something more than gratitude for dinner. And sure enough, they do the same now as the waiter arrives with the wine, and lean back and look at each other, mutually forgiven.

After the little ceremony of the arrival of the entrées and a toast simply to good appetite, he says, "What happened with you and John, if I may ask?"

She looks at him as though she's never imagined his asking such a question. "This can't go beyond this table," she says after a long silence in which her risotto commands all her attention. "The simple answer is I cheated on him, and he caught me."

"Wow," he says, and takes a swig of wine. "Caught you how?" He winces at his own question; as though that were the important thing.

"I happened to leave my phone at home one day, and he read my e-mail."

"No password?"

"He guessed it."

"Was this the CEO?"

"Yes, the CEO. How funny that you call him that."

"I don't know what else to call him."

"Robert," she says, enunciating the syllables with her prim mouth.

"Not Bob," he guesses.

"Never Bob."

"And when was this?"

Her eyes, a translucent blue, rotate upward to consult the files her brain keeps in their secret place. "It started before I met you," she says, as though this, too, were a consolation. "Before you two moved to town. It was a business trip, the usual sordid thing, except the wife was doing the cheating."

"And the CEO. Bob."

"Bob what?" she asks.

"Sorry, Robert. Robert was cheating too."

"Yes. How did you know that?"

"Because that's the usual sordid thing." He regrets it instantly, for she sees that he's in fact jealous and judgmental and not being her friend in that moment, and she falls silent, ashamed, and he wants to squeeze into the banquette next to her and put his arm around her like the avuncular old coot he's sure he's doomed to be to her.

Later on the *portal* he opens an old amaro, and they watch the Milky Way condense like celestial fog. They sit side by side on a desiccated split-log bench, their backs against a wall, the moonlight like milk on the desert below. He thinks of how often he dreamed of a moment like this with her, and now that it's here he's without impulse, becalmed. This passivity around women he loves is something he knows he should examine when his head is clearer. To prove this observation wrong, he turns to her and kisses her cheek as she's rambling on about her son who wants to go to law school and may ask him for a reference, and she stops suddenly as though he'd slapped her and turns and grabs the back of his neck and puts her mouth on his, and his hand is inexplicably up inside John Webber's white shirt, cupping the lace of a bra in whose silky filigree he detects womanly premeditation, or at least an openness to possibility. She lifts a long leg up and over his, and he holds it there for dear life, the warmth of her thigh through denim defeating any thought he had of mournful abstinence. And then they're up and gone and under the old Indian blanket on her small bed, where Sarah and he never slept, not room enough to get too imaginative, which is fine with him, missionary all the way, the way they did it with their first loves long ago. It's hurried the way it is when you're deprived or embarrassed or both, but she feels familiar, as he knew she would, the smell of her wafting up, the perfume that had scented her sympathy card, the naked arms he'd touched in passing a thousand times around him finally, the long fingers of one hand at the back of his head, the other guiding him with the practiced frankness of a wife. Which of course is what she is, still, and always will be, just as he will always be a husband. And it's there where they finally find each other fully in those moments before they lose themselves again, in that place where what they love most in each other is the love they've shown to others.

9

SOMETIME IN THE HEART of postcoital darkness he slips from the narrow bed, fetches his robe from his bedroom, and goes outside to stand in the moonlight falling like rain. The night's grown cold, uncannily clear. A pack of coyotes howl in ghostly chorus, nearer than seems civilized. Possibly they're triangulating something for the kill, possibly the white guy in his robe on the patio. Small and not-so-small pets are carried off all the time around here; owners walking dogs are stalked in broad daylight. Part of the charm of the place is that it's basically unchanged in a millennium, that this same moonlight fell on those same wild eyes before men walked the continent. They're all interlopers here.

This wish to be alone and gone following sex is one of those inextirpable male habits he'd almost forgotten, buried as it has been under years of married life when the voluptuary bed was also the bed he slept in. To this moment he can feel in his bones the posture Sarah and he assumed after lovemaking, as they drifted off to endorphin-addled sleep, her rump cozied up against his groin, his left arm wrapped around one small hip and his hand tucked under the other. Pulling her against him once, twice, once more, stilling to that vacant rest in which their younger selves might have cupped a life or two.

But before that became the norm, he was a runner. He remembers his bachelor New York days, between marriages, when he would pass an attractive woman on the street and feel a sharp pang of actual regret that she was not sexually available to him, preferably in that moment, and when he did actually manage to arrange or stumble into a liaison, after the obligatory dinner and the polite temporizing that passed in those quaint days for romance, after the dear old dance itself in which the lie testosterone had been telling him all evening was instantly recanted, he would dawdle, fighting sleep, next to his partner of the evening and silently count to sixty, then another sixty, then another, before making some excuse—he was was a big-deal lawyer *and* a single father, so he had many of these—and hightailing it out of her apartment (or hotel room, as was often the case) into the cool of the early morning streets and back to his one-bedroom on Gramercy Park to which he rarely invited anyone but Madeleine, the all-night doorman barely suppressing his knowing smirk, the apartment door snugging closed behind him like the hatch of a diving submarine; *click, click,* the bolts rammed home. Alone again, the default state from which the rest of his life was a costumed expedition. Thank God, he thinks, that those days are past. Now he sees a beautiful woman on the street and thinks, simply, *What a beautiful woman.*

And when he asked Agatha to meet him in Santa Fe, he really didn't have sex explicitly on his agenda, though he knew one can't suggest such a thing without admitting that possibility, and of course he'd wondered for years what she might be like in bed, as men will about almost any attractive woman, but he'd wondered this with the kind of detached interest with which a cosmologist might think about life on Mars—fun to contemplate, but unlikely to be verified in our lifetime.

And when the moment came he hadn't needed her, really, hadn't wanted her with that old feral intensity, had merely wanted to be with her and sit with their backs against the moonstruck wall and take it all in together. This, he thinks, is one of the liberations of a man's autumnal years; her company—that pallid word—was all he'd really wanted in that resolved moment, not the grasping need that haunted his youth and middle age, which of course can be summoned almost anytime if you're still alive and have the slightest connection to your libido. It had been a crowded little bed, each of them, he was sure, thinking in the sweet deed's midst of the other's erstwhile spouse, and of their own, those slightly different versions of the same lost people— so two Sarahs, two Johns, and them. He imagined his versions of John and Sarah as wryly benevolent onlookers, wishing them well, beyond jealousy, amused that what they'd always sensed between Agatha and him, like what he had sensed between Sarah and Felix, had been true.

After the moon has set, he goes to bed in his own room, not wanting to presume the one greater intimacy than sex, that of waking up with someone. In the morning she's up well before him, on Eastern time, has made coffee and foraged for breakfast, and he finds her on the *portal* warming her hands around a steaming mug, dressed for the day as if nothing had happened, no makeup yet, her smile slightly pained, the way you would smile as you entered a hospital room to visit an ailing relative. He walks over to her in his robe and takes her hand and bends down to kiss her wide brown forehead.

"How are you feeling?" she asks, and he says, "I feel great, how about you?" And she says she, too, feels great, and squeezes his hand in that old amen-triggered way, and in those few words what's being said, he knows, is that they have no regrets about last night but that it was enough, a complete answer to several old questions but also a final one, needing no repetition for its meaning to sink in. Repetition, in fact, would punch holes in its completeness, raise new questions for which neither one of them had any good answers.

All this is said in those few words, but they find ways to say it again over lunch in a Mexican bar in town, and again on a hike along the high chaparral above the house where there is no trail, just mesquite and manzanita, the sunlight a stern benediction, the tall grass pulling at their legs like needy toddlers.

"So what about this guy Robert?" he asks.

"What about him?"

"Do you love him?

"I do, Connie. I have to say I do."

"No need to apologize," he says.

"You'd like him," she says, puffing in the thin air as they climb, clipping her sentences. "He's kind. He loves my children. Who never visit. But he loves them. He understands me. I'm not easy." *So I've heard*, he wants to say, but doesn't. "I'm moody. Up and down. John was steady. You're steady. Robert is steady."

"How did you meet him?

"In business school. He was my professor." Another twinge of jealousy as he envisions Agatha as a lissome graduate student lingering in Dr. Bob's office after class, discussing ROI or random walks or the double-entry ledger system or whatever one studies in business school.

"It started then. And I thought it was over. But then I went back. Years later. For a trustee meeting. And that's when it happened. My infidelity." She's taken possession of it, owned it, as the kids say. It wasn't something that happened *to* her, as so many try to pretend; it was something she chose, over and over.

"But the kids. Were still young. So John agreed. To hang in there."

"How old is Robert?" he asks, still feeling competitive with this man who's known Agatha most of her adult life, preyed upon her as his student, and stole her from her benevolent if stuffy husband, Conrad's friend and fellow lawyer.

"Almost eighty," she says, glancing up to gauge how shocked he is as he helps her over a boulder.

"And I thought I was too old for you," he says.

"Never," she says. "I'd kiss you to prove it, but I can't spare the breath." And that's all he needs, he realizes, to let this whole thing go.

He makes dinner for her that night after showers and drinks, a steak Diane that Sarah always liked, corn cut from the cob and simmered in some oil with cherry tomatoes and herbs de Provence, a mesclun salad. He sets the table on the *portal*, candles all around, builds a fire and decants a good cabernet. The violet end of sunset's spectrum lingers above the hills, the stars emerging, so faint they disappear when they look for them head-on. He plays some bad Chopin on a cheap keyboard ordered from Amazon, and she applauds. She's dressed up as though they were going out, in a white off-the-shoulder peasant blouse and turquoise earrings bought that afternoon in town. And he realizes that what they each are doing there, these small acts, the making of a meal for someone you love and presenting yourself in a way that honors it, these things they always did for one another back when they were married to others and therefore just friends, these things mean as much, at least to him, at least right then, as having her the night before in that other way, the old blind way that for a moment obliterates the self and all its loves.

Sometime after midnight they kiss like siblings in the hall between the bedrooms and say goodnight and leave the doors open a crack—to let their spirits pass, it seems to him in his cheery inebriation. But he knows they've already done all that needed to be done here, and they each have homes to return to, as they always have.

10

THE HOLIDAYS LOOM, THE town already revved up, signs for the 5K Turkey Trot on every lawn, shoulder-high Christmas trees sponsored by local businesses already sprouting along the streets; Conrad knows that some fat fake Santa is preparing somewhere for his annual invasion atop a hook and ladder. Observing it all, he muses that when his granddaughter is older and falls in love with the material world, as all of us do as children and sometimes never grow out of, maybe she'll enjoy all this, the little town where her grandpa lives and they act out all the sacred fables of community. He himself couldn't care less, wishes only for the gray doldrums of January, when the world will return to synchronicity with what he knows it to be.

It's with a longing to evade it all that he's hosting a dinner well before Thanksgiving, so as to fend off expectations that he'll participate later. In this he's become kindred to Meg Franklin, who never ventures out anymore, locked in her proud perpetual mourning. Once a month he walks over to her prim Craftsman bungalow on the edge of town just to confirm that she's still alive, as he knows Sarah would if she were. If he spies Meg in her garden he turns around and goes home, mission accomplished, knowing she has no need of any chat with him or much of anyone. He admires this in her, aspires to it, but is still too much mired in the social woof and weft, has spent too many years as part of a team, to become a hermit now. A professional, he thinks, is by definition someone with obligations to others, and he's been a professional his entire adult life.

He hears from friends back in New York that Mason & Gannett is on the brink of liquidation, the pension money already gone to pay off creditors, the partners and associates scattered like refugees to other firms. In ten years no one will remember that the place ever existed. He can only be grateful that this didn't happen when he was forty or fifty. But he has Sarah's money now, the few million she received from her father's estate after they were married, carefully husbanded (a strange word he'd never utter) by him, untouched. Her father had meant it as insurance of her independence, her ability to walk away from men who might not value her as he did. But of course she met no men who didn't love her, so there the money sat, growing, for two marriages and the better part of her abbreviated life. She had meant it for her charities, on the assumption that her husband would, as wills always contemplate, "predecease" her. Naturally Conrad hadn't, and now the pile that George Bergman earned from his thousands of commutes between Philadelphia and Wall Street had fallen to a man he never knew.

Today he's cleaning out his sock drawer. He chuckles at the awareness that he's able to do this literally, if not psychologically. He's weeding out the singletons, making sure the pairs are bound together at their necks as pairs should be (another chuckle), thrilled to find old forgotten favorites like the compression socks whose manly grip on his thin calves he instantly recalls, throwing away the sorry specimens he knows he'll never wear again, if he ever did: the horizontally striped, whimsical Where's Waldo numbers from five Christmases ago, the absurdly thin silk knee-highs through which his leg hairs inelegantly sprouted, the fondly remembered wool blends from his working days that lined his wing tips and tasseled loafers and in which he wiggled his cold toes on many a Monday or Friday transcon, but which years ago developed big heel holes he doesn't know

how to repair and wouldn't if he did. He finds all this as cathartic as
six weeks of talking therapy, and hopes it's included in every widower's survival manual, if such things exist.

When he's done he takes his grocery bag full of rejected but still
useable men's hosiery over to the Volunteers of America donation bin
on Broadway, where he gently inters the contents, then ambles to the
CVS to refill his statin drug prescription, then over to the state store
on Main, as he's out of vodka. There's a pleasing symmetry to these errands, purging and prudence and wastrel provisioning in a single stroll.

He passes All Souls, and sees Father Rick ostentatiously putter-
ing in the rectory garden, wearing a black short-sleeved clergy shirt,
a flat-brimmed straw hat as though he were an Amish farmer, and
of course his collar. The priest straightens up and waves when he
sees Conrad, and makes a hip-juking motion in his direction, but
he pretends he has no time and hurries across the street before the
light changes. They haven't spoken since the memorial service, and
Conrad doesn't intend to start now.

The state store is, unsurprisingly to Conrad, one of the oldest
commercial establishments in town, situated in a nineteenth-cen-
tury storefront once used as a Rosicrucian temple. Old oak floors,
the redolence of moldy cork, the miserly array of overpriced spirits, a blandly indolent bureaucrat behind the counter who knows
Conrad's name from a thousand credit card transactions but would
never use it lest his vaguely Puritan disapproval of the whole enterprise be compromised. Conrad never enters without a quiet rush of
well-being; the very notion of the benevolent State of Pennsylvania
metering his consumption of alcohol and deigning to sell it to him is
as quaintly comforting as Santa Claus. He gets it and plays along. The
Prohibitionists, he thinks, were on to something: we are a nation of
inebriants and escapists; we love our alcohol and don't really know
what we'd do without it. It kills thousands each year, and it may have
killed his wife. No reason to be cavalier about it.

He makes his way home through the bright litter of fallen foliage and puts the vodka in the freezer. He stands next to Sarah's big mahogany table and looks around the dining room, which is otherwise devoid of furniture. College kids decorating off-campus apartments have carried off most of what they owned, but no one wanted this big old thing, partly because it's so heavy. He's glad it's still there, proof that she was.

An idea has been building in his head for weeks: this house must go. At least the house as it is. It could look the same from the outside, but its interior must change, as his has. There's no longer need for the master suite with its walk-in closet and his-and-hers vanities, no need for the three guest bedrooms (four, if he counts his office), no need for his office, surely, no need for the big family room where no family gathers. It needs to be gutted and changed, as he's been. It needs people living in it or, as he's grudgingly realized, he does.

Selling it to some young nuclear family, bursting with fecundity and debt, would only perpetuate a cultural mistake. He's long thought that the way they all lived was absurd, married off in little fragile dyads that they fortified as quickly as possible with pets or offspring and walled off from the world by spending an inordinate amount of disposable income on spaces and buildings in which to maintain that separateness, until they all grew old and the pets died and the kids with whom they conjured the semblance of a tribe suddenly departed to form their own, leaving them paired alone again in these expensive, mostly unused monuments to fleeting domesticity. And through all those decades of adult life, they're pantomiming what they really want and need by coming together constantly at dinners, parties, weddings, funerals, tailgates, commencements, campouts, group vacations, extramarital affairs and class reunions; all of them wanting, he believed, to bust out of the tidy, atomized families they'd been taught to call home and return to the broader tribe of nomads which once sat watch on the primal night, told one another stories, cooked one another's meals, and raised one another's children. He'd concede the need for some private places, true, primarily for toilets and for sex, but most of the rest of their grandiose homes were wasted on too few people too much of the time.

So his thought, here within hailing distance of the end of his days, is to start a commune and see who comes. He's heard they call it "cohousing" these days. He calls Holly Battle and tells her he won't be renewing her contract, that he's going to stay. He contacts old Bob DeForest, the local construction magnate, by now married four times to consecutively younger former clients, who is incredulous when Conrad tells him of his desire to rip out the innards of an 1830s gem like his, but who, upon hearing his budget, can see his way clear to getting together the following week to talk about it: a top floor of six equally sized bedrooms, each with its own small bath, a downstairs consisting of a much larger kitchen, a great room with two opposing fireplaces, a big lounge, a central dining island to seat twenty, and a wall of French doors opening onto the backyard where the pergola, draped in dense wisteria, already waits.

He e-mails the Sternbergers and the McCaffreys and Meg Franklin and asks them to come to dinner on the Saturday after Halloween, and to bring chairs. Madeleine agrees to fly in from New York for the weekend, and to bring little Helen; her skinny husband is in Tokyo on a deal. Megan calls out of the blue to ask if she can come to help with the baby.

"You don't have to come as the nanny," he says. "You can come as a guest. I would have asked you, but I thought you'd say no."

"Great," she says sarcastically. "Can I stay in the house?"

"I wouldn't have it any other way."

"No funny stuff, Burrell. No subtexts here, no hidden agendas. I'll just be there to help Maddie."

"I am duly warned."

"You're a hopeless romantic, you know that?"

"I do, trust me."

He meets privately with Meg, first, to tell her that she needn't live alone anymore, even though he knows it's what she thinks she wants. He assures her he's not lonely either, just the opposite, that like her he needs no one and nothing, but can choose to be with others, and for now that's how he wants to live. And that's what makes her stop her knitting and look up at him for the first time and tell him that she'll think about it.

Then he goes to the McCaffreys' big glass house and sits with Felix and Christine before their limestone hearth and watches Felix build a fire and hears how they can't afford the place anymore. They want him to buy them out of the house in Santa Fe, which he's willing to do just to keep it in the family, as they put it, but even that's not enough. Christine's treatments and therapies and the cost of the two homes have drained their accounts faster than Felix can refill them, and he doesn't want to try anymore, wants to stop traveling, be with his wife, and finally master his guitar. To Conrad's shock, he's been their inspiration in this; they see him as a business model, someone who, in the wake of crisis, can do next to nothing, say he's consulting, and make enough to live. He explains he'll be living off of savings from here on out, but that he has an idea of how they could all live "more simply," by which of course they mean more cheaply, if they're willing to put convention aside.

Finally there's lunch with Becky and Stu Sternberger, both on sabbatical from their administrative jobs at Pitt, who understand immediately what he's suggesting and to whom it appeals in an abstract, philosophical way. But they say they need to think of their daughter, who knows how to pilot attack aircraft but here on earth is still jobless and living with them in their farmhouse outside of town. He assures them there will be room enough and that they might even have a salary to offer to a full-time housekeeper and cook until something better comes along for her. They, too, say they'll think about it, which in their case he takes to be polite refusal. Their world is still much too complicated, hip-deep in the flow of work, still not done with the task of being parents but anticipating that strange precipice when they will be alone and will need to reinvent themselves as man and wife. Another big change is not what they need now, and when it comes it won't be presented to them by the likes of him. He's reminded of the night at their house when it had dawned on him that all of them would eventually drift away from each other, that the tight orbits in which they circled would decay, that they were living in a blessed interval.

Madeleine arrives the night before the dinner with little Helen on her hip, a suitcase stuffed with disposable diapers, an assortment of healthy toddler snacks in Ziploc bags, and a bottle of pinot noir. They stand in the small dim foyer and hold each other longer than he's sure they would if her husband were there, long enough that Helen starts to cry at this strange man enveloping her mother, so Conrad lets her go and kisses the little girl's curly head and extends his hands to her, thumbs up, in offering to take her to him, at which she wails all the louder. Still, she's shockingly cute, her eyes enormous teary versions of his mother's.

He picks Megan up at the airport the next morning. Behind her trails the smallest possible roller bag, a breadbox on wheels, whose austere contents Conrad can't begin to imagine. No dresses, no cosmetics, no shoes (the ones she's brought are on her feet). *What does Megan Caldwell's underwear look like these days?* he wonders. He's sure he'll never know. They hug each other ceremonially, and she turns her gray head nearly completely around to avoid being kissed. He can't be that repellent, he thinks; maybe she's taken up smoking again and doesn't want him to know. Her wild hair is drawn back in a tight silver bun, and she's anorexically thin. He puts her tiny bag in the trunk of the Mercedes and opens the passenger door for her as though they were sixteen and headed for a prom. She accepts this bizarre postfeminist gesture without a hint of amusement and climbs right in, perhaps thinking it was his habit with Sarah, which it was not, or perhaps this is what the courtly Vince Van Siclen always did, and she expects no less of him.

Watery sunlight, the trees in the forests that crowd the broad highway naked, black and spectral, waiting for the snows, not a hint that they're still living. They exit the interstate and ride a few miles in silence, past the cemetery where his father lies in his solitary grave, unvisited. His is the fate that Conrad is still trying to avoid.

"This idea of yours," Megan pipes up, sensing as she always did when his thoughts have lost their way. "About the house. Do you really think it's workable?"

"Who the hell knows? May as well find out. It makes more sense than the way any of us is living now, I'm sure of that."

"Who do you mean by 'us'?"

"Meg Franklin. The McCaffreys. Me. There could be others."

"Do you like Meg?"

He glances at her reprovingly. "She's just a friend. Single people aren't free radicals that need to be paired, you know."

"I do know, thank you."

"I can't think of anyone less interested in me romantically than Meg. Except maybe you."

She's leaning back against the passenger door, turned toward him, her gaze steady on the side of his face. "You know, our generation tried this communal-living thing in the sixties, and it didn't work out so well," she says.

"Too many drugs and not enough money," he points out. "This will be the reverse."

She smiles for the first time. "Best of luck," she says neutrally.

"You're invited too, you know."

Now she straightens up and peers out through the windshield as though his driving is making her nervous and her guidance may be required. She begins fiddling with the old analogue temperature controls on the dash, sliding levers this way and that.

"I thought we had that conversation," she says.

"That was a different conversation. You don't need to live alone in that old house."

"I'm not going to live in it. I'm giving it to Vince's kids and moving to a place nearby."

"What place?" he asks, incredulous.

"It's a nice campus run by the Presbyterians."

"Campus? You mean a retirement home? You can't be serious."

"It's called assisted living, and, Connie, it's really none of your business."

"That's not you!" he's almost yelling now.

"It's a practical solution," she says, but he can hear in her voice that it's a total capitulation, an admission of helplessness and loss of faith he can't bear in her.

"Solution to what? It's hell!" he yelps, bouncing on the frayed bucket seat.

"You're really out of line, bucko. If you don't stop, I'll get out right here and call an Uber back to the airport." She pulls out her phone to prove it.

They're quiet for a while, the tires thrumming, until he hears her sniffle and sees that she's turned her face away, toward the empty fields rushing by.

"Megan," he says, and out of ancient reflex reaches over to where she sits rigid, quivering.

"There's something you don't know," she says, muffled, her lips almost touching the glass. Always, always, something he doesn't know. And immediately he's thinking cancer, death, white hospital rooms, standing with his daughter above her mother's grave. These are the terrors we're taught to expect, the tropes of decline, the animal destinies we only evade for so long.

"Maddie and Lloyd are separating."

He's stunned and shamefully relieved. "As of when?" is all he can think to ask. "She hasn't said anything about this to me."

"She's planning to be out of their apartment by the time he gets back from his trip to Japan. She wants to tell you herself, so pretend you don't know."

"What happened?" he squawks, thoughts careening.

"Nothing dramatic. The usual. What happened to us, basically. Too much work, not enough help. Different parenting styles. There may have been some mild infidelity in there somewhere, though I doubt it. They're still too young, I think, for what they took on. Like us, as I say."

"Where's she going to go?"

"Not sure yet."

"She can come here," he mumbles. "We'll have lots of room."

At this she turns on him. "Will you for one moment stop thinking about yourself? She has a child and a job in Manhattan, you idiot. She's not moving to fucking Western Pennsylvania just so you can try to redeem yourself with her." Her lower lip snaps upward to try to stop the words that are already out, and she slams her back into the seat and looks out the window again. They're cruising up Main Street into his little town, its calm façades, its promise of sanctuary.

"That was harsh," she says. "I'm sorry."

"No, you're right. I was being selfish. Maybe I always have been."

"We all are, Connie. Some of us are just better at managing it than others."

Almost at the front door of his parents' house now, almost home.

"Did you see this coming?" he asks.

"No."

"I'm shocked."

"I'm sorry for her," she says, not sounding all that sorry. "But she'll be fine. She has friends who love her. She's an attractive woman. We'll take care of her." And with that they're parents again, partners.

"I'm not going to pretend you didn't tell me this."

"Suit yourself," she says, popping open the passenger door, one foot on the cold garage floor, looking back at him. He sees that she's waiting for something, something she can't say but wants him to. He knows her better than himself.

"Think about my idea," he says. "For you, I mean."

"Do you really mean that?" she asks.

"I do," he says. They get out and slam the old car's doors in unison.

An unseasonably warm night, then, in early November, almost two years to the day since Sarah drove off with Christine to do good deeds and never came back. He didn't pick the date consciously, but there it is. Megan is upstairs putting the baby down, the Sternbergers and McCaffreys and Meg Franklin are bent over Bob DeForest's floor plans for the remodel, drinks in hand, the women in silk and sequined sweaters and straight-legged pants and heels, the men in their button-downs and khakis and leather loafers. Party clothes, hereabouts. Madeleine doesn't know the code and is dressed in jeans and an NYU sweatshirt, embarrassed to learn that the country folk take these things so seriously. Conrad pours her a chardonnay and takes her into the empty living room.

"Your mom told me about you and Lloyd," he says, holding her arm by the elbow.

Her face begins to crumple the way it did when she was six and the world had betrayed her. "I'm so sorry, Dad," she says, and he grabs her and holds her to him.

"There's nothing to be sorry about," he says, knowing it's another parental lie in a lifetime of them. "But are you sure about this? Have you had counseling?"

"He won't go. He's too busy with his fucking job," she sobs petulantly, her tears staining his shirt. And something, against every selfish instinct in his body, makes him say, "Ask him again. Tell him you love him. Don't expose yourselves to all the regret that your mother and I live with every day. Don't give Helen the crappy half-assed upbringing we gave you."

She's half-laughing through her tears now, hitting his chest with feeble fists. "Don't you dare say that. I had a perfectly fine upbringing."

"Try again," he says. "Then try some more. It's worth it, I promise you. Take it from someone who knows what real loss is all about. Most of it you can't help, but this you can."

She looks up at him, her mascara all askew. "You're crazy, you know that? You have no idea what we've been through."

"I don't think that's true. I think I have a very good idea. Someday your daughter may go through the very same thing, and what will you say to her?"

"I don't know," she says, helpless. "I don't know what's right. I don't know anything anymore. I can't concentrate; I can't work."

He draws back a step and touches her cheek. "Ask the firm for a leave of absence and come here for a while with Helen. If you're as good as you say you are, they'll let you do it. Your mom can stay too. You can help plan the new house; you're good at that stuff. We can be a family under one roof again, at least for a month or two."

"You're crazy, Dad."

"You said that already."

"You just can't let it go."

"I've let everything go," he says. A burst of laughter from the kitchen. Megan comes downstairs and pretends not to see them as she passes down the hall. "Think about it," he says.

Meg Franklin and Conrad have collaborated on the menu: roast duck â l'orange with scalloped potatoes and string beans, eggplant parmesan for his vegetarian daughter and ex-wife. They arrange themselves around the big mahogany table, votive candles glowing in this their church, Conrad at one end, Meg at the other, the spouses carefully separated, ready in that way they've learned to extend their love to one another, Megan and Madeleine solemn and shy in their avid midst. And before he can say anything, Meg stands, imperial, and raises her glass and looks at each of them in turn before she says, "To Sarah."

And they all say it again, together.

ABOUT THE AUTHOR

© Solunar Graphics

KEITH MCWALTER GREW UP in Mexico and Pennsylvania. He is a graduate of Denison University and Columbia Law School and worked for over thirty years in the legal and investment banking worlds of New York and San Francisco. His writing has appeared in the *New York Times*, the *New York Times Magazine*, and the *San Francisco Chronicle*, and he is the author of the blog *Mortal Coil*. He and his wife live in Granville, Ohio, and Sanibel, Florida.

SELECTED TITLES FROM SPARKPRESS

SparkPress is an independent boutique publisher delivering high-quality, entertaining, and engaging content that enhances readers' lives, with a special focus on female-driven work. www.gosparkpress.com

Absolution: A Novel, Regina Buttner $16.95, 978-1-68463-061-5
A guilt-ridden young wife and mother struggles to keep a long-ago sexual assault and pregnancy a secret from her ambitious husband whose career aspirations depend upon her silence and unswerving loyalty to him.

Enemy Queen: A Novel, Robert Steven Goldstein
$16.95, 978-1-68463-026-4
A woman initiates passionate sexual encounters with two articulate but bumbling and crass middle-aged men, but what she demands in return soon becomes untenable. A short time later she goes missing, prompting the county sheriff to open a murder investigation.

That's Not a Thing: A Novel, Jacqueline Friedland
$16.95, 978-1-68463-030-1
When a recently engaged Manhattanite learns that her first great love has been diagnosed with ALS, she is faced with the impossible decision of whether a few final months with her ex might be worth risking her entire future. A fast-paced emotional journey that explores whether it's possible to be equally in love with two men at once.

Watermark: The Broken Bell Series $16.95, 978-1-68463-036-3
When Angel Ferente—a teen with a dysfunctional home life who has been struggling to care for her sisters even as she pursues her goal of attending college on a swimming scholarship—doesn't come home after a party on New Year's Eve, her teammates, her coach's church, and her family search the city for her. The result changes their lives forever.

And Now There's You: A Novel, Susan S. Etkin $16.95, 978-1-68463-000-4
Though five years have passed since beautiful design consultant Leila Brandt's husband passed away, she's still grieving his loss. When she meets a terribly sexy and talented—if arrogant—architect, however, sparks fly, and neither of them can deny the chemistry between them.